DEADLY MEETING

DEADLY MEETING

Robert Bernard

PERENNIAL LIBRARY

Harper & Row, Publishers, New York
Cambridge, Philadelphia, San Francisco, Washington
London, Mexico City, São Paulo, Singapore, Sydney

First PERENNIAL LIBRARY edition published 1986.
Designed by Jénine Holmes

Library of Congress Cataloging-in-Publication Data

Bernard, Robert.
    Deadly meeting.

    Reprint. Originally published: New York : Norton,
c 1970.
    I. Title.
PS3563.A728D3   1986   813'.54   86-45079
ISBN 0-06-080819-5 (pbk.)

86 87 88 89 90 OPM 10 9 8 7 6 5 4 3 2 1

FOR M. M.

CHAPTER ONE

Any departmental chairman, thought Bill Stratton, deserved to be murdered for holding a meeting on the last day of classes before Christmas. Let alone at five o'clock, when a self-respecting professor ought to be on his way home to put the martini pitcher in the refrigerator. Rows of bottles floated before his inner eye, but he dutifully brought his attention back to the meeting and his chairman's performance.

The big desk against which Peter Jackson leaned stood in the corner of his office. Stratton and the others sat in considerable discomfort on stainless-steel chairs around an oiled-walnut table. Jackson's right ankle was hooked over his left thigh to make a support for the folder that he was closing. "Well, there it is," he said with an ingratiating smile. "I think that's all the information we need in order to take action on his promotion." He ran his hand through his blond hair, still so thick and wiry as to belie his forty-two years. As he dropped his hand, the hair obligingly fell back into place in a shock over his brow. "Are there any questions?"

The other six men sat in silence for a time, their faces tired in the bright light that kept the December darkness at bay outside the windows. Most of the energy in the room seemed concentrated in Jackson, as if he had absorbed the strength that had slowly ebbed out of them since September. "Anything at all? Please feel free to say what you think. I do need your collective advice, and I think that however we act, we

1

must act as a department, as a unit." He put his hands on the forward edge of the desk and smiled again as he leaned confidently toward his colleagues.

The building had long since lost the smell of its annual summer coat of varnish, and the room had taken on the odor of chalk dust that seemed to seep through the walls. Stratton wondered vaguely whether academic offices all over the country smelled the same. He stirred in his seat, looked around to see that no one else was about to speak, then said, "Mr. Chairman?"

"Yes, Bill, what is it? And I think you may as well call me Peter in such a small meeting. We're here as friends as well as colleagues, I hope."

"I'm not sure that a department as small as ours can afford another medieval specialist. I don't think that Evans is a bad scholar, although I'm not as enthusiastic about him as you are, but even so, it seems to me that with Professor Moorhead here in Anglo-Saxon, and you in medieval studies, it would probably be wise to think about promoting an assistant professor whose specialty is more essential. We need someone to teach the Renaissance. Professor Fackler will be retiring in two years, and we should consider who will take his place. We certainly ought to have a senior member of the department to teach Shakespeare. Either Swenson or Rosenbloom could do that, and they are both competent to teach Milton as well. I think we ought to consider them."

"Thanks, Bill, for your thoughts. I do appreciate your point of view, believe me, but I ought to tell you that it would be almost impossible to get a promotion for either of them through the president's office, even if we recommended it. Swenson doesn't have a very impressive list of publications. If I remember correctly, only five or six articles, and that wouldn't swing it. He simply doesn't have any national exposure, and that's what we need if we are going to make this a first-rate department."

2

"He has a book nearly completed on Shakespearean comedy." Stratton turned to Fackler. "You've seen the manuscript. What do you think of it, E. W.?"

Fackler, a fat little man in a shiny serge suit, stared shyly at his feet before speaking. Forty years of teaching had never given him confidence in addressing either students or colleagues, and his manner was so retiring that only his shrewd light-blue eyes gave any initial hint of the intellect that made him the adornment of the English department. "I don't know," he said vaguely, "at least, I don't know for sure, but I do believe it is the best book on the subject that will be written in our generation. Brilliant, of course, but Swenson is brilliant." He subsided.

"Perhaps so, but we can't ignore the realities of the situation." Jackson had the patient look of a parent explaining to a stubborn child the reasons he cannot have another piece of candy. "If it were published, that would be one thing, but I can hardly talk to the president about a manuscript that may never be finished."

To Stratton's surprise, Fackler spoke again, so softly that the others had to strain to hear. "As I say, he is brilliant, and it does seem to me that perhaps brilliance is what we should be looking for, don't you think, Mr. Chairman?"

"Yes, of course, Ed, but what we want is someone like you with a big national exposure." Even after three months, Jackson still made occasional mistakes on the nicknames that he had begun to use almost as soon as he took over as chairman the preceding September. To the rest of the department, Fackler was always known by his initials, both because most of the younger men felt too much in awe of his mind to use his given name, and because even the least sensitive realized that anyone christened Edgar Winkler Fackler was not apt to be fond of that unlovely and repetitive roll of syllables.

"Then how about Mort Rosenbloom?" The question came from Tony Bongiovanni, sitting next to Stratton. He was seldom notable for patience, even with his superiors. "He's written at least as much as Evans, and he's a hell of a lot brighter. And, besides, he can teach. His classes are always crowded, we practically have to beat students over the head to get them into one of Evans's classes. I agree with Bill Stratton that we need someone in the Renaissance."

With a rueful smile, Jackson spread out his hands, palms upward. "Do I have to say it? You must know that I'm not anti-Semitic, but the president is afraid of the trustees. He wouldn't ever mention that Rosenbloom is Jewish, but, really, Tony, there just isn't a chance. I regret it as much as you do, but that's simply how it is. Instructor, yes, or even assistant professor, but they wouldn't take a Jew for a tenure position. Not to have him here for the rest of his life."

"I don't believe that the trustees are anti-Semitic, and I doubt that the president is. They put my promotion through, even if they thought that I was a Wop."

Jackson lifted his eyebrows at Bongiovanni's expression. "I'm afraid that it's either Evans or no one. I don't want to ram him down your throats, but I can't see an alternative. Perhaps Swenson in a year or two. If he ever finishes that book."

"Damn it, Evans is nothing but a publishing machine. I don't think he ever gave an exciting lecture in his life." Bongiovanni's eyes flashed with anger. "He can talk for a whole term about Chaucer without his students ever suspecting that it's poetry."

"Come, come, Tony, I think you're exaggerating. He's a scholar, not a critic, and I'm sure you wouldn't underestimate scholarship. Besides, straight criticism is more applicable to your twentieth century than it is to the Middle Ages." He turned away from Bongiovannni, who closed his mouth determinedly, as if to keep from saying more. "Anyone else? How about you, Gordon? What does our eminent Victorian

4

think about it?" Jackson took a foulard handkerchief from the breast pocket of his carefully pressed suit and blew his nose.

Gordon Thomas was the only member of the department whose appearance Jackson did not put to shame. He was fifty-five, small, still trim and neatly built, wearing the crew-cut of his undergraduate years, now gone gray, and dressed in a tweed jacket whose rumpled look and patched elbows failed signally to conceal its expensive origins and the casual elegance that still clung to it. Over the years he had acquired a quiet renown as a Victorian textual scholar. Stratton had great respect for his learning, although he had little emotional feeling for Thomas's area of specialization.

Before speaking, Thomas knocked out his pipe against a metal wastebasket that he had hauled up against his feet. Watching him, Stratton thought with amusement that Thomas was the only man present who looked like the popular stereotype of a college professor; the rest of them resembled small businessmen or doctors or lawyers, in their various stages of dishevelment. Fackler, indeed, looked like a grocer in his Sunday second-best.

"I find it difficult to state my own views, Mr. Chairman. I do appreciate your wish to maintain, or even raise, the scholarly standards of the department, at the same time that I am aware that Wilton has been famous for generations as one of the small universities with the most distinguished traditions of teaching in the country. I'm not suggesting that scholarship and teaching are antithetical, but I imagine that each of us must lean toward one ideal or the other, and I suppose I have been around Wilton so long that I incline toward its traditional goals. I think that Professor Bongiovanni has stated my own position. Evans is certainly a prolific publisher, but I'm a little worried about his teaching, and I should greatly prefer to promote either Swenson or Rosenbloom."

"I thought I had made it clear," said Jackson evenly, "that it is not a case of whether Swenson or Rosenbloom could be promoted this year. What I am asking is whether you favor promoting Evans."

Thomas deliberately put the pipe that he had cleaned into his breast pocket. "If I must speak to that, I shall have to say that I don't. I should think that my own career would indicate that I'm not opposed to scholarship, but I doubt that it is very important without a strong critical sense to back it up. Sorry, but I couldn't support Evans's promotion."

"Very well." Jackson's mouth was a hard line. "Roy, you're the only one who hasn't spoken. Have you anything to say? After all, as our specialist in Old English, you're closer to Evans's field than anyone else except me. What do you think?" His voice indicated clear confidence of support.

Roy Moorhead was a great bear of a man, heavily and lumpily built, towering by nearly a head over the rest of the department. He heaved himself together, and the steel chair on which he sat groaned with the gathering of his component parts. "Mr. Chairman, I'm aware that most of my colleagues think of me as a recluse, but perhaps I'm more interested in the department than they are aware of." Next to Fackler, he was the senior professor, and between the fat little Shakespearean and this ursine hulk of a linguist there was a long-standing friendship. For years, however, Moorhead had taken as small a part in the affairs of the department as possible, preferring work on an edition of Anglo-Saxon poetry and the tuition of his own small classes to the committee work that took up so much of the time of the others.

"You're a young man, and I have another eight years before I retire. I can't see any reason that we can't handle the older literature between us. Like the others who have spoken, I think it would be a mistake to promote Evans to a tenure position." He shifted his weight again as if to indicate that he had finished, and the sound of twisting steel once more agonized the room. But he was not through.

"And one other thing, Mr. Chairman. I am not the last to

be consulted. I don't think that Professor Benson has had a chance to speak yet."

"Yes. Sorry. Anything to add, Mr. Ben—er, Harry?"

Harry Benson, youngest of the associate professors, in his first year of tenure rank, squirmed uncomfortably. "This is my first meeting on promotions, so I think I had better pass."

Jackson had been drumming his fingers against the desk. After Benson had finished, Jackson looked fixedly at the floor between his well-polished shoes. "Frankly, I am surprised at your attitude, gentlemen. I had hoped for more support from you in my first year at Wilton. It seems to me that we have a chance to improve what has become a somewhat moribund institution, and I had hoped for more co-operation. It is disappointing." His coarsely handsome face was flushed. "Nonetheless, it is time for you to express your collective opinion by a vote, however much a formality it may be. Will all those who would like to promote Evans please put up their hands?"

Gordon Thomas intervened silkily as soon as the last word was out of Jackson's mouth. "Sorry, Mr. Chairman, but it has always been customary for this kind of vote to be taken by ballot."

"Very well, although I should think you would want to stand openly by your opinions. As the Cerberus of tradition, Professor Thomas, would you like to distribute slips of paper and collect them when the others have voted?"

Thomas stuck his empty pipe back into his mouth, and Stratton wondered whether he did so to choke back a response to Jackson's taunting words. When he had finished picking up the folded papers, he put them in a pile on the desk where Jackson sat.

"Would you count them, please, Professor Thomas?"

With maddening deliberation, Thomas opened the papers and then put them face down on the desk. "Mr. Chairman, there is one affirmative vote for the promotion of Professor Evans and five negative." He went back to his chair.

When he was attempting to control his temper, a scar at the corner of Jackson's mouth went white with effort. Now it was pale, but his voice was controlled. "Well, gentlemen, we seem to have reached an impasse. As chairman of the department, I shall still forward a recommendation for the promotion of Professor Evans. I am, as you know, required to indicate the consensus of the other tenure members of the department. That will not be difficult."

He riffled through the papers in his hand. "There are a few other brief matters. I don't want to take up your time, so I shall announce them without expecting any discussion. First of all, it is my opinion that the amount of publication in the department requires a good deal of beefing up. After due consideration, I have decided that this can be best accomplished by my not recommending to the president any salary raises for next year or any promotions from associate to full professor. I don't want you to think that this will work to your ultimate disadvantage, for next year I shall recommend raises and promotions for those whose records this year merit reward."

There was general shuffling of feet and moving of chairs. Under cover of the noise, Tony Bongiovanni whispered to Stratton, "Due consideration, my ass. He decided that just now when we didn't vote for Evans."

Jackson held up his hand for silence. "The second thing is that, as you know, the Modern Language Association will be holding its national meeting in Devonport for the first time this year. Since this is the first occasion in years that it has been held anywhere but New York, Chicago, or Denver, and since Devonport is in our own state, I think we're morally obliged to support it wholeheartedly. I expect all tenure members of the department to attend this year, without fail.

"Another thing I want to remind you of is that there has been a lot of mugging and petty thievery going on around the campus. Last night three typewriters were stolen from the offices of the psychology department. Be careful to lock your office doors when you're out. And, if you go away for part of the Christmas vacation, I'd suggest you remove any valuables from your offices. There hasn't been any trouble in this building yet, but we must be careful.

"I think that concludes our official business until after Christmas, except that I'd like to see the full professors briefly. I'd like to remind all of you that June and I are expecting you for drinks tomorrow, and I hope all of you and your wives will come. Even though I shall be seeing you then, I want to take this opportunity to wish you a merry Christmas and a happy vacation. I'll see you tomorrow and then at M.L.A."

CHAPTER TWO

"Some day I'll kill that bastard." Tony blew out the smoke from the cigarette he had lighted as they left the meeting together. "Slowly, if possible. Maybe poison. Lots of writing and groaning. Clutching at the belly and eyeballs rolling to merciless heaven. Aaaaaah!" He made a horrible face with his tongue lolling out, seized his throat in one hand, and staggered backward to lean against the wall. "I should have gone in for the Renaissance. Webster, probably, not Shakespeare." He grinned, the worst of his temper evaporated. "With all this talent, what am I doing teaching twentieth-century literature?"

"With that histrionic ability, you ought to try the stage."

Tony's face took on a look of black despair, in one of his characteristically sudden changes of emotion. "I might as well, for all the good it's doing me sticking around here. No promotions this year. Same old story." He looked apologetically at Stratton. "Sorry, Bill. I was thinking only of myself. After seven years as associates, I thought this was the time we'd both make it. Damn it, I need the money, with the kids growing so fast."

"I wish you had made it, even if I hadn't." Between them, unspoken and unresented, was the knowledge that Bill and Carrie had plenty of money of their own and no children, while Tony and Laura barely managed to scrape along as they reared two boys and a girl. "But Laura and the kids are worth hanging on for. Next year we'll make it for sure."

"What a lot of gall that guy has, demanding that we all go to M.L.A. this year. He hasn't any right to, and he knows it, but he also knows that he can swing us into line with all this crap about promotions and raises next year." Tony snorted. "I had already planned on going; otherwise, I might just thumb my nose at him. I think he's secretly scared of us."

"I doubt it. He's pretty thick-skinned. That's why the president got him here as a hatchet man."

"Nonetheless, I think he's scared of us. If for no other reason, he's supposed to be putting the needle into the department to promote scholarship, and, God knows, he's no scholar himself. He knows that the rest of us are a hell of a lot better than he is, and he's afraid that we'll find it out. Hell, we knew that all the time."

"Give him a chance. Maybe he'll simmer down after a while. If he could learn a little tact, he might even turn out to be a decent administrator. But, you know, the one I feel sorry for is Benson. What an introduction to the exalted rank of associate professor. He looked considerably disillusioned, and I noticed that he took off out of here as fast as he could go after the meeting."

"Bill, do you think he was the one who voted for Evans? I know damned well I didn't, and I'm morally convinced you didn't. Did you?"

"You know better than that."

"Then who did? Everybody spoke against it, even Fackler and Moorhead. Everybody except Benson. I'll bet that one vote was his."

Bill considered. "I doubt it. It wouldn't fit with anything I know about him. He's timid, but when he gets on a moral point, he's stubborn as an ox."

"He high-tailed it out of here, as if he didn't want to talk to anyone. But I agree that it doesn't seem much like him.

Now what do you suppose Pete the Piranha wanted to see the fulls about? He's got Gordon Thomas's back up already, and that little speech of E. W.'s about brilliance came as close as it could to telling Jackson to go to hell. Whatever he's got up his sleeve, this is the wrong time to get them to co-operate. Maybe he can count on old Roy Moorhead, but I doubt it. He doesn't like being joggled out of his rut."

The door of Jackson's office opened and Moorhead shambled out, followed by Fackler, looking half his size. Absently they said good night and went toward the elevator.

"They don't look too elated. Oh, the full professor's lot is not a happy one." In Tony's present mood, it was useless to try to cheer him up for long. "On that consoling note, I'd better go home. Have you time for a drink? Carrie would love to see you."

Tony put his hand on Bill's shoulder. "I'd better not, but thanks for the try. I ought to take this news back now. Not that it will cheer Laura up, any more than it did me."

"Why don't you wait? Get a skinful tonight. You can tell her tomorrow."

"Maybe you're right. Sorry I can't come for the drink. Love to Carrie."

"We'll see you tomorrow night, anyway. That ought to be a jolly wake at the Jacksons'. It'll be interesting to see how he carries it off."

Thank God, thought Bill as he got into his car, for having a little money. It helped cushion the shocks. The difference of a thousand or two a year that the promotion represented would make Tony and Laura's life a lot easier, but it didn't matter much to him and Carrie. Not that they wouldn't gladly trade their money for having children. Particularly Carrie. But in the twelve years of their marriage, she had never become despondent about being childless, at least not in his presence.

Their house, a beautiful but somewhat dilapidated eighteenth-century former farm, was the last on a dead-end street. He turned into the driveway. He knew he should shovel the rest of the snow off it and make room to park one car and still allow the other to get in and out of the garage. But he also knew that March would probably find the same two banks higher, dirtier, and eroded, but unmoved.

On the front steps, waiting for his whistle, sat a yellow Labrador puppy, her oversized tail switching back and forth, beating a bulge into the wire of the screen door as she whimpered with excitement. She kept her rump and front feet quiet, but she was leaning so far over the top step that she seemed to be breaking the law of gravity. If he waited until March, he would not have to put up the storm door.

"All right," he called. "Come on, Emma. Come on, girl." Before he had finished, she was halfway to him; then she put her head on her paws, her rump in the air, and barked in delirium before she dived headfirst into the snow.

She ran around him in manic circles as he started for the door, and when he opened it, she streaked into the hall to strop her muzzle on the carpet. "Emma, you dizzy bitch, why didn't I at least pick out a sane puppy while I was at it?" He bent and tickled her white stomach as she rolled over at his approach.

Carrie was sifting flour at the counter in the kitchen. "Hello, there," she called without turning around. Bill came up behind her, lifted her hair and bit her gently on the nape of the neck before sliding his arms beneath hers.

"Unhand me, you sex maniac," she said lazily, arching her neck and rubbing her head against his chin, still holding the cup of flour. Then she set it down deliberately and turned around to insert one hand between the buttons of his shirt, scratching his stomach with a floury forefinger. "I'm a virtuous woman." Standing on tiptoe, she chewed contemplatively at the lobe of his ear.

"I know. I just thought I'd try to convert you. Sorry it

13

didn't work." He bent over further, so that she would not have to stretch.

"How much time do we have before dinner?" he murmured.

"Not that long, you beast. An hour at most. Golly, I'm glad you don't wear undershirts." She scratched his stomach again.

"That's long enough."

"Not if you want this soufflé. But if you don't, I'm not very hungry anyway."

"Mmmm. Chocolate or Grand Marnier?"

"What's the matter? Are you a man or a soufflé hound? Lemon."

"If we did now, we wouldn't have any soufflé. But if we had the soufflé, we'd still have the whole evening ahead. I vote for soufflé."

"How about now and this evening too?"

"Too much for me. I'm a very ancient man, and I've had a bad day."

"Chicken." She returned to her nibbling.

"I thought you said you weren't hungry. How about taking it easy on that ear?" He pulled gently away.

"Chicken."

"A soufflé won't keep, and this will. It'll be better for waiting. Sweet, reluctant, amorous delay."

"Dr. Johnson again?"

"I just said easy on the ear, I didn't say quit. Milton. And don't get flour all over my best blue suit. I don't want my students to think I've taken up with the kitchen help."

"Come here and kiss me, sweet and twenty. In delay there lies no plenty. Shakespeare. Now, for God's sake, let's quit while I'm ahead. At least, I think it's Shakespeare."

"I didn't think you wanted to quit."

"I mean this quotation routine. Besides, I can't remember

14

any more clean ones. You've corrupted me." She kissed him on the chin and turned back to the mixing bowl. "Fix us a drink, won't you, honey?"

"Now, of course, if you'd promise me a soufflé tomorrow night . . ."

"Too late now. I give up. I thought it was supposed to be women who couldn't make up their minds. Anyway, we're going out tomorrow, and you know it."

"God, I love you, Carrie."

She turned and stuck out her tongue affectionately. "Scotch for me, please."

"Okay, wanton. Also Shakespeare, and just about as accurate as yours. I also love soufflé."

"You and all that erudition. I should have married a truck driver."

"I don't think you would have liked it. I hear they're all queer. Anyway, I'm glad I grabbed a cook while I was getting married."

"Okay, if I'm cook, you have to be houseman. Would you mind cleaning up that mess Emma made on the hall floor."

It was not until after the soufflé was eaten and the dishes stacked in the washer that Carrie mentioned the subject again. "Bad day, you say? Want to tell me?"

"Sure, or I wouldn't have brought it up." He patted the rhythmically heaving belly of Emma, who lay on her back between them on the sofa, snoring gently, her feet in the air. "I don't think this dog approves of conjugal necking. She's a prude. Anyway, I draw the line at her sleeping with us. It's that silly ass Jackson, of course. He thinks that he's livening up the department and giving it more of what he calls national exposure. But all he's doing is ruining what was a hell of a good outfit. Sometimes Gordon Thomas is too conservative, but I suspect that he's right about Jackson." He sketched for her an outline of the afternoon's meeting.

"Honey, do you mind too much about the promotion?"

He sighed. "Sure, I mind, but I think it's pride more than anything else that bothers me. It's Tony who worries me most. He's so hot-tempered that I'm afraid he might do something silly like resigning. He hates Jackson's guts, and he refuses not to show it."

"Do we have to go to the Jacksons' tomorrow night?"

"I think we ought to." He grinned sardonically. "Since we shot him down in flames at the meeting, we owe it to him to show that we don't hold a grudge. Do you mind going?"

"I can get along all right with him if he doesn't give me the lowered eyelids and the heavy breathing part. He thinks he's God's gift to women, but I can ignore that. What I really can't bear is that damned wife of his. The eyeshadow and the junk jewelry and the blonde hair. I'd like to pull it some time and see if it's a wig. If it isn't, I'd just enjoy the pulling. June looks like a tart trying to go respectable."

"You know you would hate her more if she wore tweeds and flat heels."

"Oh, I know. I suppose I'm just being bitchy. Maybe I'm jealous because she has two kids." She gloomed. "Sorry, I didn't mean that. But she is strictly Sauk Center, and she tries to be so-o-o sophisticated. She behaves as if she had been reading it all up in *The New Yorker* in the back issues before 1930."

"Come on, Carrie, don't be such a snob. She isn't as bad as all that."

"Worse. Ever since she found out that I belonged to the Colony, she's been acting as if we were soul mates. She's the snob, not me. And she treats Laura like dirt. Laura's worth a dozen of her. Twelve dozen. Maybe even a gross. Sometimes I wish I had the nerve to snub her the way Barbara Thomas does."

"Yeah, I can just see you being all prim and New England."

"I'm from Boston, and don't you forget it. I can be just as New England as Barbara if I put my mind to it."

"Maybe, but I don't think you'd be very good at snubbing anyone. Not even June Jackson."

"I'll give you ten to one that Barbara doesn't show tomorrow at the party. And five to one that ten years from now, she still won't have been in the Jackson house. Maybe I can't look as if I had smelled something unspeakable when I see June, the way that Barbara does, but I'll be darned if I don't sometimes envy the way she avoids her."

"It's damnably tough on Gordon when his wife refuses to see the wife of his own chairman."

"Between them, Barbara and Grace Moorhead have kept June out of the Thursday Garden Club. And she is dying to get into it. Maybe she thinks I would support her, and that's why she's always making up to me."

"Nice women like Barbara and Grace can certainly be bitches when they put their minds to it. The worst of it is that I'll bet they don't even realize how cruel they are."

"They aren't bitches. Grace is kind as anything, and Barbara is just a little stuffy. That's all. I think I'd be stuffy, too, if I were married to Gordon. He's good-hearted, but he's not exactly a ball of fire conversationally. All he ever talks about to me is his birds or his scholarship, and I don't even know anything about either of them."

"He's a wonderful husband to Barbara. He adores her." He frowned. "Let's quit talking about them. Why don't we ask Tony and Laura to go with us tomorrow? It might be easier for them, and I can whack Tony over the head if he gets out of hand. Peter treats him as badly as June treats Laura."

"I'll call Laura tomorrow morning and ask if we can come

17

to see the kids before the party. Then we can give them a lift, and they won't think anything about it."

Bill picked up Emma and set her down on the floor. "Quit coming between a man and his wife, you beast. It's your bedtime, anyway." He leaned toward Carrie and kissed her. "That's why I love you. That and the fact that you can cook. The soufflé was fine. How about the rest of our plans?"

CHAPTER THREE

As it turned out, Bill need not have worried about Tony. He was washed and burnished, and if he was a little subdued, that fact might owe something to his monumental hangover that morning. "I told Laura about it last night," he said as their wives preceded them up the steps of the Jacksons' big new house. "God, she's great. You'd have thought it was nothing more serious than my losing a button off a shirt."

A Negro man in a white coat, known to most of Cartersville from the parties for which he was hired, opened the door to them. "Old Petie-baby must be absconding with the money from our raises," Tony whispered.

In the front hall stood June Jackson, tall and resplendent in a long white dress with a gold stole over her shoulders. Her suspiciously blonde hair was pulled back into a long tail that she had twitched over her shoulder, so that its end hung almost into the plunging v-neck that stopped short of her navel but partly revealed her somewhat matronly breasts. "Now that's what I call national exposure," Bill murmured to Tony. "Maybe international."

"Carrie, darling, how wonderful to see you," June leaned forward to give her a peck on the cheek.

"Hello. Nice of you to ask us," Carrie answered calmly. "You do know Laura Bongiovanni, don't you?"

"Yes, indeed," said June, putting out her hand, "but I've been longing to know you better. How nice to see you, Mrs.

Bongiovanni. It is kind of you to come." Before Laura could answer, June was looking over her shoulder. "Hello, there, Bill. And Mr. Bongiovanni." Laura was left standing, her naturally pink cheeks coloring deeply with embarrassment. She was so seldom totally at ease except when with her family or a close friend like Carrie, who now took her arm and led her to the bedroom where the guests were leaving their coats.

Bill looked curiously around the room beyond. The party was in full progress. All the other senior members of the department were there, but there were no instructors or assistant professors. Rank has its duties as well as its privileges, he thought. Most of the other guests were members of the country club that the Jacksons had recently joined.

Peter Jackson was playing the heavy host in a jacket of Thai silk and pale yellow trousers. His eyes were already slightly bleary. "Hello, Bill, old man," he called. "Come have a drink." In his hand was his habitual glass of Campari and soda, the only drink Bill could remember seeing him take. "Have some booze, Tony." He waved expansively to the table where the bartender stood. "What'll it be?"

"Thanks, I'll wait until Laura gets here," Tony said. "I'm not sure what she'll want. Quite a place you have here."

"Glad you like it. I think we were lucky to find it. The Todhills had lived here only a year before he died, so we got an almost new house for a lot less than it would have cost to build it. June's done a great job of decorating, I think. She was afraid that it was an unlucky house because of Todhill's death, but she's got over that. Women, you know!" He smiled in masculine conspiracy. "Take a look around."

Tony moved away, to wait for Laura. "It's good to see everybody from the department here," said Jackson. "I like to feel that we're all one family, and this seems like a good way to get over any hard feelings there might have been yesterday. Frankly, Bill, Tony is a bit of a sorehead sometimes, and I was afraid he might not come. I knew that I could count on

20

you and Gordon, but some of the rest of the department—"
He smiled deprecatingly. "Well, they are a little rough socially. Not that it's their fault. And academia is a great le-
veler."

"Yes, I suppose it does bring together a lot of different
types." Bill turned. "There's Carrie. Excuse me, won't you?"

He and Carrie took their drinks to talk with the Moorheads, who were standing alone. Roy towered above the other
guests, mildly surveying them as if watching pygmies. Mrs.
Moorhead wore a sensible hat, a purple tweed suit that had
trouble making ends meet over her ample torso, and a fox fur
that bit its tail in a perpetual circle around her neck. She was
the only one of the departmental wives who came of "old
Cartersville" society, for her father had been president of
Wilton when she met Roy Moorhead while he was still a
young instructor.

It was Mrs. Moorhead's kindly custom to try to make new
faculty wives feel at home when they first came to Cartersville by calling on them (she was, Carrie had said, surely the
last remaining woman in Cartersville who left cards when she
called) and by inviting them to teas. No one was more assidu-
ous in presenting blankets and christening mugs to the new
babies of her husband's colleagues. Carrie and Laura were
devoted to her for her absent-minded kindness, but her attempts to welcome June Jackson had been unsuccessful, for
June was amused at her dowdiness and bored with her stories
of the old days at Wilton. Rather than take offense at being
rebuffed, Grace Moorhead had remarked to her husband that
it was probably presumptuous of her to attempt to make the
wife of the chairman feel at home; it was a new experience,
since Peter Jackson had been the first chairman brought in
from outside rather than being chosen from the English department. "They probably do things differently at Columbia," Mrs. Moorhead had mused.

"Grace, darling," said Moorhead, "I know that you are

dying to look around the house. Why don't you get Mrs. Stratton to go with you?" She and Carrie moved away. The house was built in a hollow square, and from the long window of the living room, they could look out on the snow of the flood-lit courtyard formed by the projecting wings. The Jacksons had moved into the house the previous June and spent the summer getting it into readiness. Most of the department had never been invited there before, and the cocktail party was in part a housewarming.

Moorhead turned awkwardly to Bill when they were alone. "I hope your wife doesn't mind, but I did want to talk to you a moment. I'm sorry about what happened at the meeting yesterday, about Jackson's saying there would be no promotions, I mean. I have been considering whether I might not ask E. W. to go to the president with me and tell him about the whole thing. I feel awkward saying this in Jackson's own house, but I think he made a bad mistake, and I'd like to remedy it somehow. I'm not very good at this kind of thing, but I am sure the president would listen to us. You've deserved promotion for a long time. I don't want you to wait another year."

"Thank you," said Bill, "but I doubt that it would be worth the bad feeling in the department if someone went over Jackson's head to the president. He put Jackson in as chairman, and I think he'll have to back him at least the first year. Even if he is wrong, the president would have to do that much for him."

"You know, Stratton, I realize that everyone else thinks I don't take much part in the department, but this is something that I feel strongly about. I probably shouldn't say it, but there are times when I think that Jackson is extremely silly, even stupid—" He stopped and flushed. Standing at his elbow was Peter Jackson.

It was impossible to know how much Jackson had overheard. He had had plenty of opportunity, but there was no

22

sign of anger in his face. Perhaps the Campari had dulled his nerves and hearing. Certainly he was beginning to look distinctly drunk. "Come and see the conservatory," he said. "Some of the other people from the department have to leave soon, and I wanted to show it to you. I don't know how interested either of you is in gardening and growing things, but I'm rather proud of it, so maybe you won't be bored."

Dutifully, if not enthusiastically, Bill and Moorhead followed him through the dining room into a greenhouse, perhaps ten feet square. Not quite what a Victorian novelist would have meant by a conservatory, Bill thought, but it was like Jackson to overstate his own possessions.

Carrie was already there, talking to Tony and Mrs. Moorhead. Harry Benson, looking young and unsure of himself, was with E. W. Fackler and his wife. E. W. was more than usually ill-groomed. One of the buttons of his newest—or, to be more accurate, his least old—serge suit was mismatched with the wrong buttonhole, forcing the shoulder of the suit up under his left ear. Bill smiled at the contrast between Fackler's unkempt appearance and the well-brushed but casual tweed elegance of Gordon Thomas, who was inspecting some late-blooming chrysanthemums in the company of a couple whom Bill vaguely remembered as a local doctor and his wife. All the senior members of the department were there. And all their wives except Barbara Thomas, who had not come, precisely as Carrie had predicted. And Laura Bongiovanni wasn't there, either.

The contents of the greenhouse were disappointing to Bill, who knew little about flowers. There were several earth-filled flats with seedlings just beginning to sprout, the chrysanthemums, and a colorful bank of tuberous begonias. All right if you happened to like that sort of thing, but not worth bludgeoning guests into visiting.

Jackson walked around the table in the center of the cement floor and faced his guests. "This part of the house is all that we added when we moved in," he began. Belatedly Bill realized that Jackson had probably been bringing guests into the greenhouse throughout the evening, and that what he was about to say was a little canned speech that he had already delivered several times. With the ease that comes of practice, Jackson explained and demonstrated the device that automatically raised and lowered the skylight to regulate spring and autumn temperatures, the built-in sprinkler for the seedling flats, the humidifier, and the thermostat to keep the winter temperatures constant within two degrees.

Although he was no gardener himself, Bill rather admired Jackson's passion for flowers, since he had always had a romantic notion about the essential humanity of persons who devoted themselves to the culture and care of growing things. But it was hard to maintain much interest in what became more and more openly a demonstration of Jackson's complacency. The women were listening carefully, but Tony's eyes were glazing over, Gordon Thomas was cleaning his pipe in an abstracted manner, Fackler was squinting his pale blue eyes as if thinking about an essay on *Troilus and Cressida,* and Benson and Moorhead were staring solemnly at their feet.

The doctor, whose name Bill had forgotten, had turned away from Jackson and was looking absently at the shelf behind the begonias, on which were ranged fertilizers, plant foods, hormone growth promoters, and empty pots.

"Well, there it is," said Jackson. "It's only a modest conservatory, but I'm proud of it. I'd have liked something bigger, but with building prices at this unrealistic level——" He allowed his guests to finish the sentence for themselves.

In the pause, the others began to move toward the door, making polite remarks. "Peter!" the voice of the doctor cut through the general murmur. "What are you doing with this kind of stuff in the house?" The rest of the party paused in their exits.

"What do you mean?"

"These weed killers. They're dangerous."

"Not if you can read the label and follow simple instructions. I've been using them for years. I had to get these last summer. Mrs. Todhill had let the lawn and courtyard go completely after her husband got sick. The whole place looked like hell."

"I don't mean dangerous for you. Around the children, I mean."

"Not here. I don't let the children in here alone. I don't want them to ruin things."

"There are plenty of non-toxic weed-killers. You ought to heave these out. Even if you keep the children out of them, they're bad for pets when you use them on the lawn."

"We don't have any pets, and if that damned brute of a dog next door comes over here to dig up my bulbs, I don't care if he gets a bellyache."

"Sorry to be persistent, but if you must keep them, at least get them out of the house. There's enough arsenic here to wipe out Cartersville. Haven't you got a good high shelf in the garage?"

"Is that your idea of safety?" Jackson was obviously irritated at being told how to handle his own lawn and greenhouse. "To put them out where any Tom, Dick, or Harry could get hold of them to feed to a rich aunt? Don't worry, Jerry, I'll take care of them, so you don't need to fret."

"Okay, it's your funeral, not mine. Sorry if I seemed to be interfering." The doctor shrugged and went out with the other guests. Jackson, who had been holding his full old-fashioned glass of Campari as he talked, drained his drink quickly and went back to the bar.

It was not only Jackson who had been drinking heavily. Several of the guests whom Bill had not met were beginning to have that un-co-ordinated look around the mouth that indicated too much alcohol. A full-blown middle-aged woman with red hair was sitting at the piano, ruminatively playing show tunes from the thirties. To Bill's amazement, Fackler went up and leaned over the music, and in a surprisingly good baritone sang "Night and Day" to her accompaniment. When they were finished, the woman reached up and patted his cheek before she took a drink from a glass standing on the piano. Somehow, Bill couldn't imagine that many women except E. W.'s wife had ever touched those scholarly pink jowls. "Do you know 'Begin the Beguine'?" asked the redhead and began playing it. Fackler shook his head but hummed to the music, the left shoulder of his suit still riding up under his ear.

Some distance away Mrs. Fackler sat alone, a motherly figure in a straight armchair, nodding her head in time to the piano, smiling with obvious pride in her husband. Bill went to join her.

As they talked, Peter Jackson passed with Laura Bongiovanni in tow, saying, "Come and see the conservatory, if you haven't. I was just showing your husband. It's a modest affair, really, but I'm rather proud of it."

Poor Laura. She would be bored with Jackson's recitation, but she was too shy and polite to resist. Bill felt an almost big-brotherly affection for her. In the midst of the overdressed country club set, she wore a little blue hat and white gloves, looking for all the world as if she were still an innocently pretty twenty-year-old setting out for church in the little Wisconsin farm town where she had been born. In their separate ways, both she and Tony, a second-generation Italian New Yorker, seemed a little *outré* in this New England town, but it was part of why he liked them so much. No pretense. "Yes, I agree," he said politely to Mrs. Fackler, "the popular music today all sounds alike to me, too." He wondered where Carrie was.

"Bill." At the touch on his shoulder, he turned around to see Harry Benson with an absurdly blanched face. "Bill, do you know where the bathroom is?"

Stratton excused himself from Mrs. Fackler. "I'll show you." The measure of Benson's need was his having said "Bill," for usually he was too shy to call his seniors by given name. "Feeling a little rocky?"

"Maybe I've had too much to drink." Surely the understatement of the year.

As they went around the corner, Bill pointed. "There it is." Benson started to thank him, then clapped his hand over his mouth and raced toward the door of the bathroom.

At thirty-two Benson was still so boyish that it was easy to believe that this was the first time he had ever had too much to drink. But this wasn't a normal party. Fackler singing at the piano, Moorhead confessing his dislike of Jackson, Tony brushed and combed in his best suit, now Benson being sick in the bathroom. Probably none of these unusual phenomena would have occurred if it had not been for the meeting yesterday. If Jackson's party turned into a shambles, it was his own fault. Merry damned Christmas!

As he headed back to the living room, a woman came up to him. She was about thirty-five, pretty in an overpainted fashion, with a figure that probably owed its contours to the wizardry of modern foundation garments, if he could judge by the improbably tilted breasts that pointed up at his chest. "Professor Stratton?"

"Yes." He smiled. "But I don't know you, do I?"

"No, you don't. Yet. I'm Julia Lockwood. And I want to ask you a favor. A big favor. Do you mind?"

"I'm afraid I can't answer that one until you tell me what the favor is."

"Could I possibly come to your lectures on Samuel Johnson next term at the college? I just love Samuel Johnson, and I want so much to hear what you have to say about him. Is it against the rules?"

"I don't see any reason you can't come if there are vacant

seats. There's no rule against it, but I haven't anything startling to say about Johnson. You might be disappointed."

"Oh, I know I wouldn't. I've heard what a splendid lecturer you are, and I'd just love to come. I love Johnson and the whole nineteenth century."

Bill passed a hand over his mouth to hide another smile, of a different kind. "I'm afraid I don't get to the nineteenth century. Only Johnson and the other eighteenth-century writers."

She touched her cheek in dismay. "I meant eighteenth century, of course. You must think I'm an awful fool." With her free hand she touched his sleeve. "But I did know, I really did. Thank you so much, Professor Stratton, I do so appreciate this." She paused. "I should say 'Professor,' shouldn't I? Or should it be 'Doctor'? It's so confusing."

"Most people just say 'Mister.'" Over her head he saw Carrie and Laura. If he could escape, he would join them. "Would you excuse me? I must see my wife. I look forward to seeing you at the lecture."

Her hand tightened for a moment on his sleeve. "There is just one other tiny thing I'd like to ask, if I may. I wouldn't want to take up your time, but perhaps occasionally you would have a cup of coffee with me after the lecture, to explain just what you meant. Dutch treat, of course, because it would be silly for you to pay for my coffee when you are doing me such a big favor. Would it be possible?"

"Certainly." He smiled and made his way to Carrie. Possible, but damned improbable.

Carrie smiled impishly. "Boy, what a heart breaker you are. Old Sexy. How do you like the glamorous Mrs. Lockwood?"

Before he could answer, Laura interrupted. "Would it be a nuisance if we went home now? I'm worried about the babysitter."

"Of course not," said Carrie. "Where's Tony?"

"I'll go find him. Sorry, Bill," she said in apology. Before she turned away, she gave Carrie an inquiring look.

"How did you get on with Mrs. Lockwood?" Carrie continued.

"What's the matter? Are you a jealous wife?"

"Sure. Green. She's quite a dish, and she certainly wanted to know all about you. Unfortunately, she didn't know I was your wife. She asked who you were, what you did, and then what you lectured on. So I told her and explained who Samuel Johnson was. But I didn't bother straightening out her confusion about me. She thought I was Harry Benson's wife."

"I wish he had one. At least, he's got a fiancée now. I doubt that the lovely Julia would be quite right for him. Anyway, I'd better hang on to her myself. If I don't come home after lecture some day, don't send for the police." He looked rueful. "So much for academic vanity. I thought that she really knew something about me." He turned to look for Tony and Laura. "I'll be darned, there's Harry now."

"Why will you be darned, darling?" She turned to see Benson coming out of Jackson's study. "What's funny?"

"Just ten or fifteen minutes ago I left him being sick in the bathroom. He looked like death, but now his color is all back, and he looks mad as hell. Quite a recovery."

Jackson followed Benson out of the study and closed the door. On his face Bill could see a flaming red patch surrounded by a border of white. "Honey," he said slowly, "if that were anyone in the world but Harry Benson, I'd say that he had just slugged Peter. It looks as if Peter got a good one on the side of the face. Maybe Laura's right. We'd better get out of here before the party really gets rough."

In a moment the Bongiovannis appeared. Gordon Thomas was already making his farewells as they went up to say goodnight to June. "Thank you so much, Mrs. Jackson. Barbara asked me to be sure to say how sorry she was that she wasn't feeling well."

"I hope she's feeling better when you get back." June smiled icily as Gordon went out. Probably she had not expected Barbara Thomas at the party any more than Carrie had.

"Where's Peter?" Bill asked. "We wanted to thank him, too."

"I think he just went to the powder room." She winked roguishly at Bill. "I'll tell him for you."

Bill walked with Laura to the car as Tony and Carrie preceded them. "You're a lucky girl; you must have had the short tour of the greenhouse. He kept the rest of there for half an hour, explaining all those damned gadgets."

"Mmm," she said briefly. "Can you and Carrie stay for a bite with us?"

"Thanks, but I promised I'd take her to a restaurant tonight. Why don't you come, too?"

"Sorry, but we have to let the baby-sitter go."

It was a quiet ride back to the Bongiovannis' house. "Quite a binge," Bill ventured once, but there was no response.

A bit later Carrie made an attempt. "I told you, Bill, that I'd be willing to bet that Barbara Thomas wouldn't be there."

"Right, as usual," was all he answered.

After they had dropped the Bongiovannis, he asked, "Is Laura all right?"

"I think so," Carrie answered noncommittally.

"She seemed unusually quiet tonight. I couldn't get much out of her. I hope she isn't pregnant again."

"I doubt it."

"She didn't seem to have a good time. I don't blame her if the Jacksons are too much for her. That meeting yesterday must have been a real blow, even if she passed it off for Tony's sake."

"Yes." Carrie seemed unwilling to talk, and he dropped the subject.

Not until they got home after a protracted dinner did she

mention Laura again. They were sitting on the sofa listening to Mozart's "Dissonant Quartet." Usually Carrie said nothing when listening to music and was apt to respond absently if Bill spoke, but now she broke their silence. "Honey?"

"Hmm?"

"I know what was bothering Laura tonight."

Bill said nothing. She would continue when she wanted to.

"It was Peter Jackson."

"Yes?"

"He made a pass at her."

"Oh, Lord, that's just what we need now. Did she tell you?"

"No, I'm pretty sure she doesn't realize that I know. While you were talking to Mrs. Lockwood—"

"While she was talking to me," Bill said firmly.

"All right, while she was talking to you, I thought it would be tactful if I got out of her neighborhood, so I went to the dining room to get something to eat. The door to the damned greenhouse was open a little, and I heard Peter talking. I'm afraid I couldn't resist looking around the door to see who was cornered. Peter had his arms around Laura and was trying to kiss her."

"How did she take it?"

"She was furious. Her face was red, and she had turned her head away from him. She didn't say anything, but she had her hands on his chest, pushing him away. Finally she stamped on his toes with the heel of her shoe and he let her go. She came out the door so fast she didn't see me. She was standing fuming in the living room, so I went back in there and talked to her. But she tried to act as if nothing were wrong."

"Dear Lord! Do you suppose Tony knows?"

"She wouldn't tell him. There's nothing to be done about it now, and she always tries to keep him from worrying. He would wipe up the floor with Peter if he knew. Chairman or no chairman."

"I hope he doesn't find out. He's hot-tempered, and he's jealous of Laura."

"He won't find out if she doesn't tell him. Unless—" She considered. "The only thing is that I noticed June was looking curiously at Laura when I joined her. June is so jealous of Peter that she keeps her big eyes open, and she may have guessed what happened. She wouldn't tell Tony, but I'll bet she didn't lose any time telling Peter. Boy, what a marriage that must be."

"Peter always antagonizes people, but I honestly don't know whether he does it deliberately, or whether he's just a natural-born heel. I'd swear that Harry Benson slugged him tonight. And that couldn't have been more than five minutes after Laura had tramped on his toes. Doesn't lose much time, does he?"

Carrie laughed. "You don't think he made a pass at Harry, too, do you?"

"No, silly. But I'll be darned if I can think what else would have made our mild Harry swing at the chairman. Peter doesn't like him, I know, and I think he has been intimating to him that he ought to go somewhere else to teach, but that's nothing new, and it wouldn't explain why Harry picked tonight to slug him. It's beyond me, but I'd like to know what was going on. If they don't get along, it at least makes it improbable that Harry was the one who voted for Evans's promotion. It doesn't look like a tranquil year ahead in the English department of dear old Wilton U."

"Must you go to M.L.A.? Can't you tell Peter to buzz off?"

"It's really part of my job to go and help out. We have to hire two new instructors for next year. We've already narrowed the field to eighteen men for interviews. Probably a few of them are duds, and some of them will have taken other

32

jobs before we see them, but they look like a good group, and it shouldn't be too hard to find a couple of winners. I hate the thought of all the interviewing, but, with luck, I shouldn't have to stay more than two days."

Carrie sighed and heaved a sofa cushion across the room. "I'll get along. I can always give Laura a hand with the kids. She's such a kid herself that I worry about her. I'm afraid she'll feel guilty about tonight, even if it was all the fault of that blasted Peter. I could have handled the whole thing and forgotten it in thirty seconds. But she isn't like that."

Amused, Bill held her at arm's length. "What have you been up to? Do I have to fight someone? What would you have done in Laura's position?"

"Simple. I would just have brought up my knee in a hurry and taken his mind off amorous subjects. And I haven't been carrying on, either, although I may start to, if you are going to be surrounded by gushing females like Mrs. Lockwood."

"Carrie!" He frowned. "You aren't serious about that silly woman, are you?"

"You blessed fool." She took his face in her hands. "You don't think I could tease you about her if I were, do you?"

CHAPTER FOUR

To Bill, propelled by the revolving doors into the warm lobby, the Claridge was a haven, after a street like a wind tunnel. As he walked to the reception desk, he looked around curiously. His first impression was of a sea of identical faces, not to be distinguished from the meetings of the Modern Language Association in New York and Chicago.

In all his years at Wilton, he had never before driven the short distance to Devonport. A gigantic wen disfiguring the beautiful New England beach on which it was set, it was generally ignored by anyone within a hundred miles of its chromium and cardboard splendors. But the taxes from its enormous hotels were a substantial part of the state's income. All summer its neighbors cursed the streams of cars laden with rubber mattresses and surf boards, while in the winter they lamented the emptiness of the streets through which the ocean winds whipped, depositing layers of sand upon the shuttered refreshment stands.

For the past decade there had been a determined effort to turn Devonport into a winter resort. But there were not many hardy types who liked basking in a shrieking gale, and the city fathers had turned their attention recently to securing large conventions and meetings that could not afford the more salubrious breezes of Florida and California. The Modern Language Association was their first major coup, since it would bring eight or nine thousand college professors to huddle for protection within the walls of the hotels and convention halls. Not the biggest spenders of all time, but at least a beginning.

Before Bill reached the reception desk, he greeted Charlie Hudnut from Chicago and Phil Terry from Yale, and promised to have coffee or a drink later. One of the pleasantest parts of the annual convention was the reunion with friends he had scarcely seen since graduate days. Gradually the group was settling down into individuals, but there still seemed to be an undue preponderance of large men in sober suits with large, sober faces. Sober now, but if he knew anything about M.L.A., they wouldn't all be by the end of the evening. And nuns. Like a background of black and white to the men, they were ubiquitous. Every Catholic women's college in the country must have sent a major portion of its faculty.

The original purpose of the Modern Language Association had been to give literary scholars an opportunity to exchange their views in meetings, by papers and discussions. To a certain extent this was still its aim, but over the eighty-odd years of its existence, the annual meetings had imperceptibly become equally important as the occasions for universities to hire junior faculty. "Slave market," most of the younger men called it.

Nowadays the men who read papers at the meetings tended to be either super-stars of the profession who drew audiences of a thousand or more, or earnest young men in a hurry who hoped for offers of better jobs elsewhere once they had read a paper at M.L.A. The old-timers were apt to talk in generalities so broad that Bill often suspected that their talks were left over from notes to articles they had already published, and the young men talked in such technical detail about literature (since their views were seldom very wide) that it was impossible to follow them unless one had a word-by-word recall of, say, "The Vanity of Human Wishes."

There was another reason, usually unacknowledged, for

attendance at the annual meeting. For a man who spent nine or ten months of the year teaching in Utah or Arkansas or upstate Minnesota, three days in a large city under pretense of scholarly interests were not to be despised. A token appearance at a paper on "Phallic Imagery in *Pride and Prejudice*" and one was free for the museums, theaters, or the more fleshly attractions of the city. This year attendance would probably be fairly light, since Devonport offered neither the temptations nor the anonymity of New York and Chicago.

Bill sighed. This was the first of the three scheduled days of the meeting. If he hurried, he could have a long hot shower before dinner. At eight o'clock he was due in the suite that Peter Jackson had taken. Bill and Gordon Thomas and Peter were to interview prospective instructors until ten o'clock. The full and associate professors were divided into shifts. There had been several hours of interviews that afternoon, and the whole morning and afternoon of the following day would be devoted to the same work. With luck they would have secured their two new men by then.

Interviewing was hard work, and Bill had to admit that Peter Jackson had not shirked his share of the load. He had been talking to candidates all that day, and he would be interviewing almost without stop the next.

At a quarter of eight, his stomach gurgling from the speed with which he had eaten his meal, Bill took the elevator to Jackson's suite. Peter and Gordon Thomas were already there, reading through the dossiers of the young men they were to see. Gordon looked sulky, as if he resented spending the evening in interviewing, but Peter was as fresh as if it were the beginning of the day.

"There will be four of them tonight," said Peter, handing a folder to Bill. "Williams from Stanford is first, then Leon and Scott from Harvard, and Roberts from Michigan. Williams looks weak, and Greg Newman from Yale told me at dinner that they had already snagged Scott, so I think we ought to concentrate on Leon and Roberts. Gordon has their folders, but why don't you grab a quick look at Williams's before he gets here?" Dutifully, Bill read the folder and then, since Williams was late, he began on the others.

At last there was a knock, "Come in," called Peter as he walked to the door. A pale young man entered, his eyes popping with nervousness.

"Professor Jackson?"

"Mr. Williams? Won't you come meet my colleagues? This is Professor Thomas."

"How do you do, sir," said Williams stiffly. His eyes closed for the briefest moment of recollection, then he smiled. "I've just been reading your book on the ordering of the sections in *In Memoriam*. It's a pleasure to meet you."

"And Professor Stratton."

"How do you do, sir. I've been wanting to tell you how much I learned from your articles about . . . about . . . about William Cowper," he finished triumphantly.

Bill smiled as disarmingly as he knew how. "I wish that I could take credit for those. I'm William Stratton, and it was Oscar Stratton who wrote them." There were signs of near collapse on Williams's part. "But don't worry about it; I'd be flattered if they *were* mine." Gordon exchanged glances of sympathy for Williams with Bill, but Peter looked severe. For the young not to know the major publications of the members of a department to which they were applying was a major sin in his eyes.

Whether it was because of nervousness over his initial blunder or because of the pall on the conversation cast by Peter, who had already made up his mind about Williams, the interview went as badly as any Bill could remember. Williams could hardly stammer out the title of his dissertation, and he appeared to have forgotten totally what it was about. After an agonizing twenty minutes, Peter stood up and indicated that the interview was over. Doggedly, determined to carry through, Williams shook the hands of Bill and Gordon, called them accurately by name, then went rather unsteadily toward the door.

When he was gone, Gordon sighed. "Poor boy. He may be brilliant, but he was so nervous that it was impossible to tell. I think he had tears in his eyes when he shook my hand. I wouldn't be that age again for anything."

"Nonsense," said Peter brusquely. "If he has no more self-possession than that, he wouldn't do for us."

"Peter, don't you think we might take longer over the candidates? I'd be willing to stay late tonight if we could take enough time to break down their nervousness." Bill was diffident, not wanting to offend Peter.

"If you had been interviewing all day, as I have, you wouldn't want to waste time; besides, I think we can tell all we want to know about a man in twenty minutes if we keep our eyes open."

Bill shrugged.

The interviews with Leon and Scott dragged their lengths and died. "No use in spending much time on him," Peter said of Scott. "I think he's going to Yale anyway. Roberts looks like our man to me."

To Bill, Roberts was not discernibly more brilliant than his predecessors, but for the first time Peter was totally affable in the interview, and at its end spent a considerable length of time expatiating on the pleasures of living in Cartersville. Surreptitiously, Bill looked at his watch just before Roberts's departure; nearly fifty-five minutes had elapsed since his entrance.

When the door had closed behind Roberts, Peter beamed. "Well, what do you think of him? He looks like the real stuff to me."

"He's all right," said Bill, "but why the enthusiasm? I couldn't see that he looked much better than the others.

Even," he added somewhat maliciously, "if he had nearly three times as long as they did."

"But did you see his bibliography?" chortled Peter. "Here he has gone through his graduate training in three years, and he has already published three articles. I shouldn't be surprised if he could get three or four more out of his dissertation. He's on his way up. What do you think, Gordon?"

Thomas looked noncommittal. "He's obviously industrious. I haven't read the articles, so I don't know how good they are. Have you?"

"No, not exactly. But there are three of them, and he hasn't even begun to teach yet. I think that speaks for itself."

"I suppose you're right." Thomas looked as if he smelled something faintly unpleasant. "I'm only a textual scholar, so perhaps I don't know about such things, but I have to confess that I'm not anxious to read about the account books kept by the elder Rossetti. Possibly they are significant, but I don't suppose anyone would have wondered about them if Roberts had not discovered them."

"What porridge had John Keats?" Bill murmured.

"What's this about Keats?" Peter looked annoyed, as if his dignity were being compromised.

"I just asked what porridge had John Keats."

"How would I know? That's not my field."

"I was quoting Browning. Sorry."

"He's a good scholar, too. I liked those articles of his about the political significance of *Wuthering Heights*."

Wishing he had never opened his mouth, Bill said, "I meant Robert Browning." He was afraid he was going to blush like a teenager. "The poet," he finished lamely.

"Yes, of course." Peter looked as if he thought Bill had been getting at him. "I took it you meant H. V. Browning at Berkeley. He was in graduate school with me."

Before Bill could reply, Gordon Thomas yawned hugely, so loudly as to cut off conversation. "Why don't we all go down to the bar and have a drink before bed?" Tactful old Gordon. "I certainly need one." He squinted into the empty bowl of his omnipresent pipe and yawned again.

The lobby into which the elevator spilled them was full of badges, although business at the reception desk had come to a standstill. "But we regard *our* instructors as equal to assistant professors anywhere else," Bill heard an older man proclaiming to a nervous graduate student, over whom he loomed as the young man shrank into his chair. There were few men of Bill's age to be seen. Most of them had probably gone to bed or in search of the limited fleshpots of Devonport.

Not all, however. Charlie Hudnut and Phil Terry came weaving through the chairs and carpets in the center of the lobby. They were in good humor, or, more accurately, high good humor. "When are we going to have that drink, you old Stratton, you?" called Charlie with alcoholic cheer.

Bill looked back at Gordon and Peter, who were waiting for him to rejoin them. He ought to ask Charlie and Phil to come with them, but there was something too daunting about the prospect of keeping a conversation going between his slightly tipsy friends and the already-miffed Peter. "I think we'd better try to make it tomorrow."

"Oh, come on," Phil said pleadingly. "There are lots of publishers' parties, and they need the charm of our presence and the grace of our minds."

Bill wavered a moment. Oh, the hell with it. Peter would probably sulk the rest of the evening, anyway. "Okay, wait a minute." He went back to Peter and Gordon. "Would you mind if I deserted you? Terry and Hudnut have been on what there is of the town tonight, and they might be a little too much if they joined us."

"I had hoped to talk more about Roberts, but it doesn't matter. Gordon and I can make up our minds." Peter was cool, but he didn't appear offended. "See you tomorrow morning. Nine sharp."

"Attaboy." Phil threw his arm over Bill's shoulder as he returned. "And now back into the elevator with you. Son, the papers on Cherokee linguistics have all been read, it's been established that Mrs. Hemans and Gerard Manley Hopkins were having a wild affair, the president has long since finished his speech of welcome, and the sackbuts and hautboys from the Renaissance concert have been packed away again. There's nothing to do but drink. What do you say to Helicon Press?"

"I got an invitation to their party, but it was before dinner, wasn't it?"

"It got a good start then, but the juices were still flowing half an hour ago. Come on." They stepped into the elevator. "Penthouse, please."

Normally the publishers' parties at M.L.A. were small, the invitations limited to those who had published or were about to publish a book with the firm, plus a few professors whom the publisher was trying to sign up for a future book, and, when the publisher could manage it, a big name or two to give tone to the gathering. Most of the parties were held in suites taken by the publishers, and the water for the drinks was brought by a junior salesman from the bathroom, beyond rumpled beds.

This year, however, Helicon Press had been taken over by the Stellar Broadcasting Company, and the new owners were moving into the world of university textbooks with the same panache that had put them at the top of the television and radio industry. For their introduction of the newly reorganized firm, they had taken over the entire ten-room penthouse of the Claridge. Invitations had been sent out wholesale to the English and foreign-language departments of what Stellar considered the top thirty universities of the country. Five bars had been set up to serve the guests. Among so many, it was less probable that uncomfortable questions would be asked about the old employees of Helicon who had been eased out at the time of the merger.

With the sense of direction that came from familiarity, Phil and Charlie headed straight to the nearest bar, with Bill swimming in their wake. "Scotch and water for three, please," said Charlie. "And put them all in one glass. I don't know what my companions are having." Without bothering to smile, the man behind the bar poured an ounce of whisky into a glass and covered it with ice and water before handing it to Charlie. "Thanks, old man. It's a good thing you and I are protecting the stockholders' dividends, isn't it?"

"We interviewed Scott from Harvard tonight," said Bill to Phil as they waited for their drinks. "I understand you've got him all sewed up for Yale."

"Where'd you get that idea?"

"Jackson told me."

"The truth's not in him. We interviewed Scott this morning. No go. We wouldn't touch him with a ten-foot yard-stick."

A pretty girl, not more than twenty-three, came up to them. On the shoulder of her dress was a big badge nested on bows of green ribbon, proclaiming "Helicon-Stellar." An editorial assistant during most of the year, Bill guessed, along with the other Smith and Radcliffe graduates who drifted into publishing every spring. "Good evening, gentlemen," she said brightly. "Is everything all right? I'm Ginny Cobb of Helicon-Stellar. Let me know if I can help you, or if you would like to be introduced to anyone. Let's see; you're Dr. Hudnut from Chicago, aren't you? And Dr. Terry from Yale. I don't think we've met," she said, turning to Bill. "You haven't been here before, have you?"

"Let me present Professor Howard Mumford Jones of Harvard," said Charlie with a sweeping gesture of his glass.

"Oh, Dr. Hudnut, I know that you're teasing; this isn't

Dr. Jones. I used to go to *his* lectures when I was at Radcliffe."

"All right, you win. You're too shrewd," said Charlie. "I didn't think analytical powers like that could hide behind such a pretty façade. Actually, he's John Livingston Lowes."

Not quite sure whether to believe Charlie, the girl looked at Bill for help. "Knock it off, Charlie," said Bill. "Sorry, Miss Cobb. I'm William Stratton from Wilton."

"How do you do, Dr. Stratton," she said gratefully. "Would you like to meet Mr. Rabinowitz? He's our senior editor in charge of textbooks. I know that he has been wanting to meet you." She looked around helplessly. "Oh, dear, he seems to be gone. I'd better find him." She moved quickly away in relief, looking once or twice over her shoulders and jerking convulsively as if afraid that Charlie would pinch her as she retreated.

"Dr. Hudnut and Dr. Terry, why don't you two clowns let up?" asked Bill. "I'm too far behind to catch up with you, even if I wanted to. Anyway, you're not as drunk as you think you are. Let's sit down. If you want to go disport with the young ladies, just leave me to my couch." He led them through the rooms of the apartment until they came to a deserted bedroom. "Let's sit down in here."

Charlie craned his neck to look around the door into the room, then screwed up his face. "There are only two comfortable chairs, and if one of us sat on the bed, he'd pass out. I'll leave you two old married men to talk about joint checking accounts while I go in search of vinous lechery, or at least what will pass for it with a virtuous celibate like me. See you tomorrow." He continued down the hallway.

As Bill had guessed, Phil was less drunk than hilarious. When Charlie had gone, even the hilarity wore off, and he and Bill talked soberly about their wives and Phil's children, about their respective departments, the wave of student rebellion, and at last of the interviews of that day: in short, the

43

normal gossip of two academic friends of long standing who meet but once a year.

"I wonder," mused Phil, "why Jackson told you that we had decided to hire Scott. Actually, he isn't as bad as I said, but he's no ball of fire, and I doubt that we would want him."

"Peter is a strange man, and I certainly don't pretend to understand him. Maybe he just misunderstood what Greg Newman told him, but that isn't like him. Whatever else, he's usually accurate in his information. It doesn't make any real difference about Scott, but it shows how high-handed Peter can be."

"I don't know him very well," began Phil, "but I've met him at meetings, and I have certainly never been much—" He broke off at the sound of voices outside the open door. From where they sat, they could not see into the corridor, nor could they be seen from outside. Phil grinned and held up a finger to direct Bill's attention to what was being said.

"Come on in here. We can close the door and talk in private. Don't be shy."

"I shouldn't, I really shouldn't. I don't think so." There was hesitation in the girl's voice, but Bill could not tell whether it came from reluctance to enter or reluctance not to.

"But this is so damned crowded that we can't hear ourselves talk. Come on."

Phil leaned over and whispered, "This may be a little embarrassing for all concerned." He grinned again, but Bill did not smile in return. He had recognized the man's voice.

"I shouldn't, I really shouldn't. I don't know what Mr. Rabinowitz would think if he knew. I don't think he would like it."

"All right. Why don't we go down to my room, then? We could have another drink there."

"I couldn't, I really couldn't. I'm not supposed to leave until the party is over. All right, then, let's go in here."

Before the couple entered, Bill deliberately turned his head away, so that he would not be looking at the doorway. There was the soft fall of footsteps on the thick rug, then the sound of breath quickly taken in. "Sorry. I didn't realize anyone was in here," said Peter Jackson.

"Hello, Jackson," said Phil casually. "Come in."

Reluctantly, Bill turned around. "Oh, hello, there. I didn't hear you come in." He hoped he sounded more convincing than he felt. "Hello, Miss Cobb."

Pink though her cheeks were, Ginny Cobb gallantly maintained her role as the ship went down. "Oh, Dr. Jackson, you do know Dr. Terry and Dr. Stratton, don't you? We're just looking for Mr. Rabinowitz," she added in explanation.

Peter ignored her. "Miss Cobb and I are discussing an anthology, and we were looking for a place to talk. Sorry to bother you." He and his companion were gone.

"Damn the luck," said Bill resignedly. "We haven't been getting along very very well before this, and he'll probably hold it against me now that I overheard him trying to put the make on that girl. This is not going to make for a cozy day tomorrow."

"The old goat," said Phil. "Why doesn't he leave the Miss Cobbs of the publishing world to bachelors like Charlie? Theirs is the greater need."

"I don't give much of a damn about his sex life, but I wish he had the tact to keep away from his own department when he's on the prowl. Now I don't know whether he will be more furious that I was a witness or that we were in the way of his extracurricular activities. Either way it is going to be uncomfortable." Bill yawned. "Well, no matter in whose bed he winds up, I've got to get back to my own. Alone. It's almost midnight."

The first interview the next morning was at nine-thirty, and a little after nine Bill finished a leisurely breakfast, rather larger than he usually ate, in the basement coffee shop of the hotel. One other man, wearing a badge identifying him as a faculty member of Penn State, got into the elevator with him. They exchanged glances at badges but did not speak. On the lobby level a half-dozen other wearers of badges got in, faces sour with the advent of morning. Once more there were covert looks at the other badges but no greetings.

Someone must have a monstrous hangover, Bill thought as he tried to avoid smelling the stale odor of alcohol that entered the elevator with the six men. Again they started silently upward.

The mezzanine was the nerve center of the convention, the location of the registration tables and the message exchange booth, as well as the fifty-odd booths set up by publishers to display new textbooks. Glumly the eight men watched the doors slide open. Facing them was a young nun, the shapeliness of her pretty legs enhanced by black stockings and knee-length skirt. Her arms were clasped to what Bill supposed even nuns must think of as a bosom, and escaping from her arms were dozens of publishers' catalogues, flyers of new books, her convention program, and what seemed a half-ton of other miscellaneous paper.

For a fraction of a second she stood looking around at the tired faces, in such contrast to her own youthfulness. Nine o'clock, Bill realized, must seem late in the day to a nun; probably she had already been around the booths for an hour or more. With a glance she saw that all the men were wearing badges like her own, and a smile of purest bliss came over her face. "Hasn't it all been fun!" she breathed and stepped into the elevator.

Bill wished that Peter Jackson might have seen her; it might have made him more sympathetic to the youth of the men they were interviewing. Perhaps the men weren't feeling her sense of liberation from the convent, but meeting their colleagues of the future should be at least a little fun, and Jackson seemed to be working hard to prevent that.

To Bill's relief, Jackson made no attempt to explain his

appearance with Miss Cobb the previous night. Fackler and Harry Benson were interviewing with them this morning. Just before noon a young man from California named, improbably enough, Thackeray, not only seemed pleasant and intelligent but was much interested in coming to Wilton. As he left, Jackson said, "I hope you will not make any other commitments without consulting us." After the young man was gone, Jackson continued, "He's obviously first-rate, and I could tell that you all thought so, too. With Roberts from Michigan, it seems to me that we've found the two men we need. Agreed?"

"Sorry, Peter," said Bill, "but I'm the only other person here who saw Roberts, and I didn't think he was in the same class as this man. I won't argue if you want Roberts, but I certainly think we should consider the others that we planned to see this afternoon."

"Naturally," said Peter impatiently, "but I can promise you that we're not going to find any better, and there's no point in wasting much time on them."

During the interviews after lunch Jackson spoke seldom, slouching in his chair drinking coffee, making only perfunctory comments, scarcely bothering to thank the candidates for having come. Only once did he come to life, and that was during the last interview of the afternoon, with a Minnesota graduate student named Krajewski. His grades were good, and his recommendations were enthusiastic. "I doubt that we'll find much here," said Jackson before the candidate's arrival.

Krajewski's appearance was unexpected. He was scarcely five feet tall and correspondingly fragile in build. Bill tried not to stare, but Jackson openly looked him up and down. Mostly down.

"Tell me, Mr.—Mr.—I'm sorry, but I'm not good at pronouncing foreign names—"

"Krajewski," came the answer in a surprisingly deep voice.

"Yes, of course. Mr.— Well, anyway, tell me, what is the subject of your dissertation?"

"The novels of Thomas Love Peacock."

"Hmm. I shouldn't have thought there was much interest in them nowadays, is there?"

"He's not a popular novelist, of course, but a lot of critics concerned with the form of the novel are interested in him."

"Seems a bit effete to me." Jackson leaned back again and took a sip of coffee. Harry Benson led Krajewski into a discussion of the Romantics, and Tony Bongiovanni talked with him about theory of the novel. His mind seemed even better than his dossier had promised, and Bill could not help wondering how many of his professors had been put off by his stature, as Jackson obviously was. He seemed as good as Thackeray and far more interesting than Roberts had been the night before.

When Benson and Tony had finished, Jackson sat up again. "Have you done much lecturing?"

"No. I've given a couple of guest lectures, but that's about all."

"Did you hold their attention?"

"I think so. As a matter of fact, I liked doing it."

"I should have thought it might be a bit difficult for you to—well, to be seen by your audience."

Krajewski's face reddened. "They didn't have any trouble," he said shortly.

"Tell me, what are you interested in outside the classroom?"

"Sports primarily."

Jackson looked surprised. "That's interesting. What sports?"

"Swimming. Tennis. Squash.

"Football?"

"A little touch football."

"Basketball?"

"No. Obviously, I'm too short." Krajewski looked levelly at Jackson.

"Well, it's very interesting. Anything else, gentlemen?" Jackson looked at his colleagues. No one responded, and he stood up. "Thank you for coming." He went over to the chair where Krajewski's overcoat lay and picked it up. It was the first time he had done this for any of the candidates. He held it out, just a few inches too high, so that Krajewski had to stand on tip-toe to put his arms into the sleeves. "Goodbye. If we have an opening, we'll be in touch with you. Thank you again for coming."

Krajewski turned around, buttoning his coat, then stood facing Jackson. "Don't bother. Don't bother, you big, over-stuffed son of a bitch. I wouldn't teach in the same department with you if I were starving." He turned to the others. "Goodbye and thank you. I've enjoyed meeting you." He went out the door and instead of banging it, as Bill expected, he closed it very softly.

Jackson's face was frighteningly red. "That sawed-off, feisty little bastard. I'll blackball him with every departmental chairman in the place."

"For Christ's sake, Peter!" It was Tony, unable to contain himself. "You asked for that, and you had it coming. If you try to do him any harm because of what he said, I'll personally go around after you and tell every other chairman at the meeting why Krajewski behaved that way. I'm surprised he didn't stand on a chair and take a sock at you."

It was Fackler who restored decorum. "I don't know about the rest of you," he said in his quiet voice, "but I'm too tired to stay around here talking about personalities. Let's make up our minds about which candidates we want, then wind this up."

Stony-faced, Jackson said, "I don't think there is much doubt. Roberts and Thackeray. Any objections? I want to thank all of you for coming to help in the interviewing, but technically the final decision is mine as chairman. Unless you have strong objections to either of them, I propose to get in touch with them and offer them jobs for next year. Do I hear any objections?" No one spoke. "Very well, then. I hope to see you back here at six for a drink. In the meantime, I'll get in touch with the two men and invite them, too."

As they walked together to the elevator, Bill said to Tony, "Why can't you learn to hold your temper with Jackson? I know how irritating he is, but blowing your stack won't help. Come on, Tony, simmer down."

"He hates my guts, and I hate his, so I don't see any reason I shouldn't make it clear, since he knows it anyway."

"Sometimes I feel like murdering him myself, but if you keep on at him, you're going to make a real ruckus in the department, and a hell of a lot of people besides the two of you are going to get involved."

"You're right. I know it," said Tony slowly. "I'll behave myself. Or try to." He grinned. "All the same, I wish that cocky little guy had hauled off and slugged him in the belly, or wherever he could reach. It would have made me feel so good that I think I could have kept out of trouble with our Peter for a full year just on the strength of it."

"He's certainly a bully when he gets the chance. I'm glad he hasn't got any handle on me. I think he could be damned unpleasant about it."

"Mmm," said Tony noncommittally, apparently having recovered his temper at the mental picture of Krajewski's hitting Jackson.

CHAPTER FIVE

At precisely five minutes before six, Gordon Thomas knocked on Bill's door. "Since I was down the hall, I thought I might as well stop for you on the way to Peter's suite," he said in explanation. "The two new instructors are sure to be prompt, and it would be embarrassing for them if there were no one to talk to." Behind his punctilious exterior Bill recognized Gordon's genuine kindness. Probably no other man in the department would have bothered to think about the shyness of the new men.

"Besides," he continued as they walked to the elevator, "I suspect Peter may be embarrassed at his treatment of Krajewski and Tony, and there is no need to make him feel worse."

A uniformed man from room service was arranging the drinks when they arrived. Unopened bottles of Scotch, bourbon, gin, vermouth, and Campari stood on a polished tray beside the ice bucket and glasses on a desk in one corner of the living room. He's doing the department proud, thought Bill, then noticed the Campari again. Nor forgetting himself, either. Probably no one else in the group would drink it, but Jackson had never been seen to drink anything else.

Gordon and Bill were the first arrivals. As the man finished arranging the tray and left the room, Peter came out of the bedroom, freshly shaved and dressed in his best glen-plaid suit with a plum-colored waistcoat. He was tucking into his breast pocket a handkerchief to match the waistcoat. "Welcome, welcome," he said pleasantly, "the other guests haven't come, but there is no reason we should wait for a drink."

There was no trace of irritation in his manner. The Krajewski episode might as well never have occurred, for all that it seemed to bother him now. "Gordon, what will it be? Bill?" He opened the bottles, fixed drinks, and handed them to Bill and Gordon. "From now on, you're on your own. No barman today. Perhaps you would be kind enough to see that Roberts and Thackeray don't go thirsty." He poured himself a generous portion of Campari and splashed it with soda. "Here's to the department."

Jackson downed nearly half his drink in one gulp. He was a moderately heavy drinker, but this was unusual. Bill had occasionally wondered whether Peter really liked Campari or merely thought it was a sophisticated drink. The way he gulped it made it seem improbable that he was fond of the taste. Or perhaps he was merely nervous today.

Peter laid a well-manicured hand on Bill's shoulder. "You know, old man, I was really caught off-base last night by that remark of yours about Keats and porridge. I was thinking about something else at the time. But I haven't been able to put it totally out of my mind since. Perhaps it would be a little lightweight, but I have been thinking that someone might make an interesting short piece out of it. Not for *PMLA*, of course, but it might do for *Notes and Queries*. Keats came from Hamstead, didn't he?"

"Yes."

"There would probably be lots of material in the newspaper files at Colindale. Advertisements for porridge, and that sort of thing. Of course, it would have to be done tactfully, even elegantly, or it would merely look silly. Pity he isn't your period. But you could put a graduate student onto it. It might be suitable for one of the nineteenth-century journals.

It would give a graduate student a big leg up when he goes to look for a job. Publication is always impressive."

"Yes, perhaps," said Bill lamely, and was then spared having to continue by a knock on the door. Roberts and Thackeray entered together, shaved, brushed, pressed, shined.

"Welcome to the party and welcome to Wilton," said Peter, going forward with outstretched hand. As Gordon Thomas and Bill were greeting them, Bongiovanni and Benson came in the door. A minute or so later Fackler and Moorhead arrived to complete the party.

In the flurry of introductions, welcomes, and drinks, Bill found himself talking to Thackeray, who wanted to know about housing in Wilton. "How many children do you have?" he asked.

"About two-thirds of one. Mary's expecting a baby in March. We won't need a lot of room, but we do want at least two bedrooms. Three would be nice, so that we could have a guest room or an extra room for another child."

"How do you think your wife will like New England after California?"

"She will be even happier than I am. She was born in Boston. As a matter of fact," and he looked somewhat shyly at Bill, "I believe that she is a relative of your wife. Her mother is a second cousin of Mrs. Stratton. She's younger, of course, than your wife. Well, not so much, really," he said in confusion. "Anyway, you understand that I didn't want to say anything before, don't you?"

"Of course. Carrie is an inveterate house hunter for new people, but when she hears that it is her cousin who is coming to Wilton, I think I can promise you that she'll spend weeks at finding the best place going." Over Thackeray's shoulder he saw Peter pouring himself another drink. He hoped he wouldn't get drunk. "Carrie is thirty-six, and I'm forty, so I imagine that your wife is much, much younger, isn't she?"

"She's twenty-three."

"I'm sorry I didn't know your wife and Carrie were related, but I've never been good at remembering all her relatives that I've never met."

"One thing that we are both looking forward to in New England is the bird life. The California birds never seem the same." He stopped, with the ready embarrassment of the young. "I suppose bird-watching must seem a little eccentric to you, but we both love it."

"You'll find a fellow fanatic in Gordon Thomas. He has an office on the top floor of our building, and he feeds birds every day on the roof. You'll have to talk to him."

"Did I hear someone mentioning bird-watching?" Gordon Thomas asked, coming out of the bathroom. By the time Bill had detached himself, they were already deep in the lore of the yellow-bellied sapsucker, and they did not notice his departure.

He stood watching the others in the room for a moment. He knew that he ought to go speak to Roberts, but he could hear him explaining to Tony and Roy Moorhead how the elder Rossetti had managed to buy coal at a discount, and he felt he could postpone the pleasure. Benson and Fackler looked more interesting, but as he approached them, he heard Fackler advising Benson about the advantages of publishing with university presses rather than commercial ones. That could wait, too. On mature consideration, Bill finished his Scotch and headed to the drinks table, where Jackson was pouring what Bill knew to be at least his third drink in considerably less than half an hour.

"Bill, do you know Miss Cobb?"

"No, I met her only briefly last night."

"A very interesting young woman, with much more scholarly knowledge that you would expect. Say what you will, publishing does give a person a broad view of the educational needs of universities. She was suggesting that it would be a good thing if I were to do an anthology of medieval poetry for Helicon-Stellar. She knows what is going on in the academic world. I was most impressed with her mind. Of course, she is a Radcliffe graduate. Harvard, I suppose I must say now."

"They are very lucky to have someone so well informed," said Bill equably. Then, with only the slightest touch of malice, "And she's pretty, too."

"I suppose she is. I hadn't really thought about it." Jackson looked around the room. "I think I had better talk to Roberts. We're fortunate to get him." He took a long drink. "He might be the man to work on Keats's oatmeal. He has a good mind for scholarly detail, and it's his period. At least, Browning is, even if Keats isn't. I think I'll mention it to him." Jackson went in the direction of Roberts, Moorhead, and Tony. At his approach Tony detached himself from the group and went to the bathroom.

The table on which the drinks stood was at some distance from where the guests had grouped themselves. By the look of the bottles, the party seemed either to be going well or to demand a good bit of liquid support. Both the Scotch and the bourbon were diminishing quickly. Only the gin seemed scarcely touched. Bill looked around to see who was drinking gin. He might have known; the abstemious Fackler held a nearly full glass of what looked like martini. It would probably last him through the entire party. The Campari bottle seemed to be nearly a third empty. How Peter could hold so much of it, Bill could not understand, but it was not his business. Since anyone pouring a drunk had, of necessity, to turn his back to the rest of the party and so to shield what he was doing, Peter had probably taken advantage of being unseen to give himself considerably more than was good for him.

Bill poured himself a weak Scotch, and was just turning around when Tony came to replenish his own drink. "Jesus," he said, "that Roberts! I've been hearing about Rossetti account-books until it's running out of my ears. I wish to hell he had something else to talk about. I dread being caught with him in the coffee room next year. I've heard all about the Rossettis' coal bills, and he hasn't even begun on laundry."

"Maybe by then he'll have switched to Christina and Gabriel."

"At the rate he's going now, he'll be hot on the track of the grocery bills ten years from now. Anyway, I doubt that he's ever heard of Christina and Gabriel. Right now, my own concern is with booze, not coal. Bourbon, here I come. And then I'll talk to Thackeray. I like his looks."

Bill had heard phrases like "marbled godwit" and "white-bellied booby" being thrown recklessly back and forth by Thackeray and Thomas, but they cheerfully received Tony, dropping their new discussion of the limpkin and the bufflehead. Jackson was having trouble introducing Keats into the conversation with Roberts, who was relentlessly pursuing his way through the Rossetti household accounts of the 1840s, to which he had cavalierly skipped from 1837. Peter's face was darkening, and Bill wondered whether he was beginning to regret his championship of Roberts. It would serve him right if he heard about coal bills for another decade. "And always insist on galley proofs," he heard Fackler admonish Benson.

He wished that Carrie were there to laugh with him. Why did his colleagues, who were more than ordinarily intelligent and almost hideously well informed, sound so dull when they got together? So far as he knew, all of them, with the possible exception of Jackson, were fine teachers, and all of them had the scholarly instinct developed to a high degree, but it was sometimes hard to take them seriously when one was not immediately involved in the discussion. Probably, thought Bill wryly, he was quite as boring as the others when he launched into talk of Sam Johnson in the middle of a cocktail party. Perhaps all specialists were at heart dull fellows. But give him English professors any day in preference to sociologists or mathematicians, neither of whom seemed even to speak the language with which he had been familiar since childhood. He must join one of the groups soon or it would look as if he were avoiding his colleagues, and he did not want to give that impression. It wasn't even true, for that matter.

First, he had to go to the bathroom, no matter what. He hoped it was free now. Perhaps shyness had kept Thackeray and Roberts from admitting their need, but the rest of the department had been streaming in and out ever since the party began. Cold weather? Middle-aged kidneys? Probably only the effects of drink. Anyway, the place had been like Grand Central.

When his mission was accomplished, Bill realized that the evil moment of talking to Roberts could no longer be postponed. Peter must have despaired of telling him about Keats, for he was sitting by himself on a sofa, while Roberts was regaling Fackler and Benson with the cost per hundredweight of good-quality coal in 1842. His audience look stupefied. So far Roberts appeared not even to have drawn breath. Peter's face, which had been red with irritation, now looked distinctly pale. Anger has more than one countenance, Bill thought.

Manfully he joined the group. Roberts was just taking a drink in reckless defiance of the danger of losing the floor. Seeing his chance, Bill plunged in. "Who is your choice for the love of Christina's life? I'd put my money on Cayley. How are you betting?"

Roberts reflected, as if trying to remember who Christina Rossetti was. "Actually," he began, "my interest hasn't been centered around Christina, and I'm afraid—"

Over Roberts's shoulder Bill could see Jackson trying unsuccessfully to stand up. His fists dug into the sofa cushions, as he tried to lever himself upright. When he pushed, his elbows buckled. God, Bill thought, he's drunk, and no wonder. He interrupted Roberts, "I beg your pardon," and went over to Jackson. Probably Roberts wouldn't notice, and he hoped Thackeray wouldn't either. This was hardly the ideal introduction to their new departmental chairman.

"Roberts does seem committed," he began as he sat down beside Jackson. Peter paid no attention, so he continued in a lower voice, "Are you all right? Would you like me to help you into the bedroom? It's hot in here, and if you are feeling faint, it might help to lie down."

"Oh, Christ, I feel terrible," Peter said thickly. "I've got to go to the bathroom. I think I'm going to be sick." Bill put an arm under Peter's and helped him to his feet. Without too much fuss, they got to the bedroom door, which Bill kicked shut behind him.

"Hang on, Peter; I'll get you there. You'll feel better in a little bit." But not much, he told himself. With that skinful of drink, he'd be lucky if he felt like living before morning. "I'll get some aspirin after you've been to the bathroom."

"Guess I drank too much. I've got terrible stomach cramps." Not since his own days as an undergraduate had Bill seen anyone so drunk. It would be lucky if he didn't pass out in the bathroom. All the same, Bill was thankful to close the door on him. For a moment Bill thought of sitting on the bed to wait for him, but then he realized that it would only call attention to Peter's absence. He went back to the sitting room to rejoin Roberts.

If there had ever been much chance that he could concentrate on what Roberts was saying, it was gone now. No matter how much he disliked Peter, he could not help feeling sorry for him in his present state. Harry Benson worked around to his side. "Is Jackson all right?"

"Stoned," he whispered without disturbing Roberts. Fackler was too dazed by the constant stream of information to have paid much attention to Peter. Five or ten minutes passed, but Bill had not yet heard the bathroom door open. It wouldn't be much fun, but he ought to see that Peter was all right.

He had been too drunk to think of locking the bathroom door, which opened to Bill's turn of the handle. Jackson lay on the tile floor, a pool of vomit by his mouth. Bill bent and touched his forehead. It was cold and damp. "Peter! Peter!" There was no response but a flicker of the eyelids and a low groan.

Bill snatched a blanket from the bedroom and threw it over Jackson. Then he went to the telephone. "Is there a hotel doctor?"

"No, sir. I can call one for you."

"Get him here in a hurry. A man is seriously ill. Got the room number?"

"Yes, sir."

Bill looked at Peter again. He could think of nothing else to do for him, so he returned to the living room. Peter had drunk too much, but this looked worse than mere passing out. Too much alcohol at one time is dangerous, Bill knew, but surely unconsciousness would occur before one could drink that much, at least if the alcohol were mixed with soda, as Peter's had been.

He went to Tony, excusing himself to Thackeray and Thomas. "Can you give me a hand with more ice in the bedroom?" He led Tony to the other room and closed the door.

"What's up? You've been doing a lot of to-ing and fro-ing. Petie-baby bombed?"

"I guess so." Bill pointed into the bathroom.

"Boy, is he clobbered! Shall we put him to bed? Serve the bastard right if we let him sleep it off on the floor."

"He looks seriously sick. I've called a doctor. I hope he gets here soon." Bill touched Peter's forehead again. It was colder now, and his breathing sounded like a long, slow snore. "Peter?"

There was no response.

Tony watched in disbelief. Bill pulled the blanket up to Peter's chin. "I wish to hell the doctor—" The door of the living room opened, and a man stood there, black bag in hand.

"I'm the doctor. What's the trouble?"

"I think he's had too much to drink. But it looks worse than most drunks. I thought I ought to call you."

"I haven't time to make calls to drunks. But since I'm here, I'll see what I can do." The doctor opened his bag and bent over Peter. With a motion of his head to Tony and Bill he indicated that he wanted to be alone.

When they joined the others, Fackler, Benson, Thomas, and Moorhead, as well as the recently hired instructors, faced them silently. Bill realized that they were not aware of why the doctor had come.

Fackler stepped ahead of the group. "What is it, Bill?" The others slowly set down their glasses one by one as Bill explained. Thackeray and Roberts unobtrusively moved to the rear of the group.

The bedroom door opened behind Bill. "What is the name of the man in there?" The doctor's voice was sharp.

"Peter Jackson."

"Mr. Jackson is dead." He stopped their expressions of shock with a lifted hand and looked at Bill. "How long were you with him?"

Bill told him what he had done after helping Jackson to the bathroom. "Then I called the doctor." He passed his hands over his eyes. "I mean I called for you and got Mr. Bongiovanni here to stay in there with me until you came. I don't know how long that was. Not long, perhaps ten minutes?"

"Perhaps." The doctor looked tired. "Do you know what he was drinking?"

"Campari and soda. That's all he ever drank. Why?"

The doctor ignored his question. "Where's his glass?"

Gordon Thomas pointed. "There, by the sofa. What's the matter, doctor?"

"I don't know for sure. I haven't any authority to do this, but I suggest that you all go to the far corner of the room, away from the sofa and the table. Leave your glasses where they are, please. I have to call the police now, and I think it would be wise if you all stayed together there until they come. Sorry, but I'm afraid I'll have to order you to do so."

The new instructors and the six older men moved into the corner he indicated. He pushed a couple of straight chairs toward them, on which Fackler and Moorhead sat.

The doctor picked up the telephone and asked for the police. "This is Doctor Howard Sherman. I'm in room 1517 of the Claridge Hotel. A man has just died here. His name was Peter Jackson. I believe that he may have died of poison. He was at a party in his own suite here. I've asked the guests to stay until you arrive. Can you hurry, please?"

CHAPTER SIX

Detective Lieutenant Moynahan of the Devonport force was a surprise to Bill, but since the police were not a part of his normal life, he really had no standard by which to judge. Moynahan was about thirty-five, soft-spoken, and almost handsome in a virile way. His manner was considerably more courteous and humane than Bill had expected. On arriving at the Claridge, he immediately arranged for the survivors of the party to go to a neighboring empty room. "I'll have to ask you not to use the telephone," he said, "but please make yourselves as comfortable there as you can." Thoughtful of him, but undoubtedly he wanted them out of the way, as Tony pointed out.

First Fackler was called back to the suite, then Moorhead, then Thomas, and they had not returned to join the others. Now it was Bill's turn.

He and Moynahan sat on opposite sides of the desk, which had been moved to the middle of the room. The drinks tray with its bottles and ice had disappeared, and the glasses from which they had all been drinking were gone.

When his name and address had been taken, Bill asked, "Has Mrs. Jackson been notified?"

"Not yet."

"How will you tell her?"

"We'll have the Wilton police get in touch with her."

"Would it be possible for me to call my wife and ask her to

tell Mrs. Jackson? They're not close friends, but it would be much easier to hear it from my wife than from a policeman."

"I suppose it will be all right." Moynahan sounded reluctant.

"I'll use the phone in the bedroom," said Bill, "and you can listen from the extension here." There was no use in making Moynahan think that he had anything to hide. The detective still looked a bit reluctant, and Bill wondered whether he could be embarrassed at the idea of hearing a man's private conversation with his wife. "Go ahead," he added. "I don't mind."

The quilt that had covered Peter was folded on a bed. The bathroom door was closed. Bill had no desire to open it, although he supposed that the body was gone by now.

Carrie answered the third ring. "Hello, it's Bill. Are you alone?" He thought of the telephone on the little mahogany table in the corner of the living room.

"No, I'm not."

"Can you go to the other phone?"

"Of course." One of the best things about Carrie was that you could trust her not to ask silly questions. In a moment he heard her voice again. "Bill? Go ahead."

"Something pretty bad has happened here. Peter Jackson died about an hour ago."

"Oh, my God! How? An accident?"

"Yes."

"Are you all right? Were you in the car with him?"

"No, it wasn't an automobile accident. I—I think it was poison."

"It doesn't seem possible. June's downstairs now. We've just finished eating."

"Can you tell her?"

"I'll have to. What happened?"

"I don't know. I wish I did. He must have taken the wrong

pill by mistake." He could think of nothing but Moynahan on the wire.

"Oh, darling. Poor June! She called me this afternoon and asked if she could talk to me, so I invited her for supper. She's been crying ever since she got here, worrying that she and Peter were breaking up. It will be hard, but I'd better go tell her now. Give me your phone number, so that she can call if she wants to."

"I can't, Carrie. It wouldn't be convenient now. Try to keep June there if you can. If she wants to go home, you go with her."

"Where are you?"

"I'm in Peter's suite. I'll call back as soon as I can. If I don't get you at home, I'll try her house. God bless."

Moynahan was back at the table when Bill came into the sitting room. "Lucky for her she was at your house," was all that he said until Bill sat down. Then he went on: "Why did you think it was poison?"

"Because of the way he behaved. I've been thinking about it, and I don't see how he could have been so sick if it were only alcohol. Besides, the doctor asked what he had been drinking, and he told us not to go near the glasses and bottles. It's all I could think of."

Moynahan wrote in his notebook. "And why did you think it was an accident?"

"Isn't that a natural supposition? Nothing else makes much sense."

"Why doesn't anything else make sense?"

"Obviously, I've been turning it over in my mind ever since we were put in that room. I find it hard to think it was anything but an accident because I can't imagine Peter Jackson committing—doing it deliberately. I can't easily imagine anyone killing himself, but I think he would be the last person in the world to do so."

"I can tell you this much, Mr. Stratton. Both the doctor

you called and the police surgeon feel sure he died of arsenic poisoning. We won't know positively until the post mortem, but the symptoms suggest arsenic. Whatever may have happened, it's improbable that he took the wrong pill or too many pills. What we want to know is how he took the poison. Have you any idea?"

Bill shook his head. "I don't know how he did it, but at six o'clock when I first came into his room, he seemed in good form. How long before arsenic takes effect?"

"Somewhere over a quarter of an hour. More often, perhaps, half an hour. It would depend upon how much he had taken. Say half an hour."

"The obvious thing, then, would be for it to be in his drink."

"That's what we thought, too. How do you know you saw him at six o'clock?"

Bill explained that Gordon Thomas had come by for him. "It can't have been more than a minute or two after six that we got there."

"Had Mr. Jackson been drinking when you arrived?"

"I don't know. He was just finishing dressing as he came to the door. He was putting a handkerchief in his coat pocket. I suppose he could have had a drink while he was dressing."

"What did he drink at the party?"

"Campari. That's all he ever drank."

"Was anyone else drinking Campari?"

"No. I'd have noticed it if anyone was. Peter asked me to keep an eye on the new men's glasses, and once or twice I looked around at people's drinks. I'd have noticed if anyone else had Campari. It's a different color from whiskey or gin." He flushed. "Sorry. I didn't mean to tell you what you know."

"That's all right. I want all the information I can get." Moynahan grinned. "I'm not a college professor, and maybe

I don't know everything that you think I do. Isn't Campari bitter?"

"Very."

"Then it would probably disguise the taste of something else with a mild flavor."

"I think so," said Bill slowly. Then he pounded one palm with the other fist. "I just remembered. I doubt that he had a drink before we got here. When Gordon and I came in, the man from room service was just setting up the bar, and none of the bottles had been opened. Peter opened them himself."

"Couldn't Jackson have had a bottle of his own?"

"Probably. Did you find another Campari bottle?"

"No, but it could have been got rid of."

"You know, I doubt very much that Peter had his own bottle," Bill said haltingly.

Moynahan's eyebrows lifted. "Why?"

"I probably shouldn't have said that." Bill hesitated, but the detective said nothing. "To be frank, Peter was a little stingy. I don't think he would have bought a bottle for himself when he knew that the department would be paying for drinks later. It's unkind of me, but I think it's the truth."

"Didn't you like Jackson?"

Bill looked directly into the other man's eyes. "Frankly, not much. I didn't dislike him as much as—as much as I've disliked a few other people in the past, but I'd be lying if I said that I liked him."

Moynahan frowned. "Mr. Stratton, I want you to help us as much as you can. This is probably either suicide or murder, and we want to know which. You were about to say that you didn't dislike him as much as some others did. Isn't that so?"

"Yes," said Bill shortly.

"We'll leave that for a moment. Who else knew that Jackson drank nothing but Campari?"

"Everyone else in the department, I imagine. It was a kind

66

of joke. Some of us thought he drank it because he wanted to show that he'd learned to when he was abroad."

"Who else had access to the drinks?"

"All of us. Peter fixed drinks for Gordon and me and for the two new men when they arrived. Everyone else made his own. Gordon and I fixed our second drinks."

"Did anyone make a drink for Jackson?"

"I doubt it. He was drinking rather heavily. I remember thinking that he probably put more in his glass than he would have wanted the rest of us to notice."

Moynahan, who had been taking notes, held up his hand. "Just a moment." He wrote for a minute. "Did you see either Mr. Roberts or Mr. Thackeray at the drink table?"

"There was no reason for them to go near it. After Peter made their first drinks, one of the rest of us poured more when their glasses were empty."

"Mr. Stratton, I'm no professor. Wasn't that a lot of drinking for a group of academics?"

"I don't think anyone had much to drink except Peter. Most of us probably had two drinks in an hour and a half, but that's not a lot. Maybe somebody had three, but even that isn't much for a cocktail party. Professors drink the way other men do."

"Mmm." The telephone rang, and Moynahan picked it up. "Yes. Yes. I figured as much. Okay. Thanks."

When he had replaced the receiver, he turned back to Bill. "That was the lab. There was arsenic in Jackson's glass, and there was arsenic in the Campari bottle. Enough to kill a dozen men. Have any idea where it could have come from?"

Bill shook his head, but something about Moynahan's words rang a distant bell.

"Did you go to the bathroom during the party?"

"Yes."

"Why?"

Bill could not help smiling. "For the usual reasons. I had

been drinking, and I had to urinate." He stopped smiling. "And later I went in when Peter got sick. Twice, I think."

"Did anyone else go to the bathroom?"

"So far as I can remember, everyone did at one time or another. Cold weather, I guess."

"Did everyone go alone?"

Bill laughed. "We're a close department, but we're not that close."

"Did you notice anything unusual in the bathroom?"

"Not that I can remember. What sort of thing do you mean?"

"Did you look into the wastebasket?"

"No."

"After Jackson's death, we found an empty bottle of weed killer in the wastebasket." Bill knew what had ticked over in his mind when Moynahan had said that there was enough arsenic in the Campari bottle to kill a dozen men. "The lab said there were still traces of arsenic in it." He looked hard at Bill. "Does that mean something to you?"

"Lord, yes. The other night at Peter's house a doctor friend of his said the weed killer in the greenhouse was dangerous because of the arsenic in it." He told Moynahan about the incident at the party.

"Who else was there when the doctor mentioned it?"

Bill tried to remember. "My wife and I. Tony Bongiovanni and his wife. No, that's wrong; Laura wasn't there. The Facklers and the Moorheads. Harry Benson, I think. And Gordon Thomas. His wife was not at the party."

"How about Benson's wife?"

"He's not married."

Moynahan looked back at his notebook. "In short, then, everyone who was in this room tonight, except the two new men, was in the greenhouse?"

Before Bill could answer, the telephone rang again. Moynahan answered it. "Yes? Yes, he is. I'll get him." He handed the receiver to Bill. "It's your wife."

Bill put his hand over the mouthpiece. "I'll go into the bedroom again. You can listen here."

As he walked to the other extension, Bill debated whether he should warn Carrie that Moynahan was on the wire. He decided not to. The more the detective talked, the clearer it became that he was thinking Peter had been murdered. He and Carrie had nothing to hide, and if he were to warn her, it might look as if they had. Anyway, why worry her?

The connection was poor, and Carrie's voice sounded cracked. "Bill, I'm sorry. I knew that you told me not to call, but I had to. June broke down when I told her about Peter, and for a while she couldn't say anything. All she could do was to cry. When she could talk again, she said, 'That's what I was afraid of. I knew that he would.' I asked her what she meant, and she said that Peter had been threatening suicide for a long time. Today she got a letter from Devenport, saying again that he was going to kill himself. The poor silly woman didn't know what to do about it. That's why she was so broken up when she came to see me tonight. She didn't have the sense to call him or the police or even to get in touch with someone like you. All that she can say is that it is her fault, and that she was afraid of what people would think if she got in touch with anyone else."

Even with the crackling of the connection, Bill could hear her voice break. "And the worst of it is that she's right. If she had had any sense, she could probably have stopped him. Oh, Bill, I feel so awful. Maybe it is her fault, but I'm so sorry for her. All I can do is think what it would be like if it were you."

"Carrie, darling, don't. I'm all right. You've got to help her, and it won't do any good if you break down. I'll be home just as soon as possible, and you've got to carry on until then."

"I know. You're right. I'll try. I'm not just feeling sorry for myself. I called you because I think you ought to tell the police."

"I think they know, Carrie." He felt obscurely disloyal at having not told her before. "Lieutenant Moynahan has been listening on the extension of the phone here."

Moynahan's voice broke in. "I'm sorry that I seem to be eavesdropping, Mrs. Stratton. Your husband didn't want to alarm you by telling you that I was on the wire. But his openness has helped me a lot, and I appreciate it. And thank you for calling, too. You've been a big help. Where are you?"

"At home."

"Is Mrs. Jackson there?"

"Yes."

"Try to keep her with you, please. We'll get someone there as soon as possible to see her."

"I don't see how she can talk to anyone now."

"I'm afraid we'll have to send someone. It might help prepare her if you told her that a Wilton policeman will be there in a few minutes."

When they had hung up, Bill said, "Thanks for explaining why you were listening. I'd have felt strange telling her."

Moynahan smiled with unexpected warmth. "I know how I would have felt. It was the least I could do. We're not totally inhuman, you know. Now, I've got to call Headquarters." When he had made his connection, he outlined briefly and accurately what Carrie had said. Whatever else, Moynahan was not callous, and he was certainly neither forgetful nor unintelligent. Not a detail was wrong in his account. "Better get a man over there as soon as possible."

When he was finished, he looked at his watch. "It's nearly nine-thirty. This took longer than I planned. Coffee and sandwiches are coming in a few minutes. You've not eaten, either. Why don't you stay, and we can talk while we eat—all right?"

Bill grinned. "I didn't know I had a choice." He was beginning to like Moynahan. "Sure, I'll stay."

"I may have to talk to you again tomorrow morning, to find out a little more about Jackson. Tonight I wanted to talk about what happened in this room while it was still fresh in your memory. But Mrs. Stratton's call changes that somewhat." He yawned. "I need the coffee."

While Moynahan went to the bathroom to wash up, Bill remained slumped in his chair at the desk on which the Campari had been sitting earlier that evening.

Everything took on a new aspect after Carrie's call. Peter had died from the contents of the Campari bottle: that much seemed clear without a post-mortem. And weed killer did not get into a fresh bottle of Campari by accident. However he turned it over in his mind, Peter's death had to be either suicide or murder. And neither of them made any sense. Even after what June had said.

It was unthinkable that a man of Peter's tremendous ego would ever consider doing away with himself. But if he had not done so, he must have been killed by someone in his own department, and that was even more unlikely. All of them were men whom Bill had known for years, whom he liked and respected: men with the tempers of other men but with the calm deliberation that the scholarly life tended to inculcate. Some of them, like Tony and even Harry Benson, had low flash-points; some of them, like Fackler or Thomas or Moorhead, might ponder a long time before action. But none of them had the temperament of a murderer, of that he felt sure. He could not have worked so long with five men without knowing that much of them.

And, come to think of it, none of them had known Peter Jackson long enough to want seriously to kill him. Tony boiled with fury at him, perhaps Harry had hit him in his own study: but that kind of quick anger dissipates itself without inspiring the necessary loathing for murder. Or was it

71

possible that something of which he was unaware had taken place in the last day or two that had made Tony or Harry want to kill Peter? He knew from his own experience with Jackson that he could recover his equanimity in an amazingly short time, as he had done that very afternoon following his brush with Krajewski. If there had been an incident with Tony or Harry, perhaps he could have waved it aside equally well. What was more improbable was that either Tony or Harry could have recovered his composure sufficiently to act naturally while entertaining Roberts and Thackeray. Particularly if he were planning to murder the chairman.

Anyway, he could not believe that either Tony or Harry could have carried the kind of grudge that would make one of them bring a bottle of weed killer to Devonport to use for murder.

On the face of it, Fackler and Thomas and Moorhead were men more apt to commit murder out of—out of what? Conviction? Deep-seated resentment? Long hatred? But he kept coming back to the fact that none of them had known Peter before that summer; the interim had not been long enough for them to develop the hatred required to murder a man.

But he was theorizing in a vacuum, a vacuum that excluded what was most important about his colleagues: their personalities. He'd be willing to stake everything on the fact that none of them was a murderer. He had never known one, but he was sure that, eventually, a man who is a potential killer must reveal some indication of that side of his nature. And that indication was precisely what he had never seen in any of the men he was considering.

Of course, he had known Peter no longer than the others had, so perhaps it was presumptuous to be sure that he had not killed himself. Peter's own wife thought that he had committed suicide, and she knew him far better than Bill did. All the same, suicide did not ring true.

His mind kept shuttling from suicide to murder to suicide

to murder to suicide, without being able to settle on either. In theory, there were two other possibilities, but they were even more difficult to believe. Roberts or Thackeray could be guilty. But neither they nor Peter had betrayed any recognition on meeting, and there was no reason to believe that either of them had ever known him before. And they were not even near the desk on which the bottles sat. If it were a bad mystery film, one of them might have slipped poison into his glass while he was drinking, but the stubborn fact remained that neither of them had been near either the Campari bottle or the bathroom, where the empty bottle of weed killer had been found.

In theory, the Campari bottle could have been doctored before it was brought to the room, and the seal replaced. But even that would not explain how the other bottle got into the wastebasket in the bathroom.

It was no use. Nothing seemed to fit the persons involved. He tried to concentrate on being home again with Carrie, to forget the death of Peter as he waited for Moynahan.

Moynahan came back just as Bill was letting in the waiter with the food. It was the same man who had been setting up the drinks when Bill and Gordon had come into the room that afternoon. For a moment Bill wondered at his still being on duty, and then he realized that less than four hours had elapsed, probably only half the normal shift of duty for waiters. It seemed as if days had passed.

The waiter appeared to be in a hurry to put down the tray. Probably the story of Peter's death had been passed on by the staff. Even in a big hotel like this, murder couldn't be a common occurrence. No wonder he looked worried.

Moynahan watched him. "Do you know who brought the liquor up here this afternoon?"

"I did, sir."

"What did you bring?"

"A bottle each of Scotch, bourbon, Campari, gin, and vermouth." The ease with which he recited the names indicated that he had been thinking about the matter.

"Had any of them been opened?"

"Oh, no, sir." He looked indignant. "We always bring unopened bottles."

"Where did you get it?" Clearly, Moynahan had considered the possibility of the bottle's having been tampered with.

"From the steward. He checks out the bottles and makes up the bills."

"Thanks. I'm glad you remembered it all so clearly." Moynahan walked to the door and closed it after the waiter left. He turned to Bill. "That's easily checked on. It's what I expected."

The speed with which the detective began on his sandwiches and coffee indicated that he had no real thoughts that anyone in room service would tamper with food and drink. To his surprise, Bill found he was as hungry as Moynahan.

"Now, Mr. Stratton. You said earlier that you didn't think Jackson had committed suicide. Does your wife's call change your mind?"

Bill put down his sandwich. "I don't know. All I can think is that if it isn't suicide, it would have to be murder. And I can't believe that." He told Moynahan of what he had been thinking in the detective's absence. "But," he said in conclusion, "I really haven't much right to make a judgment."

"What is it that seems so inherently improbable about suicide? Lots of men have committed suicide."

Bill looked at him with a quizzical expression that changed to an amused smile. Moynahan's face showed both puzzlement and annoyance. "What's so funny?"

"Sorry," said Bill, "but I couldn't help being surprised when you said 'inherently.' I didn't know detectives talked like that."

To his relief, Moynahan grinned in return. "Okay, professor. Don't make fun of us poor illiterates. I read a book once.

And now, what's so improbable about Jackson's committing suicide?"

"There are a number of things. First of all, he didn't seem to me to know what was wrong with him before he went to the bathroom. At one point I think he said that he had drunk too much. I suppose he had, but that wouldn't make a man forget that he had just taken a lethal dose of poison. Right?"

"There's something in that," the detective admitted. "But it's also true that if he wanted to commit suicide, he would want to keep anyone else from knowing what was wrong and applying first aid or calling a doctor before it was too late. We can't know, perhaps, but that's at least an equal possibility."

"I hadn't thought of that." Bill considered. "I don't really know much about suicide, but there are some kinds of suicide that Peter couldn't have committed. For instance, he wouldn't have been the sort who is pleased at the thought of how sorry everyone else will be when he is gone. I think he knew he wasn't generally liked and that probably there wouldn't be many sincere mourners over him. Even if he didn't realize that, he took too much pleasure in being around when he triumphed over another person."

"What else?"

"I doubt that he was very worried about money. He told me once that he had inherited a good bit, and though he lived well, he certainly never seemed to be in any trouble over it."

"What happens to his money?"

Bill made a wry face. "I haven't any idea, but it's funny you should ask, because I should probably know very soon. You see, I'm the executor of his will, I think."

"You think?"

"I'm not sure. Shortly after he came to Wilton, he told me that he was changing his will and he asked my advice about banks or lawyers who might act as his executors. He had just come from New York, where he had been teaching at Columbia, and he had to have an executor resident in this state. I told him that my lawyer was my executor, but for some reason he didn't want to name him. He asked if he could designate me as executor temporarily, until he was more familiar with local people, and could name a permanent executor. We didn't know each other very well, but I agreed. I'm afraid he may never have replaced me. I felt awkward, but it would have been rude to ask him to hurry up. One never believes that death is imminent, so it didn't really make any difference to me. I suppose that his wife and children get the money."

"We'll find out soon enough. Any other reasons that suicide is improbable?"

"I've heard that some persons kill themselves because they feel inferior or inadequate. Not Peter. He was both conceited and insensitive to the opinions of others who might have a low opinion of him."

"What did the rest of the department think of him as a chairman? Was he good?"

"No, I don't think so, and I doubt that anyone else thought so. Probably the president of the university thought he was good, or he would have replaced him. Anyway, I don't think he could have felt inadequate."

"Possibly not professionally. How about sexually?"

"Good God, no! He thought he was heaven's gift to women." Bill stopped. Moynahan was too good at listening. "I shouldn't have said that. He's dead now."

Moynahan rubbed his nose thoughtfully. "Do I have to remind you that this is either suicide or murder? You're too intelligent to believe it is a good thing to hold back information from the police, out of some kind of superstitious regard for a dead man. Tell me the truth about what you think."

"Actually, I don't know that he thought he was irresistible, but he certainly acted as if he thought so."

"Any examples?"

Reluctantly Bill told him of the scene the night before with Miss Cobb. "And I think that he sometimes made passes at other women." There was no use in adding the story of Laura Bongiovanni's discomfiture to make a point.

"What other women?"

"I don't remember now. I only mean his air of being too attentive to women."

"What did Mrs. Jackson think about that?"

"My wife thought she sometimes resented it, but I never saw anything to prove it."

"Do you know of any women with whom he was more serious?"

"No, and I doubt that he was. Too much smoke for there to be much fire, if you see what I mean. Real seducers probably don't put on such a show. He was probably just trying to prove something to himself."

"Something like sexual adequacy?"

"Maybe." He looked up and caught the ghost of a smile on the detective's face. "Okay, you win. Maybe he did have feelings of inadequacy. I guess I denied that too quickly."

Moynahan allowed himself the luxury of looking self-satisfied as he drank the last of his coffee. "Just one more thing, and then I must see the others. How did Jackson happen to be chairman when he was so new to Wilton?"

"Our former chairman resigned last year to go to California, and the president brought Peter from Columbia to replace him."

"That must have created some hard feelings among those of you who were already there, didn't it?"

"Lord, no. Maybe it's hard for someone who isn't academic to realize, but no one wants to be chairman. Or at least damned few men do. It means giving up teaching and research, the very things that make men want to be professors. We were all relieved to have someone brought in from outside. We weren't totally pleased with the way he ran the department when he got here, but at least we didn't have to take on the job."

"If the position had gone to someone in the department, who would have been chairman?"

"Probably it would have been offered to Fackler, but he's too close to retirement. Besides, he's not interested in administration. After him in seniority come Moorhead and Thomas, but neither of them would be any good, and besides, they both make no secret of hating administrative work."

"You've been very helpful. I greatly appreciate what you've told me. I'll want to talk to you again tomorrow morning, so please stay where I can get in touch with you. Now I must see the rest of the men. It looks like a late night for me. Get to bed yourself. Good night."

As Bill was going out the door, he turned back. "Surely you have thought about examining the weed killer bottle for fingerprints, haven't you?"

"We didn't forget that. The lab man reported on it when he called. There were no prints except those of Jackson, and they were all over the bottle. Good night, Mr. Stratton."

CHAPTER SEVEN

Bill's second interview with Moynahan the next morning was an anticlimax. For half an hour he repeated that no one in the department had liked Jackson, that several of them, including himself, had probably said on one or more occasions that Peter deserved killing, and that there was no reason at all to believe that any of them had meant it literally.

Over the familiar ground they went: departmental disagreements, resentments at Jackson's authoritarianism, even Peter's pawing of Laura and Bill's suspicion that Harry had hit him at the cocktail party. After Bill's halting retelling of the scene when Harry and Peter came out of the study, Moynahan made a note, but he seemed unperturbed by, almost uninterested in, most of the information, and Bill concluded that the detective could find nothing more suspicious in it than he could himself. When the interview was finished, Moynahan told Bill that he was free to leave whenever he wished.

He left Peter's suite just before noon. He had intended, when he first arrived at the meetings, to stay for a paper on Smollett that afternoon, to be given by a scholar visiting from England, but the prospect of waiting until three o'clock to be told, in an impenetrable accent, about the novelist's scatalogical obsessions was too daunting. The news of Peter's death had appeared in the paper that morning, and he disliked having to talk about it to everyone whom he encountered. For the moment he didn't even want to meet his Wilton colleagues. In the future, there would be far too much discussion of the fatal party. If he could avoid it now, so much the better.

Instead of going down to the lobby, he took an elevator to his own room, where he threw his clothes into his suitcase. Fifteen minutes later he had checked out of the hotel and was driving out of the garage where he had left his car. In another hour he was shouting "Down!" while Emma hurled herself at him in disobedient welcome.

Carrie had kept lunch for his arrival, and they sat at the kitchen table, taking advantage of the sunlight streaming through the window. Emma retired to a corner and began assiduously digging at the tiles of the kitchen floor, in preparation for the burial of a dog biscuit, while Carrie and Bill talked of Peter's death and of the shock to June.

"Did she stay with you last night?" Bill asked.

"No. She felt she had to go home to the children. She wasn't going to tell them about Peter until this morning. I offered to go with her, but she said she had to get used to being without Peter, and that it made sense to begin at once."

"Maybe, underneath all that silliness, she is more sensible than we thought." Bill checked himself. "That's uncharitable. I do feel sorry for her, even if I don't like her. Did you talk to her after the policeman had seen her? How did you take it?"

"Better than I expected. I was with her while she talked to him. I thought they would want to see her alone, and that she wouldn't want anyone else around. But she was so shaken up that she asked me to stay. The policeman didn't object, so I didn't, but I wish I hadn't been there. It's not pleasant to know that much about someone else's marriage. Particularly a bad one."

"Did she have to go into all that?"

"Practically everything you can imagine, plus a lot you couldn't. What a mess they've had."

"Women?"

"Women and more women. June said that she knew he had been unfaithful to her at least a dozen times, and probably she didn't even suspect a lot of others. It has been going on for years. Finally she couldn't stand it any more. While he was still at Columbia, she told him she was going to divorce him. He talked her out of it, and when the offer from Wilton came, he promised to make a new start if she would stick with him. She still loved him, so she gave him another chance."

"Did he reform?"

"What do *you* think? Of course not. The same old thing again, even before they left New York. It was too much. This time she was really going to leave him. He insisted he couldn't live without her, and that if she divorced him, he would kill himself. She didn't believe him, but she did agree to come to Wilton with him. She knew he couldn't handle the job if she left him. They got here in June, and by August he was on the prowl again. He was sneaking off to New York, sleeping with a young pianist they knew.

"She decided the only way to make him behave was to threaten him with something worse than divorce, so she told him she would go to the president of the university if he got out of line just once more. Even if the president didn't get rid of him for adultery, there would have been a howling scandal, and Peter couldn't face that. He threw a big scene, crying, begging her to forgive him and give him just one more chance. The works. He swore that if she went to the president, or if she left him, either way he would commit suicide. He couldn't live without her, and he couldn't face up to the scandal if she exposed him. She was so furious she told him he'd better get ready to cut his own throat if he got out of line one more time, because she would go to the president. If he committed suicide, that would save her the trouble of leaving him."

"Did she tell the detective all this?"

"It took him a long time to drag it out of her. I don't think he was half as startled as I was at the whole story."

"Had she told you any of it earlier in the evening? Why did she want to see you, anyway?"

"She needed a shoulder to cry on. Poor woman, I don't suppose she has any real friends. She couldn't have if she picked on someone she knew no better than she knows me. She told me at supper that Peter had been unfaithful, and that their marriage might go smash, but that's about all. She didn't have time for much more than that, she was crying so much. Later on, she really had something to cry about."

"But how about the note from Devonport? Did she tell about that?"

"Of course. It seems that the day after the party at their house, he said he had to go to New York to see a publisher, and he might have to stay overnight. She didn't say anything, but she suspected that he was back with the pianist. She went to New York herself and went to the woman's apartment. Sure enough, there was Peter. She didn't make a scene, but just turned around and came back home. When Peter got back, she wouldn't speak to him. He tried to explain, but she just walked away from him whenever he tried to talk to her. It went on like that right through Christmas.

"Peter went off to M.L.A. with things at a stalemate. She had written a letter that was waiting at the hotel for him, to say that this was the end, and that as soon as the president came back after New Year's, she was going to go to him. Peter tried several times to talk to her on the telephone, but she refused to talk, so he sent her a letter from the hotel. It was just a note saying that he was going to kill himself so that she wouldn't go to the president."

"Did you see the note?"

"She had it with her in her bag. She showed it to the policeman, and I saw it. There wasn't even a salutation, just a couple of lines, and his name."

"What did it say?"

"I don't remember exactly, but it was something like 'I can face death better than your going to the president. Peter.' Certainly, it didn't say any more than that, even if I haven't got the words just right."

"Great God," said Bill. "Want some more coffee?"

When he had finished filling their cups, he sat in silence for a moment. "Why do you suppose he was so afraid of her going to the president? A scandal wouldn't be any fun, but there have been worse ones than that. The very worst the president could do would be to suggest that Peter resign as chairman and say that it would be more convenient if he left Wilton. That's rough, of course, but it isn't enough to make him commit suicide."

"You know the big front of the perfect gentleman that Peter always put on. A big scandal would certainly tarnish that."

"There wouldn't have been a big scandal. The president wouldn't be anxious to advertise it. And besides, Peter always put on such a big Casanova act that I don't think he would be hurt much if it were discovered that he had actually been making out. Anyway, not enough to account for suicide. All he would have to do would be to give June a divorce and marry the pianist, and he'd be respectable again. People forget things like that fairly quickly. Or stop being shocked by them, at least."

Carrie laughed for the first time since Bill had arrived. "Oh, honey, you don't understand feminine psychology very well. I think Peter did. He knew that June wouldn't give up that easily. She's the sort who would show up at the next place he got a job and spread the word around. It wouldn't be a good prognostication for another marriage, either."

"You're probably right. I don't pretend to understand what makes women tick, and I certainly didn't understand much about Peter."

Carrie walked around the table, bent, and kissed Bill on the nose. "Thank heaven you don't try to understand women. Just put up with me. That's all I ask."

After dinner that evening they went to see June. "I know you don't want to, but we really should," Carrie said. "It's the least we can do. She doesn't have any near relatives, and she shouldn't be alone now."

But June was singularly composed. She was pale, as if she had had no sleep, and her face, innocent of its usual makeup, was puffy. Her hair was pulled back carelessly. For the first time that Bill could remember, she looked like the competent housewife she undoubtedly was under her normal layers of slightly vulgar sophistication. Immediately he liked her better. Strange that widowhood lent natural dignity to even the most unlikely women.

"The detective from Devonport, Moynahan, was here this afternoon," she said after Bill had offered his sympathy. "He told me what you did for Peter. Thank you, I do appreciate it. I hate to think that he was in such pain, but if anything could help at a time like that, he must have been grateful for your consideration." She looked down into her lap but kept her composure. "Dying must be the loneliest moment of one's life, and one doesn't want to be totally alone."

"I really didn't do anything," said Bill inadequately. "I only wish I had realized how ill he was and had called a doctor earlier."

With a look of sympathetic wisdom of which Bill would have guessed her incapable, June said, "I don't imagine he wanted you to realize that." Bill remembered Moynahan's words on the subject. Perhaps he had repeated them to June. If so, they seemed to be a solace to her. "I loved him, you see, whatever had happened. It may have been my fault for not understanding him better, or for not being more patient. I don't know now. I didn't believe he would do it. He was probably no happier than I was, but I was so angry that I

84

didn't realize it. And now he will never know that I'm sorry for having been selfish."

She blew her nose while Bill got up to poke the fire to help her hide her embarrassment. "Sorry," she went on, "but there is something else, Bill. I talked to the lawyer today. He said that Peter's will named you as executor. I hope you will take it on. It would be a big help to me. Peter kept his affairs in good order—" then she added too quickly, "his financial things, I mean, and I think there shouldn't be much for you to do."

"Of course, I will." There was nothing else to say, however much he disliked the idea.

"I don't know when the funeral will be. The detective said that it might not be for a few days. They have to do things to—to the body, I think." Once more, she looked as if she were about to break down, but she gave a watery smile. "Sorry, I'm not a good hostess tonight. Won't you have a drink?"

"No, thank you," Carrie and Bill answered together.

"Oh, please do. I'm sure you would like one. To tell the truth, I want a drink myself. I don't like drinking alone. Maybe I shouldn't want one now, but I do. Won't you, please?"

Bill got up. "I'll make them. What would you like?" For a fraction of a second, he could not help remembering the drinks in Peter's suite.

"Who will be the new chairman?" asked June when he sat down again. "Do you know?"

Bill was taken aback. "I haven't the slightest idea. Maybe Fackler will be acting chairman this year." He was probably wrong about her seeming insensitive. Probably she was only making the kind of inconsequential remark that people sometimes do when suffering from shock. He felt ashamed of his hasty judgment.

"It would be nice if you were."

"Oh, no, don't wish that on him," Carrie blurted out. Then, as if realizing that she might seem to be deprecating Peter, she added, "Bill hasn't even taken the screen door down yet. I don't think he would be a good administrator like Peter."

"Carrie's been holding that screen door against me since September, so don't pay any attention. But she's right all the same. I wouldn't want the job, even if I were asked, which is pretty improbable."

After a little more desultory conversation, Bill and Carrie left. In the car Carrie said, "Well, I managed to stick my big foot in my mouth, as usual."

"What do you mean?"

"Acting as if being chairman were the worst thing in the world, and then, when I tried to cover up, I had to say how good Peter had been. We all knew I was lying. You've got a tactless wife. Just the same, I wonder who is going to be chairman. I hadn't thought of it until now."

"Stop worrying about it, or I'll ask the president if I can be chairman, just to spite you. It would be bad enough for you to have to manage the social affairs of the department. What's worse, imagine Emma trying to manage the canine affairs. She doesn't even understand English."

CHAPTER EIGHT

The remainder of the holidays slipped away almost unnoticed. Because of Peter's death there were few big parties on New Year's Eve. No one could pretend to miss him much, but it would have been unduly callous for June's acquaintances to carry on as usual.

Bill and Carrie, who preferred a bottle of champagne and bed by eleven, felt a guilty pleasure in having an excuse not to accept an invitation for the evening. What had happened since Bill's return from Devonport had been more depressing than they envisioned.

The day after he and Carrie had seen June, he had gone to see Mr. Fairweather, the old lawyer whom Bill had recommended Peter retain to make his will. After the preliminary greetings, Bill asked directly, "All right, what did you mean on the phone that the will was puzzling? I probably can't be much help if you don't understand it yourself."

"It's not that I don't understand the provisions; I don't understand what lies behind them. I may as well confess that I tried to talk Professor Jackson out of one of the provisions, but it seemed to me such an intimate matter that I could not say much, and he was obdurate. Actually," and he smiled in a wintry fashion, "if he had not been a client, I should say that he was remarkably stubborn. And callous to his wife's feelings."

"What's the provision?"

"The will, although there is a good bit of property and money involved, is basically simple. In the normal course of things, the entire property would be left to the widow. However, Mr. Jackson insisted on putting in a provision to say that if he predeceased his wife as a result of either murder or manslaughter, she would receive no more than the mandatory quarter of the estate that the law allows the widow. The remainder in such a case would be put in trust for his children."

"Great God!" Bill said.

"Exactly. You can see why I am upset with the will. When I drew it up, it seemed unlikely that such a provision would ever have effect. Now we can do nothing about the will until the police have completed their investigation. It is most annoying."

"I should think a lawyer would try to talk a man out of a silly thing like that."

"I *did* try, Mr. Stratton, but he refused to listen. He told me curtly that I was paid to carry out his wishes, not to question them." The lawyer brushed an imaginary piece of lint from his trousers, then looked back at Bill. "The truth is, many of my clients act erratically when they are making their wills. I believe that there are many reasons why this is so. Some of them are sufficiently egocentric to want to run the lives of their families and friends from the grave. Many more, actually, than you would credit. And many of them hate so much to think that one day they will be dead, that they become irrational about the fact. Lots of persons, for example, want to have provision made for special examinations of their bodies, to make sure that premature certification of death is not made. Some think they are being neglected by their relatives, and that they may die from such neglect. The human race does not face death nobly.

"Once or twice before, I have had clients who worried about unnatural deaths, but I have been able to talk them out of putting that fear into effect in their wills. I couldn't this time, but even so, there was nothing stranger about Mr. Jackson than there is about half of my testatory clients."

"Did he seem—afraid of Mrs. Jackson?"

The lawyer shook his head. "As I remember, not at all. Aside from the provision itself, nothing to draw one's attention. Actually, I couldn't ask a man whether he was afraid of his wife. I think you can understand that."

"What did Lieutenant Moynahan say when you told him about the will?"

"Not much, except that he expected to know in a few days whether any action would be taken about Mr. Jackson's death. This state does not require an inquest. If the police undertake an investigation, it may hold up the settlement of the will. If not, they give permission for the burial of the body, and we can proceed, since it will be irrelevant whether Mr. Jackson died by his own hand or by accident."

"How much will the estate be worth?"

"I should guess a bit in excess of a million and a half."

Bill whistled. "Dollars? I had no idea Peter had that much money."

He had the opportunity himself to talk to Moynahan about the will that very day. After leaving Fairweather, he went to his own office and began marking papers. He was interrupted by Moynahan's knock. "Sorry to bother you," said the detective, "but I thought I'd take a chance on finding you here. I was afraid it would be vacation for professors as well as students. If I may talk to you a few minutes, it will save me an extra trip from Devonport."

Bill waved him to a chair. "What can I do for you?"

Moynahan looked as if he found it difficult to begin. "I want to ask your opinion about Jackson's will. I've talked to the lawyer about it, but he didn't know the Jacksons personally. Since you are the executor, and since you knew Jackson as well as anyone else around here did, maybe you can help."

"Shoot," said Bill. "Not that I think I can help much."

"First I have to give you a little more information, and I am afraid that it must be confidential. After I had seen Fairweather, I went to Mrs. Jackson and talked to her. She didn't know yet, or at least said that she didn't, what the provisions of the will were, and I had to tell her."

"Hadn't Peter told her?"

"She said that he had told her a couple of months ago that he was going to put something of the sort in his will. It seems that she was threatening to leave him if he didn't behave himself. Once, when they were quarrelling, he said that he would commit suicide if she left him, and he would make his suicide look like murder if he did. And then he told her that he was going to put this provision in the will to embarrass her."

"Nice," said Bill with distaste.

"She said she thought her husband was just trying to keep her from leaving him, and that he wouldn't do anything of the sort. One of the things I'd like to ask you is whether you think he was the kind of man who would threaten his wife like that?"

"I don't know," said Bill slowly. "I didn't know him well, and what goes on between a man and his wife is one of the most difficult things to guess. But I suppose I'd have to say that he seemed to me to take such delight in the discomfiture of other persons that it is possible. Not pretty, but possible."

"I should have thought so, too, from what I've found out about him. But if he did not threaten her with the provision, then we have to face the even less pleasant prospect that he might really have been afraid of his wife. And even the possibility that she was somehow concerned in his death. What do you think?"

Bill looked sardonically at his visitor. "You ask the tough ones, don't you? June is sometimes a little—" He stopped as he tried to think of the right word. "A little hard, I suppose I mean. But I've never seen anything that would make me think he was afraid of her. Physically, I mean. I don't doubt that she took a kind of pleasure in frightening him with threats of leaving him and exposing his carryings-on. But I doubt that he was really afraid of her. If I were to choose between the possibility of his being nasty enough to want to threaten her with the will, and the possibility of his really being afraid of June, I'd say that the former is the only one I could even take seriously."

"I think it is more probable, too," said Moynahan. "But the fact remains that if Jackson's death was a suicide, Mrs. Jackson will have a million dollars more than she would otherwise."

"Are you suggesting that she had something to do with his death? That's silly, I think."

"I'm not suggesting it. I'm merely trying to consider all the possibilities. And a million and a half dollars is a lot of money."

"Well, forget it," said Bill. "She was with Carrie all evening when Peter died. That lets her out."

"Of course it does, so far as actually killing her husband. But what if she were working with someone else? Someone who was in the hotel room when her husband died. Who were her best friends in the department?"

Stiffly, feeling his face redden as he spoke, Bill answered, "I suppose that I know her as well as anyone in the department, and that is not very well. And, if it comes to that, it was in my house that her alibi for the evening was established, if you want to put it like that. Is that why you came to talk to me today?" To his surprise, he felt more anger than fear.

"Oh, for Christ's sake, Mr. Stratton, calm down. In the first place, I don't have any reason to believe that Mrs. Jackson had anything to do with her husband's death, even if I do have to consider the possibility. In the second place, I don't suspect you, and that's precisely why I came to you today instead of going to anyone else in the department. Besides, I was operating on the assumption that you were a sensible, intelligent man to whom I could talk in the expectation of sensible, intelligent answers. Okay?"

"Okay." Sheepishly, Bill said, "Sorry about that, but I'm not used to this kind of situation, and you are. Don't forget that other people may be sensitive about being suspected of murder."

"I hadn't forgotten. And now, may I ask again about the people she knew best in the department?"

"Honestly, I don't think she was close to anyone. I knew her as well as any of my colleagues did, and that was only because she seemed to like my wife and made a point of seeing her frequently. Probably no one else even knew her well enough to call her by her first name."

"Didn't she know any of the department before she and her husband came here?"

"Not that I know of. I'm sure she didn't. And she didn't make much effort to get to know the university people after she arrived, either. I think some people resented that."

"Why didn't she? I thought that was part of the job of the chairman's wife."

"Normally it is. But June wasn't the usual chairman's wife. She was more interested in the country-club set in Cartersville."

"I'm surprised. I wouldn't have taken her as coming from a social background."

"I don't think she does. But she is as ambitious socially as her husband was academically."

"Are you saying she was a climber, Mr. Stratton?"

"Perhaps. But that isn't relevant, is it?"

"I suppose not. But not much does seem relevant in this case." Moynahan stood up. "Thanks. I guess that winds things up. This isn't official, because the final order will have to come from the Chief at Devonport, but I think you can tell Mr. Fairweather to go ahead and begin the probate of the will. And it might be a kindness if you were to tell Mrs. Jackson that the body can be buried tomorrow or the day after. I'll call her officially after I've talked to the Chief. But I am sure he will take my recommendation."

"Can you tell me what the autopsy showed?"

"Not more than you would expect. Death by a massive dose of arsenic."

Bill sighed. "I suppose I'm glad that it is all over. Certainly, I'll be relieved for June Jackson. I'll be damned if I can think of any alternative to suicide, but it still doesn't seem right to me. Not right because of Peter's personality, I mean. There isn't a possibility that someone else sent the note from the hotel, is there?"

"Not a chance. It has been examined, and there isn't the slightest doubt that Mr. Jackson wrote it. To tell the truth, the whole thing doesn't smell quite right to me, but the evidence certainly points to suicide, and I have generally found it safer to follow evidence than personal hunches." He stuck out his hand to Bill. "You've been very co-operative, Mr. Stratton, and I appreciate it. I hope we'll meet again under pleasanter circumstances."

The next two days passed uneventfully for Bill. Peter was buried at a private service attended by June and a few distant relatives who stayed for the day only. There was to be a memorial service in the university chapel after the opening of the second term. In the meantime, Mr. Fairweather began the necessary preparations for probate of the will, and Bill started winding up the financial affairs of the estate.

It was not until after Peter's funeral that the blow fell. Bill was preparing to leave his office when the phone rang. "Professor Stratton, the president would like to talk to you," said the familiar voice of the president's secretary. "Hello, Stratton," Bill heard in a moment, "this is John Grover. Are you going to be in your office for a few minutes?"

"Yes, I had planned on staying for a while," Bill lied.

"I'll come over to see you if that's all right."

"Of course."

"I'll see you in five minutes then."

Bill speculated, as he waited, on why the president was coming to his office, rather than calling him to Old Main, in the customary way. Something fairly serious must be in the air, since he was coming in person.

"Damned bad business about poor Jackson," said Grover as he came in the door. "You were there, weren't you?" It was obvious that the difficulty of dealing with the situation in the university would outweigh any personal sorrow that he felt for Peter's death. Grover was a cold man, but at least he was not a hypocrite, and he wasted no time in pretense.

"Stratton, I've come to ask a big favor of you. Will you become the chairman of the English department, to replace Jackson?"

"Oh, no!" was Bill's involuntary response, then he caught himself. "Frankly, President Grover, I think it would be better if you were to ask someone else. Fackler, for instance."

"To tell the truth, I've already asked him, and he has refused. He feels that he is too old for the job, and that he doesn't have enough energy. I can understand that."

"Then how about Gordon Thomas? Obviously, it ought to be taken by a full professor."

"You're embarrassing me. Thomas has turned it down, too. And don't suggest Moorhead; we both know that he is a good scholar but no administrator."

"Then I ought to be as honest with you as you have been with me. I don't share your ideas about running the department. At least, I didn't agree with Jackson in his policies, and I think they weren't counter to your own ideas. My belief is that Jackson was on the wrong track in his way of trying to improve the department. To me the mere counting of entries on a bibliography is almost simple-minded. Fackler said some time back that excellence is what we ought to be looking for, and I subscribe to that entirely. Scholarship is certainly a large part of excellence in an academic, but so is teaching, and the most important thing is the whole quality of what the man is."

"I may have been wrong in appointing Jackson. I don't think you and I would disagree very often, so don't worry about that. I'd support you in every way that I could. I agree that the head of the department ought to be a full professor. Your promotion would be effective next autumn. It's true that I asked Thomas and Fackler to take the position, since they were the senior men, but I really believe that you would make a better chairman than either of them. What I want is a man of intelligence who is a scholar himself, but who also can pull together again a department that has been churned up in the past year. I'm asking you as a favor. How about it?"

Bill pulled a lock of hair and twisted it, as he was apt to do when thinking hard. Then he walked to the window and looked out over the quiet campus. The offices and seminar rooms of the English department were on the top three floors of the seven-story building, and he could see over a large open space to the frozen river beyond. At last he turned back to Grover. "I love this place, and I have a lot of affection for the department, so I suppose I have to do what I can to help, but I really don't like the idea. And I don't want my promotion to look as if it were a favor from you."

The president smiled. "I think it's better this way than if you had to forward your own recommendation for your own promotion later on, don't you? Would it help if I were to see that Bongiovanni was promoted at the same time? I know more about what goes on in the department than you think. And the normal raises for next year would be in effect."

In his turn Bill grinned. "You're a good man at bribery.

All right, then. If I am going to take the position, I'll try to placate my wife, but she may be after your scalp. I want to ask one other thing for the department."

"Ask ahead."

"Peter's death means that we are going to be even more understaffed than we have been already this year. If I could find someone to come for the second term, would the university pay his salary?"

"I think that would be feasible. But would it be possible to find someone at this late date? No other university is going to release a man on such short notice to let him come here as a visiting professor."

"I'd like to try. The department is already hard pushed. But it won't be easy, and the price may be high. Would that be all right?"

"Of course. Anything to help out the department." Then, with a reversion to presidential caution, Grover added, "But do try to keep the cost down, won't you? The budget is in bad shape this year."

CHAPTER NINE

Modern furniture was all right, but Bill had scant enthusiasm for it in an academic setting. When Winthrop Hall, the building in which the English department was housed, had been built five years before he had managed by alternate supplication and threat to keep the furniture from his old office, to the obvious disgust of Buildings and Facilities. Dr. Johnson might not have been ill at ease had he survived until the age of stainless steel chairs, but Bill, being of weaker stuff, felt the incongruity too much. He, for one, could never write a book about Johnson on an "executive desk." Probably his battered furniture was more suitable for a study of Ruskin, but that anachronism was easier to take.

His outdated desk now replaced the splendid walnut affair at which Peter Jackson had worked. On it stood the heavy crystal ashtray that Bill was particularly fond of, the gift of a grateful graduate student two years before. The long seminar table with uneven legs and the rickety chairs whose arms were carved with the initials of generations of undergraduates looked as much at home as they had in his former office. And though he could not do much about the wall-to-wall carpeting, part of it was covered with a frayed Oriental rug that Carrie had turned out of the house ten years before. At the far end of the room stood the Coromandel screen he had inherited from his grandmother. His own eighteenth-century engravings had replaced Peter's reproductions of Klee, and his books were shelved at last.

"It does seem a shame," said Mrs. Watkins at his elbow as he stood surveying the results. "All that nice furniture for some instructor. Maybe I could get Buildings and Facilities to give you a piece of broadloom instead of that old rug."

"Never mind," Bill said. "This will do me nicely." At least it didn't look like the office of a too-prosperous dentist. He was surprised that Peter had not sported a plastic philodendron in a redwood pot in a corner of the room. "I'm sorry I made so much ruckus, but I like having my own things around me." Besides, he hoped not to be chairman long, and if he left his furniture in his old office, he was sure it would be replaced overnight by stainless steel.

"At least you still have the file cabinets," Mrs. Watkins said as she went out of the door into her office. She was an efficient secretary but scarcely decorative. Occasionally Bill wondered what her home life was like. She left every day at exactly five, having worked seven hours without ever mentioning her husband. It had been the whim of an antic parent to call her Rosamund, and though she was never addressed by the faculty by anything but her married name, they all referred to her in private as "Rosie."

Yes, he still had the file cabinets: three large constructions with four drawers each, in which were kept the confidential records of each member of the English faculty, clear back to 1887, when it had first been lopped off the Classics department.

Bill turned to the pile of mail on his desk. Most of it was addressed to the Chairman of the English Department, but some bore Peter's name. There was no way of telling which was personal, which official, and it had been accumulating ever since Peter's death. He began reading it. Here it was Friday, and classes began again on Monday. He sighed.

As he read the letters, he sorted them into piles for answering. Many were requests for teaching positions, written by graduate students from all over the country. He would dictate individual letters to each of them, regretting that there were no openings; nothing was more discouraging to a young man than a form letter of rejection. There were a half-dozen routine requests for information from the president's office; Rosie would have to help him with those. A seventh-grade girl in Lima, Ohio, was writing to ask whether Bacon had written Shakespeare's plays. That would take some tact, too.

Near the bottom of the pile was an envelope with a direction in unformed handwriting to "Professor Peter Jackson, Department of English, Wilton University." Bill hesitated a moment before opening it, then turned it over to look at the Chicago address engraved on the back. It was obviously expensive stationery, suitable for personal, rather than business, letters. Still, there was no indication on the envelope that it was private. In any case, if it were, it would surely have been sent to Peter's home. Probably it was one of the many crank letters that any university received, or perhaps another request for information like that of the Lima schoolgirl. He opened it.

The first words that he saw were "Darling Jack." He folded up the sheet and put it back into the envelope. But instead of going on to the next letter, he sat in thought. He ought to give the letter to June without reading it. He knew that, but he also knew that June was already badly upset by Peter's philandering, and if this were a love letter, now was certainly not the time to give it to her. It would be better to destroy it. On the other hand, there might be a perfectly innocent reason for the salutation. An aunt, a cousin, or even a sister of whom he had never heard.

As he unfolded the letter again he consoled himself by thinking that he was Peter's executor as well as his successor in the department. He looked at the bottom of the single sheet to the signature. "With all my love, Mama." He had never heard either Peter or June speak of Peter's mother, and he had assumed that she was dead. At least, she had not come to the funeral. At the top of the sheet was engraved "Mrs. Giacomo Petrocelli, Sr.," with the same Chicago address as that on the envelope.

"How are you?" the letter began. "I have been pretty well, but my arthrites has given me a pretty bad time. I have been taking aspurun for it, which helps a little. Mrs. Carlucci down the street died the other day. A heart attack they say. I wish I could come to see you and June and the kids but I don't think I could stand the plane ride. Father Fiore said a Mass for Papa yesterday. Thank you for calling me on Xmas. And thank you again for the house coat. It is nice and warm. I'm glad you liked my presents. Write often. And come to Chicago this summer if you can. With all my love, Mama." Bill's eyes misted at the childish letter. And now Peter was dead.

Mama. Mrs. Giacomo Petrocelli, Sr. Jack. Jackson. Petrocelli. Peter. It seemed neat enough, but perhaps there was another explanation. There was no possibility that the letter had been put in the wrong envelope, since Mrs. Petrocelli had mentioned June and the children. Bill looked at the date on the letter. The twenty-sixth of December. She was writing to thank Peter for her Christmas present, and the letter had probably arrived in the office the very day of Peter's death.

If Peter's mother had remarried after her husband's death, her name would be different from Peter's. That still left "Jack" unexplained. But it would be a natural nickname for an Italian-American boy whose real name was Giacomo.

In no way that Bill could think of was it any of his business. If Peter had changed his name, presumably there was a good reason, and if he had been ashamed of the name that he had been given at birth, no good would come of revealing now the secret he had kept in life. But it was puzzling.

Feeling slightly ashamed of his curiosity, Bill stepped out into Rosie's office. Behind her desk was a bookshelf holding the New York telephone directory, a copy of *Who's Who in America*, the *Oxford Companion to English Literature*, the useful list of addresses published annually in *PMLA*, and a few other reference books of particular use to Rosie. Bill pulled down volume two of the *Directory of American Scholars* and carried it into his own office.

There it was. "Jackson, Prof. Peter, b. Chicago, Ill., Aug. 3, 26," followed by the universities at which Peter had been educated and where he had taught, and the scanty list of his publications on medieval subjects. Nothing about Petrocelli. He had been born in Chicago, but so had millions of other people.

What was important was the letter itself and its disposition. If June did not want it known that Peter's name had once been Petrocelli, she would undoubtedly worry if she saw that the envelope had been opened. Perhaps there was not much affection between June and her mother-in-law, since there had been no mention of love sent to June. The fact that the letter had been sent to his office rather than to Peter's home seemed to corroborate his guess. Once her son was dead, Mrs. Petrocelli would not worry about whether he had received her letter, and there was nothing of importance in it for anyone else to see. The best thing would be to destroy it and say nothing. Bill tore off the heading, shredded the rest of the letter, and threw the scraps away.

He returned to the remainder of the correspondence. The last envelope was addressed to "Prof. William Stratton, Chairman of the Department of English." Someone was certainly up-to-date in his information. It was from Roberts, the obnoxious expert on the domestic affairs of the Rossettis. Count on Roberts to know the latest dope. Surely, he couldn't be so gauche as to write to congratulate him on the chairman-ship. Or could he?

"In view of the unfortunate events at the Claridge Hotel," the letter began, "I think I need not feel myself bound to a previous commitment with Wilton, since the offer was made by Professor Jackson. I am afraid it might be injurious to the reputation of a young scholar to be associated with Wilton any further than was necessitated by my presence at the aforementioned unfortunate event." The pompous son of a bitch! "You may be interested to know that I have accepted an offer as assistant professor at the University of California. The salary is considerably more than Wilton was prepared to offer, so I am sure that you will wish me well in my new position."

With a close approximation of the authentic movie cowboy sound, Bill shouted "Yip-pee!" at the top of his voice, wadded the envelope into a ball, and threw it at the window, where a sparrow took wing in terror.

Rosie stuck a startled head through the door. "Are you all right, Mr. Stratton?"

"Never better. Sorry for the explosion. You'll have to get used to my being a little eccentric. And while you are here, would you please see if you can locate the telephone number of a man called Krajewski, a graduate student at the University of Minnesota? It ought to be in his folder with his application for a job here."

"How do you spell that?"

He told her. "And you'd better learn it, because if I have any luck, he is going to be teaching here next year." Fifteen minutes later Rosie had reached Krajewski. He admitted that he had not yet found a position for the coming autumn. In another five minutes the offer had been made and accepted.

Before he hung up, Krajewski said, "I guess I made a damned fool of myself with Professor Jackson at M.L.A.

I've felt sorry about it ever since I heard about his death. But the truth is that I couldn't have come to Wilton while he was chairman."

"Forget it," said Bill. "Nothing can be done about it now."

There was a sound of pleasure from the telephone. "Gosh, sir," said Krajewski, forgetting for a moment that he was an adult, "this is the best news I've had in a long time. If you don't mind, I'll hang up now. My wife is at the laundromat, and I want to go tell her."

Thank God, neither he nor Tony would have to listen to the domestic accounts of the Rossettis in the departmental coffee room next year. And it would be stimulating to have the peppery little Krajewski around. Whatever else happened, this was one bright spot in his first full day as chairman.

He spent another hour at the dictaphone answering the letters of the applicants for a job and that of the Lima schoolgirl. All the time that he was dictating, however, he could not rid his mind of the letter from Mrs. Petrocelli. When he had finished, he picked up the telephone, amused at his own curiosity, and called an old friend, Don Newman, dean of men at the North Shore university in Chicago where Peter had been an undergraduate.

"Don," he said after the conventional preliminaries were finished, "I'm calling with a funny kind of request. I want some confidential information about Peter Jackson. . . . Yes, that's the man. I'm the executor of his will." That was true, however misleading. "He was an undergraduate at your university. Could you look up his record and, if possible, the material on his admission as a freshman?"

"Sure," said Newman. "The records office will have it all. What do you want to know?"

"I believe that he changed his name, and I wonder if you have any information about it. I'm not sure, but I think his name used to be Giacomo Petrocelli."

103

"Sounds easy. How soon do you have to know?"

"As soon as it's convenient for you, but don't rush. Either call me person-to-person here or call me at home, could you, please?"

Newman did not return the call until after dinner that night. "Long distance," said Carrie, handing Bill the phone.

"Sorry I couldn't call before," Newman said, "but I just managed to get to the records office before they closed. You're right about Jackson. He was Petrocelli during the first three years he was here, then at the beginning of his senior year, he changed his name. I think he had just become twenty-one. I've met him a couple of times at meetings, and he had certainly left the Petrocellis far behind."

Bill thanked him. "Any time," Newman said. "Goodbye, Bill. With a name like that, he must have left a lot of money for you to take care of." The receiver clicked.

"Okay, Hawkshaw," asked Carrie, "what was all that?"

Before answering, Bill considered a moment. Strictly speaking, it was not his business, and it was probably even worse than prying to tell what he had found out. But he knew that Carrie was trustworthy. He told her the whole story.

"It doesn't surprise me," she said. "I always thought he was a phony. I don't care if he changed his name, but I don't like the way he covered it up. It sounds as if he kept his mother under wraps. She was probably worth a dozen of him." She laughed. "No wonder he didn't like spaghetti."

"Maybe it's why he didn't like Tony," Bill added.

Carrie returned to her book, and Bill took up the rest of the term papers he had to mark. Emma lay on her side, her flanks heaving rhythmically in her sleep as she digested the last of a rung she had chewed from Carrie's best Chippendale chair. After a quarter of an hour, Carrie broke the silence. "Bill?"

"Mmmm?" he said, finishing his comments on the paper and circling the C −.

"Did you say Petrocelli?"

"Uh-huh."

"Jack Petrocelli?"

"Yes. Why?"

"You're always laughing at me because I like to read about gangsters and the Mafia. But I remember that name. I'm sure there was a gangster in Chicago with that name. Something happened to him, but I can't remember what."

"He's dead. Mrs. Petrocelli had a Mass said for him."

"I think—" She considered. "I think he got rubbed out by the mob."

"Watch your language, moll."

"I can't remember just when it was, but I think when I was a kid. About the time I got interested in gangsters. I must have been about thirteen or fourteen. Sometime during the war, probably."

"Maybe that's what Don meant when he said that Peter ought to be rich with a name like that." Bill got up and went over to Emma. She woke up, gave a snort, and thrust her nose up his trouser leg to lick his bare calf. "Don't you think this animal needs a ride?"

"At nine o'clock in the evening? You're mad." She squinted questioningly at him. "All right, what are you up to? Where do you want to go?"

"If you insisted, we could go to the library."

"Stop being so mysterious. Why?"

"We could look up Mr. Petrocelli in *The New York Times Index*, couldn't we?"

The essential facts about Peter's father's death were easy enough to find. Both newspapers and the weekly magazines gave long accounts of how he had been eating among the Louis XIV costumes and flaming spits of an expensive Chicago restaurant with his wife and their only son, Giacomo, when three masked men brushed aside the headwaiter and riddled the gangster's body with bullets. One other diner had been killed and two badly injured. Without undue haste the three gunmen had then left the restaurant, unidentified, never to be seen again.

Petrocelli was a member of the Chicago underworld, first a minor muscle-man collecting protection from brothels, then working his way up by brain rather than brawn. From protection he turned to the better-paid but more dangerous practice of blackmail, in a city where there were plenty of leading citizens who were not anxious to have either their financial dealings or their amorous lives made public. The demands for money were made by underlings, but it was Petrocelli who conducted the investigations that made them possible. He was almost uneducated, but he had a talent for ferreting out unpleasant details that would have made him famous, although probably less rich, if he had been working for the police or the district attorney.

At the time of his death it was widely believed that he had turned his attention to the past of a highly placed public official, whose connections with the underworld were closer than even Petrocelli had realized. The killers were never traced, the public official continued to prosper, and in a few weeks the case was forgotten by almost everyone except the proprietors of the restaurant, who redecorated it in Bavarian style and installed a Tyrolean band.

"I can't say that I blame Peter," Carrie said, dusting her hands as she pushed the last volume back onto the shelf. "I think I'd have changed my name, too, and left Chicago, if I had been in his place."

"He seems to have hung onto the money," said Bill ungenerously, then added, "It must be tough on his mother, though. Her husband murdered, and now her only child a suicide. I suppose I've been too hard on Peter. Even with a million-or-two bucks, he probably had good reason for not being a particularly nice guy."

CHAPTER TEN

It was even harder to find a visiting professor in medieval literature than Bill had feared. He and Moorhead made up a list of medievalists the day after the president had asked him to be chairman. As soon as he was installed in his office, he began placing calls throughout the country. There was only a month until the opening of second term, and it was too late to write letters and await replies. But it was no use. After five days, there was still no one to give the graduate seminar.

"I'm sorry, too," Bill said. "If you have any ideas, give me a call. Goodbye." He hung up the telephone and made a grimace at Moorhead, who was sitting on the other side of the desk. "That's number seventeen. And not one lead so far. There isn't even anyone willing to come for one evening to give the seminar. If you weren't already giving an extra course, I'd ask you to help, but I couldn't do that. And don't offer to give the seminar, because I wouldn't let you. But I'll be damned if I know what to do now."

"I should have thought," said Moorhead, "that at least one retired professor would like to make some extra money the second term. I don't know how many hundred million people there are in the United States, but you'd think that somewhere there ought to be one good medievalist we've not thought of, who would like to come to Wilton."

"Roy," said Bill thoughtfully, "we're too provincial. How about an Englishman? There always seem to be plenty of them who would like to milk a few dollars out of our slender gold reserve."

Moorhead's face brightened. "What about old Millicent Hetherege?"

"We wouldn't stand a chance of getting her, would we?"

"Why not? She's over seventy, but there's still a lot of mileage in her. She retired a couple of years ago as Principal of St. Agatha's in Oxford, and she might be interested in coming to this country. I doubt that she has ever been here. So far as I know, she hasn't been writing much since her retirement, but she still knows more than almost any ten other medievalists I can think of."

"How could we get in touch with her?"

Moorhead smiled. "I thought I was supposed to be the man of retiring disposition in this department, not you. Phone her, phone her." He looked at his watch. "It's three o'clock, so it's only nine in Oxford. I saw her in the British Museum just after she retired, and she said that she was going to stay on in St. Agatha's. They've given her rooms there. Unless Oxford has changed more than I think, it will be vacation, and there won't be many of the fellows of the college there, so they won't have a big dinner, and she will probably be back in her rooms. It's worth a try at least."

Bill rang for Rosie. "Would you put through a person-to-person call to Miss Millicent Hetherege of St. Agatha's College, Oxford, please?"

Moorhead intervened. "Better make it Dame Millicent Hetherege. She was be-damed or whatever they call it, just before she retired."

To Bill's surprise, his buzzer sounded within five minutes. He picked up his phone and heard a booming voice, unmistakably English, berating Rosie: "If Professor Stratton, whoever he may be, wants to speak to me, put him on the wire. I'm a busy woman."

Bill cut in and apologized, then explained who he was.

"Yes, yes, what is it?"

Bill outlined the situation at Wilton and told her why he was calling. She did not interrupt him, and when he finished, there was a long pause before she spoke. "How much?"

There was no use in trying to bargain with a woman of Dame Millicent's distinction. With a gulp Bill said, "Fifteen thousand dollars." It was nearly as much as most of the full professors made in a year.

He could have sworn he heard the click of a calculator as he waited for her answer. "I think that's six thousand, two hundred and fifty pounds, isn't it? If there are a few odd shillings or pence, we won't worry. Not bad. How about traveling expenses?"

"Normally, visiting professors pay their own travel."

"If you add a thousand for my trip, I'll come, provided you have university housing for me. I don't want to waste my money on rent, and I hear that it's desperately exorbitant out there."

If he had not already called seventeen other scholars, Bill would have refused on the spot. He would have to fix it with the president later. "Very well."

"And that is one seminar of approximately three hours for post-graduate students. Right?"

"Yes."

A note of cunning crept into Dame Millicent's voice. "I'd give two for twenty-five thousand. That would be quite a saving for you. No extra travel money."

"No, no; no thanks," said Bill faintly. If he didn't hang up soon, the university might have to mortgage Winthrop Hall. "One will be just right."

"Very well, then. Meet me at Idlewild, or Kennedy, or whatever, on the thirty-first. I'll let you know what time I'm arriving. B.O.A.C., of course. Goodbye."

"Whew!" said Bill with feeling. "That was like being put through a blender. She's decisive, at any rate. I wonder what it will be like having one of those acidulated Oxford academic women around the department."

"I think," said Moorhead as he went to the door, "that you've got a few surprises coming."

Bill looked at his watch. He was beginning to understand why the chairmen of departments at Wilton seldom had an early dinner. In a few minutes he was to see a graduate student who had asked for an appointment, and in another hour there was a meeting of the full and associate professors.

The buzzer sounded. "Miss Englander to see you." There was a note of disapproval in Rosie's voice. A moment later she opened the door for a young woman.

"Yes, Miss Englander, what can I do for you?" Bill asked as she sat down in the chair Moorhead had occupied.

"It's about a supervisor for my dissertation. You see, it was Professor Jackson. And now it's almost a week since classes began again, and I still haven't been told who my new supervisor will be. I'm sorry to bother you, but I'm sure you understand how I feel." She smiled brightly at him.

Since it was small, Wilton had comparatively few graduate students, and the faculty of each department knew most of their own students moderately well. Susan Englander was one of the four women in the English department, but there was probably more conversation about her among her teachers than about the other three together. In the first place, she was one of the most intelligent graduate students in the department for some years. But hers was not a lovable mind. It was hard, driving, and so arrogant that she had few friends among the students with whom she had shared seminars. Armed with a formidable background of reading, a seemingly infallible memory, and the capacity to make intellectual connections between the discrete aspects of her knowledge, she would ruthlessly destroy the seminar papers of her fellows. What was most maddening to them was that they were unable to retaliate; a bit of sniping at her papers, which she would systematically demolish, and she would walk away with the honors. And, for all their admiration of her, there were few of her teachers who thought of her with anything approaching affection.

This, however, was not all that made her so much noticed by both graduate students and professors. Although unusual, her kind of intelligence was far from rare. Incongruously, Susan Englander's mind was housed in a breathtaking body, so beautiful that it defied the habitually nondescript clothes that she wore. It was a body that spoke, even shouted, of magnificent sensuality, but preferred to attempt to hide itself unsuccessfully under slightly long skirts, high necklines, and baggy sweaters. Her face, at odd variance with both body and mind, was that of a schoolgirl, although she was nearly twenty-five. Innocent gray eyes, the delicate cheekline of a twelve-year-old, a rather too-small mouth, all combined with a quiet voice to mask totally to strangers the pitiless clarity of her mind and her ruthless determination.

What obviously fascinated everyone who knew her was the impossibility of synthesizing the disparate elements that made up Miss Englander. In conversation the little-girl face and childish voice predominated. In intellectual competition the crystalline mind blotted out everything else. It was generally known, however, that the beautiful body had a life of its own, one that had in the past included a wide assortment of graduate students from other departments and probably a young instructor in English who had resigned unexpectedly a year before. Even the grayest of heads could not always refrain from speculating on what this combination of Aphrodite and Athene would be like without the dowdy draperies.

"I'm sorry," said Bill, who against his will had found himself slipping into the common speculation, "but Professor Jackson's death was so sudden that I've not had time to do anything about re-assigning his students. Is there anyone with whom you would particularly like to work? I can't promise that I could give you your choice, but it's useful to know your preference."

"Who are the possibilities?"

"I imagine that the best person would be either Professor Moorhead or Professor Evans."

She thought a moment. "Professor Moorhead."

"Professor Evans is a good bit younger, of course, but he is more interested in the medieval romance than Professor Moorhead is. As you know, Professor Moorhead is basically a linguist."

"Yes," she said unequivocally, "Professor Moorhead. I don't think I'd get along very well with Professor Evans. And Moorhead is more distinguished. He would be more help in getting me a job. Besides," smiling up at Bill like a Dresden shepherdess, "he's so old he'll probably keep his big greasy hands off me. I'm tired of being pawed by my supervisor."

In spite of himself, Bill's eyebrows shot up. "That's a fairly serious accusation, Miss Englander." If Peter had been playing around with graduate students, he did not really want to know, but he could not let her statement pass unremarked. "Do you really mean it?"

Her face shining with innocence, she shrugged. "It isn't an accusation. It's a fact. But what difference does it make now? I just don't want any more of it. I guess I'm not fast enough on my feet for dissertation conferences with another supervisor like him." She dropped her eyes demurely. "He was a bastard. I didn't care if he made a pass at me, but he kept confusing courtly love and his own libido. But, as I said, what difference does it make now? I just want a supervisor who will keep his eye on the text."

It was hard to think what to say. There was every reason in the world that a man and a woman put in close proximity over the study of literature might feel attraction on one or both sides, but in theory the professor-student relationship was one in which the teacher, at least, kept his eye on the text, as Miss Englander had put it. The ancient taboo was occasionally violated, but the violation was little countenanced. "I'm sorry about that, Miss Englander, and I can promise you that nothing of the sort will happen again."

"Don't get me wrong, Mr. Stratton. I wasn't shocked, but it was inconvenient. After all, he was my supervisor and he was chairman of the department. I couldn't brush him off without worrying that he might take it out on me by not passing the dissertation or something like that. Anyway, I think he was less interested in sex than he was in finding out graduate student gossip about the faculty."

The interview had already gone too far. Bill stood up. "I'll speak to Professor Moorhead about taking you on as his student, and I'll ask him to drop you a note if it is agreeable." He knew he sounded stuffy, but he couldn't go on listening to this kind of talk from a student.

When she was gone, Bill sat in thought. He disliked the idea of Peter's relationship with Susan Englander, but he was not totally surprised. Whether Jackson's passes had progressed into more than that, was not clear, but whether he and Susan Englander had shared a pair of sheets or not was less important than Peter's breaking the unwritten compact that kept a professor's interest on a cool, intellectual plane. Ultimately, however, it was even more disturbing that Miss Englander's last words indicated that Peter had used her as a source of gossip about his own faculty. That was unforgivable.

Bill grimaced. It was never pleasant to know too much about another person. What he had been finding out about Peter made him realize how little he really knew of his colleagues. How many of them did he really understand? It was improbable that beneath the smooth surface of their routine, academic lives there was as much seething as there had been beneath Peter's exterior, but he could no longer feel sure. He had told Moynahan that he knew them all too well to believe that one of them was a murderer. Perhaps he had been wrong. Certainly, Peter was beginning to seem more and more the kind of man who asked for trouble.

He called Moorhead and arranged for him to take Susan Englander under his supervision. "Thanks, Roy," said Bill. "I do appreciate it. I'll see you at the meeting in half an hour."

He hated going to a meeting of his colleagues when he had suddenly realized that he really knew none of them. It was not a good frame of mind in which to hold his first meeting as chairman. Peter's death left the department short-handed in medieval studies, even if Dame Millicent came for a term, and Tony had suggested that they might want to reconsider their lack of enthusiasm about Evans's promotion. "Not that I want him, even so," Tony said, "but it puts a different light on things. For instance, Moorhead said that he and Peter could handle the older literature together. But he won't want to do it alone, so perhaps he would be more favorable to Evans now." With his usual mercurial change of mood, Tony grinned. "It's strange to find me in the position of wanting to give Evans another chance, isn't it? But there was one vote for him last time, and perhaps there would be more now, so I suppose I ought to be more flexible." Bill had agreed, and the full and associate professors were to convene in another thirty minutes.

Personally, Bill had not changed his mind about Evans. He was not surprised that Susan Englander had preferred Moorhead as her supervisor, although her reasons were not what he had expected. Whether the others would feel that Peter's death was reason to promote Evans was unpredictable.

The notes were all ready for the meeting; there was little to prepare for it, since everything had been assembled by Peter for the meeting before Christmas. Rather than stay in his office, Bill thought he would get a breath of fresh air after a day in the building. He put on his hat and coat and went out the side door of his office that led directly to the corridor.

He pushed the button for the elevator, opposite his door. As he did so, he looked at the glass arrows that were supposed to light to indicate the direction of the elevator. They remained dark. He pushed again. Nothing. The elevator had never worked well, and the undergraduates delighted in baffling the mechanism that responded when one pushed a button. It seemed as if it were being repaired every week or so. Ordinarily it wasn't important, but Bill felt too tired to walk from the fifth floor to the first, and then make the return climb in a few minutes.

He was about to go back into his office when he thought of the rooftop. He pushed open the door to the stairwell and walked up two flights to the seventh floor. The stairs were meant primarily as a fire exit, and although the doors could be opened from the hallway of any floor, they could not be opened from the stairs without the passkeys given to the faculty.

On the seventh floor Bill took out his key and opened the door to the hallway. It was a nuisance if one wanted to go quickly between floors and had forgotten one's key, but it meant that at night a single watchman was sufficient for the whole building, since everyone but the faculty had to use the elevator in going between floors. One man by the main floor doors of the elevator would thus have a rough surveillance of the entire building.

Across the stairs was the office of Gordon Thomas, whom Bill could see through his open door, working at his desk. He looked up at the sound of the stair door. "Hello, Bill. What are you doing up here? I thought we were going to have a meeting in your office in a few minutes."

Bill looked at his watch. "Another twenty-five minutes, and I wanted a little air. How about coming up and showing me your birds?"

"I want to finish this paper, if you don't mind going up alone. It won't be much of a show at this time of day. You ought to come at feeding-time if you want to see birds."

Gordon looked preoccupied, so Bill waved and went toward a door at the end of the hall. The main staircase stopped at the seventh floor, and a small interior stair led from the corridor to the roof.

A rough wind blowing from the sea whipped at him as he opened the door to the flat, pebbled roof. He threw up a hand to hold his hat and walked out of the shelter of the superstructure of the stairs. The cold made his eyes smart, and his lungs hurt when he breathed deeply, but it was a welcome antidote to the stuffiness of the overheated building in which he had been working, and to which he must return in a few minutes. He ran across the pebbles to get into the lee of the elevator housing that took up the center of the roof. In the clear, frigid light of mid-afternoon he could hear an occasional shout blown up from the river, where a group of undergraduates were skating, their caps and jackets bright against the dull blue of the ice.

It was a peaceful scene. Huddled figures hurried along the walks that crisscrossed the campus, but at this distance there seemed no urgency in their flight from the cold. Soiled snow covered the ground, but Bill could not see the winter grime from his observation point.

Winthrop Hall was the only tall building in a big sprawl that included everything from the delicate Queen Anne administration building, through Georgian, Federal, Greek Revival, Victorian, and the cautious Gothic of the twentieth century. Bill regretted the passing of the original Winthrop Hall, with its wide steps, sandstone towers, rutted floors, and the holes beneath blackboards through which friendly mice listened to lectures. Modern architects were very severe about mixing Ionic columns and rusticated Tuscan balconies, but he had found it a comfortable jumble, and he faintly deplored

116

the seven-story glass and concrete structure that had replaced it.

The tower on which he stood was not ivory; it was white concrete, and the peace that he contemplated was, he knew, illusory. Student rebellion; the deep alienation that only three years before had made a junior throw himself into the river; the frustrations of the faculty; the hectic, painful love affairs of the students; the constant awareness of both teachers and taught of how far short they fell of the past that they studied. The pain and exaltation that lived side by side on the campus were little different from those felt by the rest of the world, either in intensity or in quality. The men whom he was to see in a few minutes differed little from the rest of mankind except in their intellectual interests. Hatred, lust, envy, avarice: they were as much a part of a professor's makeup as intellectual clarity, the dispassionate judgment of evidence, or the driving curiosity of the born scholar. Bill was more than usually aware of the darker side of the complex pattern of man.

To warm himself before going back to his office, he jogged around the rooftop. A low parapet two or three feet high ran around the edge; the rest of the surface, broken only by the superstructures of stairs and elevators, was empty, the snow blown away by the winds that whirled across the top of the building. Gordon had been right. It was a bad day for birds. Bill didn't care. His invitation to Gordon had been a formality, for he knew little about birds and cared nothing for them. There was a miserable specimen pecking on the gravel, a black bird about seven inches long, but what its species was Bill had no idea. A few droppings, a little scattered food at which the lonely bird was grumpily pecking, and, near the head of the stairs, a big bag of food covered with a plastic sheet: aside from such scanty evidence, there was no indication that Gordon came here regularly at least once a day to scatter provender. At feeding time the roof was alive with their wings; now most of the birds had disappeared.

With relief Bill plunged into the doorway, gasping in the warm air. Gordon came out of his office as Bill passed. "I'll come down with you," he said. "Any birds today?"

Bill shook his head. "Anything the matter?" he asked. Normally Gordon showed an imperturbable face, but today he looked drawn and worried. Once he had asked, Bill wished he could withdraw his question. Gordon's reserve never invited intimacy.

This time, however, he surprised Bill by his look of gratitude. His answer was in his usual reserved tone. "Not really. I've not been sleeping well. Peter's death upset me more than I expected. And Barbara—" He stopped. Even to mention his wife's name, as if things were not going well with her, was as surprising in Gordon as a frank talk about his marriage would have been in another man.

As if to indicate that he did not want to pursue the matter, Gordon began speaking of departmental affairs as they walked down the two flights of stairs. On the fifth floor he excused himself and went to the men's room.

As Bill approached the English office, Rosie came out, propping the door open behind her. "I'm just going for coffee," she said, "and I thought I'd leave it open, since you're expecting the tenure members for the meeting. Professor Benson has already gone into your office."

Bill walked across the thick rug with which Buildings and Facilities had supplied Rosie. He stopped to look at the "Out" basket on her desk, to see whether the letters he had signed were ready for the afternoon collection. She was a good secretary, but occasionally she forgot to send out letters.

There was a slight jarring rattle of metal from his own office, and he looked up. The door stood open, concealing his desk from view, but through the crack against the casing he could see Harry Benson standing in front of the personnel files. As he looked, Harry pulled hard at the handle of one of the files, and Bill heard the metallic sound again. The files were locked, as they usually were when he was not using them.

Curious, he went into his own office, the rug again muffling the sound of his shoes. "Anything I can do for you, Harry?"

Benson stopped tugging and spun around to face Bill. He flushed deeply as he said, "Sorry, I was just admiring these files. They seemed a little out of place with the other furniture, but they're fine workmanship, aren't they?"

"They're the best thing Buildings and Facilities has given us for a long time." Bill spoke nonchalantly, but he could not help being surprised at Harry's action. It was unlike him to be nosy.

In another five minutes the others had arrived. "I realize that we have already discussed the case of Evans, and that we have voted against his promotion," Bill began the meeting. "But Peter Jackson did not forward a recommendation before his death, as he intended. I've asked you to come here today to see if there is any disposition on our part to change our decision in the light of what has happened, and, if it meets with your approval, to take another vote." The constitution of the group was the same as that which had met a month before in the same office, except that Jackson was not there.

The discussion was desultory. Everyone seemed to think that he had made his point during the previous meeting. There were a few suggestions about young men who might be approached about coming to Wilton if Evans were not promoted, but no new opinions appeared. At last Bill handed the slips to Gordon to pass out for the vote. When the ballots were counted, there were five negative votes.

Bill was startled. What had happened in the past month would seem to make votes against Evans less probable, not more so. Probably someone had changed his mind in order to

119

make the vote unanimous; the administration did not like split votes on promotions, and was apt to suggest crossly that the department ought to make up its mind. There would be no trouble about this vote.

"That's that," Bill said. "Peter Jackson had intended, as he said, to recommend Evans's promotion, even without our backing, but I don't intend to do so. I'll begin finding out about the men you have suggested. Any other names you think of would be welcome." He looked at his watch. "Since this took such a short time, I'd like to ask the full professors to remain a few minutes."

When Tony and Harry Benson had left the room, he turned to the others. "This is just to tell you that the president has said that he intends to promote Tony Bongiovanni and me for next fall. I'm sorry that I couldn't call a meeting to discuss it with you, but I think you'll agree that it would have been awkward for me, as an associate professor, to preside at the meeting on Tony. And intolerable if I were under discussion." He watched them warily, conscious that they might resent their privileges being usurped.

To his relief, they all seemed spontaneously pleased at the news and congratulated him heartily. Fackler lingered after the others had gone. "I couldn't be happier; I know we can't mention this to Bongiovanni yet, but I wonder if you and your wife couldn't come for a drink in celebration this evening. Just the four of us."

"Sorry," said Bill. "We have a dinner engagement." He was genuinely disappointed not to be able to accept. The Facklers were not inhospitable, but they seldom gave informal invitations. There was no one whom Bill respected more than Fackler, and it was heartening to know that he approved of the promotions.

"I'm sorry, too," Fackler said. "Anyway, let me congratulate you on the conduct of your first meeting. You've been put on a tough spot, and I know it."

As he walked to his car, Bill thought with warmth of the department. His department, as Peter would have said. Good men, sound, generous, and intelligent. Was it possible that there was anything sinister in that group of six men who had just disbanded?

CHAPTER ELEVEN

The endless paper work was enough to keep any scholar or teacher from wanting to be chairman of a department. A proposed budget to be submitted to the president in the early spring; a revised budget in the fall; an accounting for expenses, due at the same time as the proposed budget for the following year; repetitive analyses of the efficiency of teaching hours; judgments of each course offered; and daily requests for information that had not been thought important previously. Probably it was all necessary, but when it was combined with the hours spent on committees, it added up to more than a man could bear, particularly one trained in literature, not accounting.

The problem that faced Bill this morning was an eight-page report in triplicate on Tony Bongiovanni to be submitted to the president's committee on promotions. Rosie had spent an hour showing him how to fill it out, but he had to do the work himself. For the life of him, he could not understand why he had to repeat every item of information that had gone to the president's office each year since Tony had begun teaching. At least, those details of education, courses taught, promotions and raises in salary, and publications of the past could be copied from last year's report. But his scholarship and teaching had to be evaluated (how could he possibly make an accurate estimate of how another man taught?), and suggestions had to be made about scholars in his field to whom the committee could write for an independent judgment of his scholarship. All this, plus the reasons for the necessity of his promotion to full professor. It was too much.

With a groan of protest, Bill unlocked the personnel file cabinet and reached for Tony's folder at the back of the drawer marked "Current Tenure Faculty." The folders of the full professors were filed alphabetically in front, followed by those of Benson and Bongiovanni. Peter's folder had already been sent from the president's office and put in its alphabetical place among those of every man who had taught in the department for some eighty years. The whole professional history of English at Wilton was filed in those drawers. Wryly, Bill noted that in 1900 a fifty-year career was contained in a quarter-inch of paper. Tony's file was already over two inches thick. Heigh-ho for bureaucracy.

Everything was there, from the letters of recommendation when Tony first applied to Wilton, to last year's evaluation sheet when he was recommended for an increase in salary. Even the candid remarks made by his superiors when he was being considered for promotion were carefully filed. Bill had already been asked to send his own folder to the president's office. That was tactful, for it would have been asking a lot of his discretion to expect him not to read the folder, and it might have been embarrassing. The president, he supposed, was making out a sheet about him, as he was doing for Tony.

He wanted to finish the report before lunch, so that Rosie could type it that afternoon. When it was completed, he put it into a drawer for her. As he assembled Tony's file, a piece of yellow paper slipped out of the back and fell to the floor. He bent to pick it up and saw in Peter's handwriting: "A. R. B., Englander," with the date "25 March" two years previously. Below, in a different ink, was "19 December," and the year that followed was the one just past.

"Englander" would have been enough to catch Bill's eye, even were it not for the interview with the enigmatic Susan the previous day. He didn't know whether Tony had ever taught her, although it was probable in such a small department. But he couldn't remember Tony's ever speaking about her. He started to replace the paper when he noticed the second date again. A quick glance at the calendar showed that it had been the first Monday of vacation, two days after the party at the Jacksons' house.

Could Miss Englander have been asking for a change of supervisor? That made no sense, since Tony's specialty was contemporary literature, not medieval romance. Bill took another look at the dates and put the folder away. He was late for lunch. The paper was faintly puzzling, but he had no time for speculation.

He ate alone at the faculty club, and after a quick look into the lounge, he decided to skip coffee, since there was no one he particularly wanted to join. As he was picking up his hat and coat in the cloakroom, Tony came out of the lavatory.

"Hi, Bill, I'll walk back to the office with you."

It was not until they were almost at Winthrop Hall that Bill asked, "Does the date of March twenty-fifth mean anything to you?"

"The Feast of the Annunciation?"

"How about March twenty-fifth two years ago?"

Tony turned dark red. "What is this, College Bowl? It was a week after Bo-Bo was born, if that's what you mean. What are you getting at?" His voice was hard, and for the first time in the years of their friendship, Tony's ready anger seemed about to leap out at Bill. "What business of yours is it?"

"None at all."

"I want to know why you asked," Tony's face was unfriendly. "What are you up to?"

"I'm sorry as hell, Tony. I didn't mean to ask anything personal. It's just that I was wondering about a paper I saw this morning."

"One of Peter's papers?"

"Yes." There was nothing to do but tell the truth. "I was curious, and I had no idea that it would make you angry. Let's just forget it. I'm sorry to be a blunderer."

Tony's face softened. "I should have known that you weren't trying to get at me. You're not that kind of friend. Maybe I'd better tell you about it. May I come to your office?"

Nothing more was said until they were sitting in Bill's office, the door to Rosie's office carefully closed. Tony lounged in an armchair, his long legs sprawled out. "I wish this hadn't happened, but if I didn't tell you now, you might think it was worse than it is.

"The twenty-fifth of March was a week after Bo-Bo was born. Laura had a hard time, and she had to stay in the hospital nearly three weeks. The other kids were off at their grandmother's because I couldn't get anyone to take care of them. The house seemed so damned lonely without Laura. You know what I mean, don't you?"

"Sure. I go stir-crazy when Carrie is away."

"That year I had a seminar on Wednesday nights. On the twenty-fifth of March I gave back their first papers to the students. They had all turned in carbon copies except Susan Englander. I explained that we kept the carbons in the files, and that we didn't give back the originals until the carbons had been turned in. I started to walk home after the seminar and ran into Susan again. She said she knew I'd have to pass her apartment, so she would walk back and get the carbon for me.

"It was a wet night, and she asked me to come up out of the rain. When I got upstairs, she gave me the paper and then asked me to have a drink. She must have known that Laura wouldn't be waiting for me. Anyway, one Scotch led to two or three."

Tony frowned. "There's not much point in going into the rest of it, except to say that when she brought back the second drink, she sat down on the sofa with me, and finally I stayed the night."

Bill wanted to say something comforting, Tony's discomfiture was so obvious, but he could think of nothing. "Maybe you can't understand this, but it was because I was lonely for Laura that I stayed. It's the only time I've been unfaithful to her, and I didn't intend to be then. The hell of it was that I didn't even like Susan Englander much, but she was available. That's all."

"My God, Tony, I know how you felt. I have felt like that lots of times, and it was only luck there wasn't a Susan Englander around at the right moment. It's crazy how much we need someone just to hold. Does Laura know about Susan?"

"No, of course not. She would understand that it meant nothing important—I mean, nothing about Susan—but it would make her feel like hell. I don't want her to know."

"How did Peter find out?"

"Evidently the efficient Susan keeps a diary. Or at least some kind of record of what she does. When I found out that Peter knew, I went to her, and she admitted she had told him. She even had the guts to say that she was afraid not to, since he was her supervisor. She didn't actually say so, but she made it clear that he was considerably more than that."

"When did you find out that he knew?"

"All that weekend after the meeting when he told us that we weren't going to be promoted, I kept getting madder and madder, so I went to see him the next Monday and asked for more money because I was strapped. He said it wasn't possible, which only made me madder. Finally, when he told me that he didn't see much future for me here, I blurted out what was really bugging me at the time, and told him to keep his distance from Laura or I'd beat the hell out of him." Suddenly, with the self-deprecation that endeared him to his friends, Tony laughed. "If I wasn't going to stay here, it would have done no harm to take a poke at him.

"And don't look innocent. I could tell that you and Carrie knew Peter was pestering Laura at their party. Carrie can't hide what she's thinking. She's like me. When I told him to keep his hands off, he said that I didn't have much to complain about, since I seemed to like sleeping with my students. He suggested that it would be wise if I were to start looking elsewhere for a job before I got into a real scandal. The son of a bitch! He even had the nerve to pretend that he wanted to spare Laura any pain.

"I stomped out of the office, mad as usual. If Peter had lived, I would have resigned as soon I could find another job. When he died, you can understand that I wasn't anxious to say that we had quarreled."

"Don't be a damned fool, Tony. Nobody who knew you would think that you would do more than lose your temper and storm out."

"Well, our friend Moynahan didn't know me. I don't think anyone else knew about the quarrel. I doubt that Peter told Susan. Anyway, please don't say anything about it." Tony blushed again. "I'm sorry. I know I don't have to ask you that."

"I promise," said Bill.

As soon as Tony had gone, Bill went to the drawer where the current files were kept. He took out Fackler's folder. At the back of it was a sheet with initials and dates, similar to that which had dropped on the floor when he was working on the report about Tony. Without trying to figure out the meaning of the scrawls, he put the paper back into place and went on to Moorhead's folder. There he found the same kind of sheet. Quickly he looked for and found similar pieces of paper in the files on Thomas and Benson. With Tony's folder, that took care of all the full and associate professors, except himself, and his folder was in the president's office.

He took out Evans's folder, which he had casually put back into place the previous afternoon; no sheet of initials and dates there. It could have dropped out, either when he was using the folder or when Peter had used it the previous month. A close search of Swenson's folder, as well as those of Rosenbloom and the other assistant professors, and the thin folders of the instructors, revealed nothing.

If the other sheets were cryptic records of discreditable incidents in the lives of the full and associate professors, as Tony's had been, it must mean that Peter had been practicing some kind of blackmail. Like father, like son, Bill thought. But it was improbable that he had been blackmailing for money. More likely that he would use his knowledge as a lever to implement his own wishes for the department. The desire for power could be as corrupting as money. Particularly if one already had money.

But to leap to the thought of blackmail, Bill realized, was to put too much importance on what he knew now about Peter's father. One mustn't assume that a blackmailer's son would automatically follow in his father's footsteps. There might be an innocent explanation of the pieces of paper. The dates and initials meant nothing to him. It was premature to assume that they indicated something scandalous.

What he had not considered, he realized, was his own folder. It was improbable that it would be the only one without such a sheet. But if it were a record of something discreditable, he could not think what it would be.

He phoned the president's secretary. "Professor Stratton here. I believe the president has the confidential folder about me in your office. Could you look in the back, please, and see whether there is a yellow sheet with a date or two on it?" As he waited, he tried to think of what in his past he would most hate having revealed.

The President's secretary came back on the phone. "Yes, there is a sheet. Would you like me to read the figures?"

"No, thanks, but I'd like to have the paper. I can stop by for it."

Well, that made it complete. All the full and associate professors. But he couldn't guess what he would find on the paper. Probably everyone in the world could, if pushed, think of a hundred discreditable things he had done. All the same, he couldn't remember much in his own life that seemed worthy of blackmail. That ought to be something dramatic, not just an inability to get out of bed in the morning, or picking one's nose, or even the fact that he sometimes had a piece of pie in the middle of the afternoon, in flagrant defiance of his diet. He had not been unfaithful to Carrie, and, in spite of what he had said to Tony, he had hardly been tempted. Thanks to a decent inheritance, his financial affairs were in good order. If he had ever committed plagiarism in his books, it had been done completely without volition. And he had never yielded to the temptation to kill, as he was beginning to believe someone in his own department had done.

Before he had met Carrie, he had had several relationships (they scarcely merited the name of affairs), of varying passionate intensity, with other girls. One of them, a Boston schoolteacher, had been close to hysteria when they broke up, but that was the best in the way of melodrama that he could muster. Anyway, Carrie knew about his previous girls, and since there was no one else who would be interested in them, they would be unsatisfactory stuff for blackmail. He would have to wait and see.

He ripped the envelope open as soon as he left the president's office. All that was written on the yellow sheet was "27 November" of three years previously. It meant nothing to him. His memory for dates was not good, and three years was a long time. Whatever it referred to had not impressed itself on his memory.

When he got home, he asked Carrie whether she remembered the date. "I don't think so," she said. "Is it important?"

"It could be."

"Maybe I can dig up something. I've kept stacks of old engagements calendars in a desk drawer ever since we were married."

She returned brandishing a limp blue book that she threw to Bill. He turned to the twenty-seventh of November. "'10:30, coffee, Laura,'" he read aloud. "That's not very exciting. How about this: 'Dentist, 2:30.' Boy, what a wild life you lead. '6:30 Outing Club.' Do you remember what that was?"

Carrie looked puzzled for a moment, then laughed. "Do I remember! and so should you, although I understand why you don't. It was the Todhills' Thanksgiving cocktail party. Remember now?"

"Oh, no!" Bill winced. "Not that. How could I forget?"

"Honey, if I had been as drunk as you were, I certainly would want to forget."

"I told you the truth then, that I had only two weak drinks. It was the effect of getting up after a couple of weeks of flu."

"Well, whatever caused it, you kissed Barbara Thomas, and I still think it was you who pinched Betsy Todhill. The poor man's Casanova. I'll bet no one but Gordon has kissed Barbara in twenty years, and unless it's just my nasty feminine instinct going wrong, I'm sure that Betsy's bottom isn't often a mass of bruises. Now, that *was* a night. It's a wonder you didn't have a relapse."

Bill looked serious. "Did I behave scandalously? Did I embarrass you badly?"

"Don't be silly. Everyone knew the drinks hit you because you'd been sick. Even Barbara was amused. It's always funny when a solid citizen suddenly gets out of hand. Not that you really did; probably you didn't even pinch Betsy. You're not worried about it, are you? There's no reason to be."

"What I did wouldn't be grounds for blackmail, would it?"

"Are you kidding? My God, Bill, you *aren't* being blackmailed?"

"I found a paper on which Peter Jackson had put my initials and that date. What else could it be for?"

Carrie looked incredulous. "If he thought that was a piece of dirt that would make you squirm, he wasn't much of a blackmailer."

"I'm not worried personally, but I think he was collecting material on the whole department. Maybe for blackmail."

"It sounds like his father. And look what happened to him."

"I know. I wonder whether it is a case of like father, like son."

That evening Bill went to see Tony. "I want you to reconsider asking me not to say anything about Peter and you and Susan Englander," he began. "I may as well tell you that I think Peter was collecting information on all the senior members of the department, and I'm afraid it had something to do with his death. I can't act as chairman of a department in which there may be a murderer, and that's precisely what I'm afraid of." He told Tony about the yellow slips in the folders. "Even my own," he said, and explained about the Todhill party. "It's beyond my province now; I'll have to go to the police."

"I see," Tony said haltingly. "But I'd hate to have the whole thing come out. It would hurt Laura terribly. And I wonder if it wouldn't look suspicious to the police that I had quarreled with him. Even so, I can't stand in your way."

"The fact that you told me about it proves that you're innocent, so stop worrying. After all, no one else even knew that you had quarreled with him. You didn't have to tell me."

"All right, then." Tony took a deep breath. "Go ahead."

"Thanks. I knew you would agree. And now I've got to ask you to keep this quiet. If one of the department had something to do with Peter's death, we shouldn't tip him off that the police know what Peter was up to."

"Okay. When are you going to tell the police?"

"If I may use this phone, I'll call now."

Bill was put through to Moynahan at the Devonport police station. "I'm sorry to bother you, but I've come across something that might have some bearing on Jackson's death. Could I talk to you soon?"

"Can you tell me now?"

"I'd rather not. How about tomorrow morning? At my office, if possible, because what I want to show you is there. As early as you can, please."

"I'll be there at nine."

All that night a procession of names marched through Bill's head. Fackler, Moorhead, Thomas, and Benson. One of them might be a murderer. Fackler, Moorhead, Thomas, and Benson. When he slept, they reappeared in his dreams. Fackler, Moorhead, Thomas, and Benson.

He was tired when he got to Winthrop Hall. It was five minutes before nine, and the office was not yet open, but Moynahan was waiting.

Sitting across the desk from Bill, he made an occasional note while Bill told what had led to his telephone call the night before.

"That's all I know," said Bill as he finished. "Maybe it was silly to call you, but I felt I had to."

"I'm glad you did. You may be onto something. May I see the papers?" He studied them, then looked up. "Do you have any kind of photocopier in the office?" Bill nodded. "Can you copy these without giving them to your secretary?"

"Easy. We all use it in place of carbons when we type something ourselves. Wait here." He came back a few minutes later with the yellow slips and photographs, and handed the lot to the detective.

Moynahan gave the originals back to Bill. "Please put them back in the folders, just as they were. These are all I'll need. Who else has a key to the files? The secretary?"

"No. Only the chairman."

"Where do you keep it?"

"In the back of a desk drawer, as Jackson did. I found it there before his furniture was moved out."

"Keep it with you, and don't leave it here in the office. No point in asking for trouble. And be careful; if someone killed Jackson to protect his reputation, he'd have no scruples about getting rid of you."

"Thanks, I've already thought of that."

"And don't leave the slip here that Jackson put in your folder. Anyone who had seen the others would realize that you had been/looking at them if he came across your own taken out of its folder. Why not give it to me?"

"Why not destroy it?"

Moynahan smiled. "Surely, you've read enough thrillers to know that the police don't destroy evidence. Now, Mr. Stratton, you're in a difficult spot running the department; you are also in a position to find out a lot the police can't. You know all these men, you know your way around the university as we don't. I don't know whether the case will be formally re-opened, but I'm certainly going to do some snooping around. I'd like your help. A lot of investigation we can do better than you can, but there are things you can do better than we can. If you help us, we may find out more about Jackson's death faster."

"I don't see how I could refuse."

"Then I'll be level with you. I'm going to give this piece of paper to a handwriting expert, and if the writing on it is the same as on the others, we're in partnership."

Puzzled, Bill asked, "What do you mean?"

"If you had killed Jackson, it would have been for something more serious than his knowing that you had too much to drink. And if you had killed him, it would not be difficult to substitute this paper and the date for something more incriminating. Then you would have a perfect alibi. Understand?"

Bill let out a tiny whistle of relief. "That's encouraging. I hope you do the same thing with the other papers. Most of all, I want you to clear Tony Bongiovanni."

Moynahan nodded. "You're probably right about his innocence. That leaves four other men. In your frank opinion, which of them is the most apt to commit murder?"

"I can't answer that question better than I could in Devonport. None of them seems like a murderer to me."

"Fair enough. Then, which of them might be covering up something in his private life?"

Bill slowly shook his head. "They're all reserved. I know them and like them, but I don't know much about their private lives."

Moynahan stood up. "I've got to get permission from the Chief to go ahead with this, but in the, meantime keep your eyes open and let me know anything that happens. And be careful of yourself. I don't want anything to happen to you."

"May I mention this to my wife?" Bill asked. "She's completely trustworthy."

"I'd prefer that you said nothing, because the fewer the leaks there are, the better. But if you are sure she won't mention it, at least it would keep her from accidentally telling anyone what you are doing. And she'll probably keep a close eye on you to keep you out of danger. That's not a bad thing in the circumstances."

CHAPTER TWELVE

For all his protestations of being willing to back Bill to the hilt, the president had been furious when he discovered what Dame Millicent was to be paid. It had taken an hour to placate him.

A late January morning was not Bill's notion of the ideal time to meet her, either. He was feeling balky at having had to drive three hours to Kennedy, but decency required that he meet an elderly woman on her first visit to the United States. Other transportation to Wilton would have been difficult. And it was true that she was really doing the department a favor by coming on short notice, however much the salary she had demanded. Guiltily, Bill realized that the reason he was grumpy was that he had miscalculated the drive and was nearly an hour early, and he hated sitting in airports.

He bought a newspaper and retired to the balcony of the International Arrivals building. There were no empty seats. Many of those that should have been so were taken up with luggage. As politely as he knew how, Bill asked a woman if she would mind putting her poodle on the floor. Muttering, she yanked the animal away and held him on her lap. The dog leaned toward Bill, and in an attempt to make amends, he reached to pat it. With a vicious lunge it snapped at his hand, but he snatched it back with nothing worse than a flesh wound. The woman glared at him and shifted the poodle away from his contamination.

People were inconsiderate when traveling. The woman across from him, for instance, occupied three seats. On either side of her was a pile of suitcases and untidy parcels, which she patted occasionally as she read. To be sure, anyone sitting next to her would have been sufficiently crowded by her open coat made of the fur of one of the commoner mammals, and by her generous figure. As Bill looked at her, she took out a cigarette and fitted it into an incongruously long holder. Equally improbable was the tiny hat of cherry red that perched atop a pile of gray hair that clearly had not been adequately disciplined in its youth, for it now led a rebellious life of its own. There was something about her ill-advised but generously applied lipstick that brought to mind a decayed gentlewoman making an honest living as the madam of a brothel.

As he opened his *New York Times*, Bill heard his name called on the public address system. He sighed, folded up the newspaper, and went toward the stairs. By the time he got back, the poodle would be in possession of his seat again.

When he identified himself to the girl at the counter, she said, "An English lady, a Dame Hetherege, is waiting for you." She pointed up at the balcony. "There she is." Following her finger, Bill saw the woman with the cigarette holder striding next to the rail.

"Good Lord" was the best he could manage before he thanked the girl.

"Dame Millicent?" he asked as he caught the woman just swinging around in full career.

"Professor Stratton? Where have you been? I've been waiting for you."

"I thought your plane was not due for another forty-five minutes."

"But I altered my flight, and I have been here nearly an hour," she boomed. "Or did I forget to let you know? Good heavens, I believe I did. I *am* so sorry. What a silly old woman you must think I am. But now that you are here, won't you help me with my bags? You wouldn't *believe* what a porter asked just to carry them for me. We'll save money this way. That will show them."

Staggering toward the car with three heavy suitcases, Bill had to admit that she was doing her share, carrying two packages of duty-free liquor, a hat box, two handbags, and a number of brown paper parcels, from one of which hung what looked suspiciously like a corset of formidable dimensions. Given the choice, he would have taken the suitcases any day.

"Well," she said as she eased herself into the front seat and fumbled with an inadequate seat belt, "I am looking forward to this. It is my first visit out here, and I am sure I shall find it fascinating. Do tell me again your university. I'm afraid I've forgotten again."

When Bill had mumbled Wilton's name, she said with an exuberance that frosted her side of windshield, "Of course, of course. The place where Professor Jackson was murdered."

"Actually, it was suicide."

"I know the police said that. I read all about it in the *Times* of New York. But they didn't fool me. Murder, I'm sure. It would have to be. And almost certainly by a medievalist. One who had read those articles of his. Sorry as I am to say it, they deserved murder. Yes, I'm afraid it was murder."

As factually as possible Bill told her a slightly censored story of what had happened in Devonport, making it as undramatic as he could. It was bad enough that he thought it was murder himself, without unleashing this torrent of English energy onto the case. When he had finished, he tried tactfully to turn the conversation. "What kind of project are you working on, now that you've finished the book on Iseult?"

"Oh," she said with pleasure, "do you know about that? I wasn't sure that anyone out here had read it. The royalties would not indicate it. Good, isn't it?" For a moment the flood stopped, then she laid a hand on Bill's right arm that nearly made him swerve off the road. "I hadn't really intended to tell you this, but what I've been doing since I retired at St. Agatha's is very different. Very. I've become, that is, I'm Deirdre Desiree." She sat back, obviously pleased to have given away her secret.

What was clearly a tremendous revelation was lost on Bill. "I'm afraid I don't know what you mean."

"Don't you read *anything* besides scholarly works? Suspense novels?"

"Not often," Bill hedged.

"*The Mistress of Muddlethorp Hall* or *Terror at Trantingham Castle* or *The Affair at Havingham House* or *Masquerade at Midnight?* There are two others that won't be published until spring, but those are the ones you might know. *That* is what I have been doing," she said with pride. "And they pay a lot better, I can tel! you, than books on Iseult of the White Hands."

Bill took the coward's way out. "I imagine that my wife knows them. As a matter of fact, I'm sure I've heard her mention them."

"I don't mean to boast, but I did want you to know that I was not speaking as an amateur when I said that I was positive that Professor Jackson had been murdered."

With relief Bill slowed down for a toll booth, carefully avoiding the lane for motorists with exact change, even though he knew that he had it in his pocket. He handed a ten dollar bill to the attendant and waited for the change with his head out of the window. By the time they were moving again, he was able to steer the talk toward Dame Millicent's seminar. The energy with which she talked of medieval literature was not less than that expended on airplanes and thrillers, but Bill felt better able to cope with it, once they were off the subject of Peter's death.

138

It was hard to believe that the woman beside him was thirty years his senior. He shuddered at the thought of keeping up with her, had he known her, in years past when she still had her youthful vigor. It didn't bear imagining. But she was entertaining, likable, and clearly immensely knowledgeable. At least she would be a change in Wilton. As Moorhead had said, there had been a surprise waiting for him at Kennedy. Or Onassis, as she now insisted on calling it.

When he had carried the last parcel into the furnished apartment the university was providing for her, she removed the animal with which she was draped. "I hope you enjoyed motoring here as much as I did. A splendid run. I do enjoy conversation with an intelligent man." Bill wondered how she had formed her opinion, since he had scarcely had a chance to speak. "And now, won't you have a drink with me? I brought six bottles with me. I had some difficulty with the customs officer, but in the end he saw the light of reason. It's all *bourbon*," she said proudly, giving the word its French pronunciation. "I'm sure this flat will provide at least two glasses."

Before Bill could answer, she was in the kitchen, opening and closing cupboards. She returned with the glasses. "You may have ice if you wish, but I recommend it straight." She poured two-thirds of a tumbler full and handed it to him. "Cheers. It *is* a good drink, isn't it? And so expensive at home."

A bit worse for wear, Bill stood up when he had worked his way through the bourbon. "Before I go, I want to ask if you can come to our house tomorrow. My wife and I have invited the full and associate professors to meet you over drinks, and we hope that you will stay for dinner with us afterward."

"What a lovely invitation. I look forward to meeting Mrs. Stratton, and meeting the others will give me a chance to see if I can find the murderer. You know, I feel confident that I shall be a great deal of help to the police. It really is fortunate that I've come just now, before all the clues are cold. Don't you feel that?"

"I'm certainly delighted that you could come now," Bill said diplomatically.

As he went out, she said in a conspiratorial whisper that shook the door frame, "Be sure you don't tell them about Deirdre Desiree."

There were times the next day when Bill wished for the omniscience of a suspense writer, even though he was glad that Dame Millicent was busy settling into her apartment, so that he was safe from her further suggestions. He and Moynahan sat in his office, once more looking at the photocopies of the papers from the personnel files. "I haven't had much time to work on them, but I'll be damned if I can find out anything from these initials and dates," the detective admitted gloomily. He spread out the copies and looked at them. "Jackson must have had a good memory. At least, he didn't put much on paper." He picked up one of the sheets and threw it down before Bill. "What do you make of that?"

At the top of the photocopy were Fackler's initials, and under them "October 21, 1964." Bill went to the file and pulled out Fackler's folder. "He was teaching then; he wasn't on leave, so whatever it means, it must refer to something that happened here at Wilton." He riffled through the thick folder. "Here's his teaching schedule for that term. Not that it shows much. I didn't even know what day of the week the twenty-first of October was. Wait a minute." He took a piece of paper and wrote figures on it. After scratching for a minute, he crossed out what he had written. "Damn it, I forgot about Leap Year." He wrote again. "There. It was a Wednesday."

"What did he teach that day?"

"An undergraduate lecture on Shakespeare at eleven, office hours from two until four in the afternoon, and a Milton

140

seminar in the evening, from eight until ten-thirty. A big day, but he likes to load some days so that he can have free ones."

"It doesn't sound like a big day to me," said Moynahan lazily. "Five and a half hours. I frequently work ten or eleven a day."

"No doubt," said Bill shortly, "but you don't have to spend ten hours getting ready for every hour that you count as work. It's a hell of a big day, actually." He saw that Moynahan was smiling. "Sorry, I didn't realize you were joking. I'm getting over-earnest. Still, I don't think this tells us much."

"Maybe he spent the night with one of his students, as Bongiovanni did, after the seminar."

Bill snorted. "I doubt it. Maybe nobody knows much about anyone else's sex life, but I'm sure he's not inclined that way. I'd be surprised if he has much sexual drive."

"All the more reason for him to be upset, and hence liable to blackmail, if he did kick up his heels."

"I don't buy that one. Have you tried the local newspaper files?"

"Every issue for a week before that date, and a week after. Not one blessed mention of Fackler. None of the police blotters anywhere near here have anything on him. Blank. How about this one?" He gave Benson's sheet to Bill.

The notation was simply "H.B., March 28, 1959." Bill shook his head in discouragement. "I haven't a clue. He must still have been in graduate school then."

"Where was that?"

"Columbia."

"Didn't Jackson teach there before he came here?"

"Yes, but I don't think they knew each other. I'm not even sure Peter was there at the same time." He flipped through the files. "Harry finished his work at Columbia in the spring of 1961, and Peter went there the following fall. So they just missed each other." He looked quickly through the letter Benson had written applying for a teaching position. "Not much here. He took his general examination in April 1959, just a month later. He passed them with considerable distinction. Benson's a bright guy, but I doubt that he would have done so well if something was pressing heavily on his mind. I'd guess he was getting ready for the exams on the twenty-eighth of March."

"He's a very buttoned-up young man, I thought," said Moynahan. "What's your impression of him?"

"Intelligent. Maybe not much sense of humor. Hard-working. Friendly in a shy sort of way, but I don't think he has many close friends except the girl he's engaged to. I like him a lot, but I don't know much about him personally."

"Who's the girl?"

"A schoolteacher in upstate New York. He's known her a long time, but they didn't get interested seriously until last year. Girl's not quite the word; she's Harry's age, in her early thirties. They went to high school together in Albany."

"What did his teachers at Columbia think of him?"

"He passed his generals with distinction, and that usually means they thought well of him. Afterwards, even if they didn't before."

"How about recommendations when he applied here?"

Bill handed four letters to him, and he skimmed through the first. "Admirably scrupulous in his research. . . . Dissertation on Byron. . . . Highest moral character." He handed it back to Bill and took up the second. "Distinguished work in my seminar on Shakespeare. . . . Quiet, though forceful, lecturer. . . . Scrupulously moral." He picked up the third letter. "Superlative paper in my seminar. Deserves to be published. . . . Highest integrity."

"Superlatives get a little boring," Moynahan said as he reached for the last of the recommendations. "Brilliant mind. . . . Unimpeachable character."

He put the letter down. "God seems to have a rival on His hands. Are all recommendations like that?"

"Professors don't often go in for moderate praise when they are helping a graduate student get a job; even so, these are unusual. But so is Harry."

"The one thing they all comment on is his morality. Is that usual?"

Bill frowned. "Harry is such a good man that it didn't seem strange as you read the comments. But I think it would ordinarily be taken for granted."

"It's almost as if they were protesting too much," Moynahan said. "Do you know anyone at Columbia who taught him?"

"Both McCracken and Lawrence, who wrote the first two of these letters."

"Could you tactfully find out whether there was a particular reason they were so insistent on his morality? In the meantime I'll see whether he has any kind of police record in New York City. And then we can go on from there. If you can't ask them easily, I could go ask them myself. But I'd prefer to keep it from looking like an official investigation."

"Academics are a funny race," Bill said. "Most of us feel more loyalty to our students than to the law. If you said murder, I think they would talk, but short of that, they would probably feel they were protecting the privacy of a friend and colleague. Better if I did the asking. I'll see what I can do."

"Then let's go on to Thomas's file."

Bill lifted his eyebrows at the entry, "G.T., September 30, 1939." He looked at Moynahan. "He reached a long way back for this one. Peter couldn't have been more than a teenager then."

"Anything in the files about Thomas?"

Bill searched for ten minutes, then shook his head. "Nothing about that date here. He studied at Oxford through the spring of 1939, and began graduate work at Chicago in February 1940. There's nothing to indicate where he was in between."

"Did he get a degree at Oxford?"

"Evidently not. I can't remember, but I think he was a Rhodes Scholar. I'll get *Who's Who*." When he brought the volume back from Rosie's office, he put it on the desk and the papers flew on either side. "My God, that's heavy."

Running his finger down the fine print, he read, "Student (Rhodes Scholar), Oxford U. 1937-39."

"Why do you suppose he left without a degree?"

Suddenly Bill knew what had been ticking at the back of his mind. "Of course. He once told me he had been there when the war broke out, and that he had to leave without a degree. He was doing a full three-year course for a B.A. Lots of American students used to do that. They repeated an undergraduate degree there before going on in graduate work here. England went into the war early in September 1939, so whatever this date refers to must have happened after he got back to this country."

"Let's have a look at that book, if you can lift it again." Moynahan put on his glasses to read. "What's that date again?"

"September 30, 1939."

"Here's a funny coincidence." Moynahan pointed to the fourth line of the entry, and Bill read, "M. Barbara Rewlett Proctor, Sept. 30, 1938."

"Do you know where they were married?" Moynahan asked.

"England, I think."

"Is his wife English?"

"Good Lord, no. Bostonian as they come."

"Why did they get married in England?"

"I think she went over there to marry him while he was in Oxford."

"Something drastic must have happened on their first anniversary. I wonder." He continued scanning the entry, then read aloud, "l dau., Cornelia Proctor."

"What do you make of that?" Bill asked.

"Enough to wonder whether I ought to cable to London to verify the date of their marriage."

"Why?"

"It smells fishy, that's all."

"Connie is married and lives in California, but she comes here occasionally to visit her parents."

"Where was she born?"

"Probably in Chicago. I think she was born when Gordon was a graduate student."

"It should be easy to get a copy of her birth certificate."

"What do you want that for?"

"The usual reason people claim to have been married an extra year is that they have an eldest child born inconveniently soon after they were actually married."

"How would Peter have known about that?"

"God knows. What I have to find out first is whether my suspicions are justified."

Bill smiled ruefully. "It would be embarrassing enough for any woman to have it known she had to get married, but it would be murder for Barbara." His smile faded. "Sorry for murder. Figure of speech. But she is one of the starchiest women I know."

"Starchy enough for her husband to kill someone to keep it quiet that she was pregnant before she was married?"

"Lord, no. Or even if she were, that doesn't mean she could talk Gordon into murdering Peter. Anyway, we don't even know that they had to get married."

"We ought to find out in a couple of days." Moynahan yawned and looked at his watch. "Moorhead's slip is last. And if you think Jackson reached a long way back for Thomas, take a look at this. 'February 12, 1913.'"

"Personnel files won't help on that one. He was only six years old then. He may have bitten his little brother or stolen some candy at the corner grocery or wet his pants in kindergarten, but that's about all."

"Perhaps something happened in his family. If one of his parents had been convicted of a serious crime, that might explain it. Funny how long afterwards people are ashamed of things like that. What do you know about his family?"

"Nothing." Bill picked up *Who's Who in America*. "Here's his entry. Born in Reading, Pennsylvania, the twenty-sixth of June 1907. His parents were Roy Henry and Orpha Ann Metcalf Moorhead. Undergraduate work at Harvard. Want any more?"

"Not now, at least. What would you do if this were a problem in literary biography? Suppose you wanted to find out about the family of a writer in whom you were interested, and you couldn't ask him or his wife."

"I'd probably put a letter in the *New York Times* book section and one in the *Times Literary Supplement* in London, to ask for help. But that doesn't apply in this case."

"You'd probably only start a long series of bad-tempered correspondence in the *Times Literary Supplement*. No, that won't do."

Bill carefully closed the reference volume, folded his hands on it, and started at Moynahan. "It's not my job to ask questions, but this is too much. I told you in Devonport that you didn't talk like a detective. How do you know about literary biography, and how in the name of God do you happen to be so familiar with the correspondence in the *T.L.S.*?"

Moynahan blushed deep red for the first time since Bill had known him. "It doesn't matter." He fidgeted, then put his glasses back into his pocket. "To tell the truth, I majored in English at Yale, and I got an M.A. at Rutgers. But for the love of heaven, don't tell anyone. I'd hate to have the other men on the force find out about it."

"Okay," said Bill, "but you can bet that I'll write this down, and when things are rough, I'll use it for blackmail."

"Cut it out, Mr. Stratton," said the detective, reverting in embarrassment to the tones of an awkward undergraduate. "Let's get back to Moorhead. How do we find out about him?"

"I'd probably go to the library in Reading and throw myself on the mercy of the librarian, for a start."

"And I'd probably check with the police there. Willing to make the trip with me?"

"Oh, no!" Then Bill added resignedly. "When do you want to go?"

"Saturday?"

"Fair enough. And you can talk about literature all the way. How many chances will I ever have to talk to a cop who majored in English at Yale?"

CHAPTER THIRTEEN

Had he felt positive of the meaning of the word, Bill would have said that he boggled at the sight of Dame Millicent when he picked her up. "I know that sherry—I mean, cocktail—parties are very common out here, so I bought what Marshall and Snelgrove called a cocktail gown. Will it do?" She turned around for him.

"Admirably," Bill murmured in a stunned voice. "Cocktail gown" it certainly was: shimmering blue satin that glinted purple in the light, cut low in front and held on by narrow shoulder straps. Its hemline was a few inches above knees sculpted in one of the heavier architectural orders. But the skimpiness of the dress, which would have been uncomfortably drafty in the rigors of a Cartersville winter, was compensated for by the beige woollen sweater that she wore under it. The long sleeves and high neck of the sweater projecting from beneath the dress gave her the appearance of a superannuated schoolgirl trying out for the hockey team in a blue satin gym jumper.

"I'm so glad you like it," she said as she put her red hat on top of her hair, which had clearly won hands-down over attempts to subdue it. "I thought it would be suitable."

Carrie did not so much as blench when Dame Millicent came in the door. She was seized by a fit of coughing, but there was nothing to indicate to their guest that anything was disturbing her but a cold. "Sore throat, I see," said Dame Millicent. "Try vinegar and honey. Old-fashioned, but it works. I'm delighted that I'm the first to arrive, Mrs. Stratton. I want to ask about the others. I realize that you have nothing but the amateur's approach, but I wonder if you have noticed anything to indicate who the murderer is."

"Murderer?" asked Carrie dubiously. "I don't know what you mean."

"Come, come. Don't try to put me off. One of your department must have killed Professor Jackson, and I mean to find out who it was. Has any of them changed recently? Nervous tics? Wringing of the hands? Or a sleepless look? The mind, as the psychologists tell us, has its own way of betraying the body. Lady Macbeth, you know."

"No, I'm afraid I haven't noticed anything of the sort. But, of course, I hadn't been looking," Carrie answered guilelessly.

Dame Millicent turned first to Bill, then to Carrie. "I know that I talk like an old fool, but I'm not. Don't make that mistake. And you are not fools, either, so don't pretend you haven't thought of murder." She went to the fire and rubbed her hands before it. "Very well, if you don't want to talk about it, I refuse to push you. It's a great deal colder in Cartersville than I had expected."

Laura Bongiovanni stayed home, nursing a cold. Tony arrived at the same time as the Moorheads, at whom Dame Millicent smiled and waved. "Professor Moorhead and I have known each other for years," she explained to Carrie, "although we have not often spoken. Most of the scholars who regularly use the North Reading Room at the British Museum know each other. It's a kind of freemasonry." She advanced toward the Moorheads. "We shall be colleagues at last! What a pleasure!"

"Sorry your wife is ill," she said to Tony. "Mrs. Stratton

has a cold, too. Terribly prevalent out here, I think. Probably because you don't heat your houses sufficiently. Tell her to try honey and vinegar. The only thing." She smiled in open tribute to Tony's good looks and went with the Moorheads into the dining room, where drinks were being dispensed.

"There is nothing," said Tony, shaking his head, "or at least nothing that I can think of, like a Dame. Wow."

Half an hour later the party was in full swing. "Bill," said Carrie, coming up to him, "would you be a love and talk to Margaret Fackler? It's difficult to get her into the party."

As she usually did at parties, Mrs. Fackler had selected a comfortable straight chair, put her purse between her sensible shoes, and sat nursing her drink as she regarded the others with a bemused and motherly air. Bill sighed silently. It was never easy to chat with her. She was completely pleasant, and grateful for a man to talk to, but she normally returned nothing but a smile to his conversational gambits. On only two subjects had he ever succeeded in drawing her out: her husband and her interest in the theater. He had little left to say about E. W., so he chose the alternative.

"Have you been to New York lately, Mrs. Fackler?"

"No, I haven't. I want to see the Genet play very much, and I am hoping that we can go during Easter vacation. But I did get to Boston last month to see the new production of *The Importance of Being Earnest* before it goes to New York. I know it's not fashionable any more to like it, but it is really such a splendid play. The production is good, but I still think the Gielgud troupe was the best I've ever seen. I hope you don't think I'm hopelessly out of date in liking Wilde."

"Outside of Shaw," Bill said sincerely, "it's certainly the best theater of the last hundred years." Her reference to Genet was hardly what he expected.

There were more surprises to come. "Isn't it silly, all the fuss that everyone is making about nudity in the theater? You'd think no one had ever seen a naked body before. Personally, I think it's very pleasant to see a well-built young man without his clothes, and the girls console me with the memory that I wasn't always shaped like this." She made a rueful gesture toward her generous hips. "And why everyone is so shocked at a few four-letter words is beyond me. We have all been reading them for years. As a matter of fact, not infrequently, when I burn my hand on the oven or hit my thumb with a hammer, I say—"

Mrs. Fackler's favorite expletive had to remain a mystery, for at that moment Harry Benson brought his fiancée to introduce her. As soon as he decently could, Bill excused himself and went to the dining room to see that the bartender was keeping the drink flowing.

At the bar he met Carrie, with the same idea. "Good party, darling," he had a chance to say before Barbara Thomas bore down on them.

Although some of their friends found Mrs. Thomas frigidly Bostonian, Carrie and Bill had always got on easily with her. It was disconcerting to see that she looked more drawn than usual. Bill remembered Gordon's hint that all had not been going well in their marriage.

"I'm glad I caught you together," she said. "I've been feeling terribly selfish ever since I came. I see Mrs. Jackson isn't here tonight, and I only hope that it isn't because you know I'm not fond of her. I should hate to feel that you hadn't invited her because of me."

"Of course not," Carrie answered. "We thought of asking her, but since this is a party for the department to meet Dame Millicent, we thought she would feel uncomfortable. It would only remind her of Peter."

"I'm glad," Mrs. Thomas said. "I can't tell you how I have regretted—well, snubbing her. She must be terribly lonely, and I wish there were some way I could make it up to her. I can't just invite her to my house; it would be too obvious that I was trying to make amends." The first tears that either of them had ever seen in her eyes were forming slowly. "It must have been a terrible shock to her. I didn't like her husband, but she seemed to love him." She blinked. "Sorry."

Impetuously Carrie took both her hands. "I doubt that friendliness is ever resented, even if it seems to be offered in amends. Why don't you invite her? She is a very lonely woman. I must ask her as often as I can, too."

"You're right, and I thank you. I think I'll stop at her house on my way home. That would be better than writing or telephoning. I've been feeling guilty, too, because I didn't want her in the Garden Club. Perhaps I can support her for membership."

Bill faded away tactfully, to join Dame Millicent, who was talking to Grace Moorhead and Gordon Thomas. "He sounds a thoroughly unsuitable type," he heard her saying. "I should have guessed it from his scholarship in any case, but today a young woman named Englander came to see me about her dissertation, and it seemed clear from what she said, that he had been rather more friendly than the duties of a supervisor strictly require. In Oxford, at least, supervisors are not expected to behave like that. Thoroughly unsuitable. Not that I'd guess he was without provocation. Miss Englander reminded me rather of the lady in Malory who tried to seduce Percival."

Dear God, thought Bill, I must get her off that subject any way that I can. But before he could speak, Grace Moorhead had begun on her favorite topic. "Of course, I think it's contrary to nature to have women graduate students." She stopped, afraid she might offend Dame Millicent. "I mean at Wilton. My father was a professor of English before becoming president, and he was resolutely against them. He was conservative, I know, and I am probably as old-fashioned as the bustle, but I agree with him. At Harvard or Princeton or Yale, perhaps. But not here. What do you say, Gordon? I count on you to support my reactionary views."

Thomas sucked on his pipe before answering. "I'm not sure I totally agree, Grace. I used to, but perhaps not now. I remember when I first came back to this country from Oxford—"

"Oxford!" Dame Millicent boomed. "Of course! I've been wondering where I had seen you. At first I thought it was at the B.M., where I knew Professor Moorhead, but that didn't seem right. I felt sure I had seen you or met you, and Professor Bongiovanni's face seems familiar, too. Oh, I *am* glad I remember. What college were you?"

"Trinity," Thomas said. Bill was amused to see his face turn pink with apparent pleasure.

"Of course you would be. Now, where could we have met?"

"Actually, I used to come to your lectures. But I didn't suppose you would remember. It's so long ago."

"Nonsense. No longer for me than for you. I remember perfectly well. I'm in an advanced state of decrepitude, but my memory hasn't totally gone, thank heaven. I suppose Oxford's where you got interested in bird-watching, isn't it?"

"No, I've been doing it ever since I was a boy."

"You must show me your birds some time." She looked hard at him. "Were you a rowing man? I seem to remember you that way."

Gordon was as flustered as one of his own undergraduates. "I did row in Torpids. I didn't realize you were interested in rowing."

"Interested? I haven't missed an Eights Week since the end of World War I. What did you row?"

Grace threw a look of amusement at Bill, and they left the others to a discussion of rowing styles, of why Cambridge so often defeated Oxford, and of the shame that the old barges had been replaced by boat houses.

Since it was a weeknight, the guests left early. As he said good night to them, Bill could not help thinking that among them was a murderer. Fackler, Moorhead, Thomas, and Benson. The list haunted him.

It was after eight when they were all gone. Bill and Dame Millicent waited in the living room for dinner. Although she was already well primed, Dame Millicent gratefully accepted another bourbon. Emma, released from the durance of the kitchen, where she had been confined during the party, raced into the room, took one look at the expanse of blue satin lap, leaped into its middle, and settled down to rest after her exertion. "Don't you dare move her," said Dame Millicent. "I love dogs and she knows it."

Apparently totally untouched by the amount of alcohol she had taken aboard, she launched into a discussion of her seminar. Bill was so interested that he forgot to be grateful that she had not brought up Peter's death again. Deirdre Desiree might be a fool, but as she had said, Dame Millicent Hetherege was certainly not.

The old woman's enthusiasm was so infectious that Bill and Carrie found themselves talking more at dinner and over coffee than they had expected. It was a surprise when the clock struck eleven. "Good heavens," Dame Millicent said, "I *am* a rude guest. I had no idea it was so late. Sorry, Emma, I shall have to put you down now and go home."

As he went out the door, Bill said to Carrie, "I'll stop at the office on the way home and pick up some work, so that I won't have to go in tomorrow morning. I should be back in half an hour, but don't worry if I'm not."

Before she got out of the car at her apartment house, Dame Millicent asked, "Are you sure Professor Bongiovanni has never been in England?"

"Positive," said Bill. "He's never been abroad."

"Then I was wrong about my memory still being accurate. I could have sworn I had seen him before. Ah, well, I may as well accept old age gracefully. He was most interesting tonight about the crime wave here in the university."

"Not really," Bill said. "A few offices have been broken into, and some equipment has been stolen. But that's not unusual in any university. A community this large is bound either to have thieves in it already or to attract them."

"Possibly," Dame Millicent answered, "and I suppose it is even more probable out here. This is a violent country, I should think. What I find still more alarming are the attacks that he has told me about. Innocent persons being hit and robbed on the campus at night. 'Muggings,' I believe the word is. Do be careful when you go to your office, won't you?"

"In a university community a professor is safe from muggings," Bill said, "because everyone knows he has so little money."

"Nonetheless, do be careful," she warned as he took her to the door.

The woman was mad on the subject of crime, he decided as he drove to Winthrop Hall. It was her King Charles's head. The building was dark except for the light in the entrance hall. The night janitors had finished, and the guard at the entrance had locked up at eleven. So far as Bill could see, no one else was working late. In the parking lot a few cars stood, probably left illegally overnight by undergraduates too tired to go to their own parking spaces.

On the side of the building was a small door that could be opened on the outside only by the keys given to the faculty, although it could be opened from the inside by pushing a long bar that extended the width of the door. Bill unlocked it and felt around the dark interior for the switch. He flipped it, and lights sprang up on the stairway stretching above his head.

Leaving the lights on, he went into the main hallway. The night light was enough for him to find his way to the elevator. He pressed the button, and in a minute he heard the elevator come to rest at the main floor. When the doors opened, he stepped in and touched the button for the fifth floor. Going up, he focused on what had been pushed to the back of his mind for an hour or so: all the conversation with Dame Millicent meant that he had not had an opportunity to go to the bathroom. Drinks before dinner, wine, and coffee after. First things first. He could get the papers later.

He knew it was craven of him, but he had never liked being alone in the big empty building at night. As a boy he had often had nightmares about being locked into a huge cathedral after dark, and something of the old terror returned when there was vast, uninhabited space around him. Several floors of empty offices, all locked and deserted. But bodily need was more pressing than boyhood fears. The men's room first of all.

Stepping out of the elevator on the fifth floor, he went briskly across the hall to the light switch. The corridor materialized, and he smiled at his momentary fears as he went to the men's room. A couple of minutes later he came back into the corridor. The elevator doors still stood open. As he looked, they closed, and he heard the sound of the elevator's descent. For the briefest of moments he felt his spine prickle again. It was nearly midnight, and no one else should be coming into the building. Then he relaxed as he remembered the timing device that automatically returned the elevator to the ground floor when it stood empty.

Most of the visitors to his office entered it through the room where Rosie held sway, but there was also an unmarked door opening from his office to the corridor, convenient for the times when he wanted to leave without going through the main office. He unlocked the private door and was about to go in when he thought once more of the elevator. It had not been on the ground floor when he arrived. That must mean that someone else was in the building.

He switched on the lights, and the inchoate darkness took

form again. He took two books from the shelves near the door, then walked to his desk to get the notes for a lecture that he was preparing. Suddenly he stopped, aware that something was subtly wrong with the room, although he could not at first make out what it was. Then he realized that his desk chair had been turned around and pulled over to face the personnel files behind the desk.

Afterward, he was to wonder how he knew so quickly what the intruder had been after. Without stopping to consider, he unlocked the drawer containing the folders of the current faculty and pulled out the front folder, Fackler's. The yellow sheet with E. W.'s initials was gone. Quickly he went through the others in order: Moorhead, Thomas, Benson, and Bongiovanni. The sheets were gone from each folder but Tony's. That was just as he remembered it. In a quiet fury he slammed the drawer and relocked it.

He was halfway to the door of Rosie's office, to see whether that had been disturbed, when he heard a sound from the corridor, a scarcely audible click as if a door latch were being carefully closed. For a moment animal fear overtook him. The yellow sheets had obviously been stolen by the one person who would most fear their discovery, Peter's murderer. And, if his ears had not tricked him, the murderer was probably still on this floor.

Unheroically, he could think of nothing for a moment but to lock himself in the office. Wedge chairs under the door handles. And then phone for help. But he discarded the idea almost as soon as it came into his mind. He might have imagined the sound of a door. But that didn't explain the elevator. What a figure he would make, locking himself into his own office and calling for the police!

The flash of ironic amusement was enough to restore a little courage. Taking a deep breath, he stepped out into the corridor. It was exactly as he had left it. All the doors were closed, no one was visible, and there was no place for anyone to hide. He must have imagined the sound. And the elevator had probably taken a late-working faculty member to one of the other floors.

In any case, he was not going to turn off the corridor light. That could burn all night, so far as he was concerned. For a moment he stood irresolute. If he rang for the elevator, he would have to wait for its return from the ground floor. He preferred going down the stairs. To hell with dignity; he would run, and he was sure he could run as fast as any other member of the department. Besides, he would have the advantage of running scared. At the bottom of the stairs he had only to lean on the bar that opened the door and he would be safely out of the building.

He turned away from the elevator and opened the stair door. The lights he had left burning when he entered the building had been turned off, and he could see nothing but the railing of the landing on which he stood. Beyond that the stairs plunged into darkness. He turned on the lights and looked up and down the stairwell. So far as he could see, it was reassuringly empty. He began sprinting down as fast as he could go, holding onto the rail to make a flying turn at the corners. If anyone else was running after him, the sound of his feet was covered by Bill's own shoes hitting every second or third metal-tipped step.

As he jumped down the last three steps to the ground floor, he stopped for an instant. There was no sound but the noise of his own panting and the pulse in his ears. Whoever had turned out the stair lights had not pursued him. All that remained was to walk to the door and out into the reassuringly cold night air.

More deliberately now, he walked across the open base of the stairwell toward the door. In the air above him he heard a faint susurration. Instinctively he jumped sideways, and, as he did, something hit the floor where he had been, landing with a frightening thud.

He raced to the door and, pushing the bar, looked back. Behind him, separated from the pages that littered the floor, lay the cover of *Who's Who in America*.

CHAPTER FOURTEEN

"He would have been killed if that book had hit him," Moynahan said, taking coffee from Carrie. "It weighs five or six pounds, and it would be lethal dropped from the fifth floor. I ought to scold you, Mrs. Stratton. I've already given your husband the devil, but you should have kept him from going there at midnight. That's why I let him tell you what was going on, hoping you would keep him out of trouble."

"At least," Bill said, "I'd have the distinction of being the first person murdered with a copy of *Who's Who*. That should have been a consolation in your widowhood, Carrie."

"We know now," said Moynahan, "that Jackson's murderer was willing to kill you to avoid being caught. But we still don't know who he is."

"It's my own fault we don't," Bill said regretfully. "If I had only had the sense to stay where I could see both outside doors, I'd have seen him when he came out. But my only thought was to get in touch with you and the university police. By the time I got back with them, he was gone. They spent nearly two hours combing the building."

"It wasn't your fault. He was probably watching out of a window, and he would have stayed until you were gone. Anyway, he might have gone out of a ground floor window on the other side of the building."

"He had to use one of the outside doors," Bill said. "The whole ground floor is taken up with the offices of the classics department, and our keys don't fit their doors."

"What you did was the only sensible thing," said Moynahan. "Stop worrying."

"Did you look for fingerprints?" Carrie asked.

"Yes, but there were only Jackson's and your husband's on the files. We have Jackson's prints from the time of his death. There were plenty of other prints all over the outside office, but not in the inner one. The prowler probably wore gloves. He'd be wearing them on a cold night, anyway. No luck there."

"I suppose you've already found out where the others were last night." Bill was ashamed of suggesting the obvious course of action.

"Yes," Moynahan answered. "Not only the four you mentioned, but Bongiovanni, too. All of them except Benson have alibis of a kind. Not water-tight but fairly good. The funny thing is that I think Benson is the only one who has absolute proof that he didn't leave home last night, but he won't give it to me."

"Why not?" asked Carrie.

Moynahan chuckled. "The fact is that I've found Fackler, Thomas, and Moorhead all have their own bedrooms. None of them shares a room with his wife. And all of them had dinner at home, read a while, then went to bed in their separate rooms. And their wives substantiate their stories. Mrs. Fackler heard her husband go to the bathroom some time in the middle of the night, but she has no idea what time it was. Unless one of the wives is lying, all three men went to bed at eleven o'clock. But any one of them might have got up and gone quietly out of the house without his wife being aware of it."

"How about Tony? He and Laura have a double bed."

Carrie sounded indignant. "He couldn't have gone out without her hearing him. And she wouldn't lie about it."

"Unfortunately, they didn't sleep together last night. Mrs. Bongiovanni had a bad cold and went to bed early. Her husband came up about eleven to say good night, then spent the night on the couch in his study, so that he wouldn't catch her cold."

"How about Harry Benson?"

"He said that he—." Moynahan broke off. "What time do you normally go to bed, Mrs. Stratton?"

"About eleven. Why? Naturally, I waited until Bill got home last night. I was clearing up the dinner things."

"Doesn't anyone in your department ever go to bed at ten-forty-five or eleven-fifteen or midnight? Benson said he went to bed at eleven, too, but that he had no one to corroborate that, since he lives alone."

"Then why do you think he has a good alibi?"

"Because he blushed like a schoolgirl when I asked him what time he went to bed. I suspect he didn't spend the night alone. A little later I asked him what time he took his fiancée back to her hotel, and he said ten-thirty. But the desk clerk at the hotel doesn't remember seeing her come in. He could have been mistaken, but I don't think so. She didn't drop her key at the desk when she left the hotel to come here, so he couldn't tell from that. But I think that Benson will turn out to be in the clear. I can push him on the matter, and when he realizes that he will be a suspect if he doesn't tell me, he'll probably come clean about his girl."

"I can ask Janet Coulson about it myself," Carrie said. "No woman would refuse to admit that she had spent the night with her fiancé if she thought that his misplaced chivalry would make him suspected of being a thief. This isn't 1900. I'll bet she doesn't even know he lied about it."

"You're probably right," Moynahan said. "Would you do that tomorrow?"

"I don't see," said Bill, "why you are so certain it couldn't be the campus prowler, who has been in the other offices."

"It has to be someone who has keys to Winthrop, to the English office, and to the files. They could be stolen, of course, but I doubt it. And the thief in the other campus offices had to break in. All the members of the department have keys to the building and to the main office. The door between that office and yours was unlocked, so it was easy to go from one to the other. And any member of the department could easily have had a key made for the files, simply by taking Jackson's key out of the desk any time between his death and the time that I asked you to keep it on your ring. It's as simple as that."

"Then," said Bill, "whatever Janet Coulson says, I think it must have been Harry. The way he was tugging at the file cabinet when I walked into.my office the other day wasn't natural. Even if Janet says he wasn't out of the apartment, she could be lying."

"Possibly, but I doubt it. Bongiovanni actually has the weakest alibi. It would have been easy for him to leave the house after he said good night to his wife."

Carrie looked angry. "It couldn't have been Tony. If it had been, he would have taken the sheet from his own folder."

"I don't think that proves much," said Moynahan. "You know the order they were in: Fackler, Moorhead, Thomas, Benson, Bongiovanni. He could have been going through them in order from the front and not finished before your husband interrupted him."

Carrie shook her head. "But if he were trying to get rid of evidence that Peter had been blackmailing him, he would surely have taken the paper from his own folder before he even looked in the others."

"No, darling," said Bill. "Even I can see the flaw in that. He and I had talked about the sheet in his folder, so he knew that I would notice if it were missing. His own sheet would

163

not be the most important to him." He looked at Moynahan. "I can't see any reason why Tony would have wanted to steal the paper after he knew that I had seen it. That doesn't make sense."

"I'm afraid it could make sense," the detective said slowly. "My own guess is that he intended to steal all the papers, but you interrupted him and he didn't have time to finish the job. But there is also the possibility that he didn't intend to take the sheet from his own folder. As you say, that would have called your attention to the fact that the files had been rifled. Anyway, he had already explained what the initials and dates meant on that sheet. What he doesn't know is that you have seen the sheets in the other folders, or that you even suspect that they are there.

"Let's suppose for a moment that what he told you was true, but that it wasn't the whole truth. In other words, that he did stay overnight with Miss Englander once, but that Professor Jackson had something even more serious on him. The best way for him to keep you from suspecting that Jackson was an out-and-out blackmailer, not just jealous about Miss Englander, would be to remove any sheets in the other folders. That seems at least a possibility why he would rifle the others but leave his own folder untouched, doesn't it?"

"I don't see how he could have known that the sheets were in the other folders," Bill said reflectively.

"You told him yourself that you had found his sheet in his personnel folder. It wouldn't be hard for him to guess that Jackson might have put something in the folders of the other men."

Bill shook his head stubbornly. "Just the same, Tony is my best friend, and I know him better than I do anyone else in the department. I know, positively know, that he wouldn't have tried to kill me. He likes me as well as I like him."

"That's the most telling thing in favor of his innocence. I agree it's not likely that he would try to kill you. Let's change the subject for a moment. What did you tell the department this morning about the prowler?"

"Only that I had discovered a prowler in the building, and that he was probably the one who had been burgling other offices. I said nothing about his stealing the sheets from the files, or about his trying to brain me. And I asked them not to use their offices in the evening until the whole thing was cleared up. I don't want anything to happen to someone else."

Before Moynahan could answer, the telephone rang. Bill picked it up. "Yes, Harry.... Of course you should.... Yes.... Mmm.... Of course not. Why would I talk about it? I don't want to embarrass either you or Janet. And I think you were wise to call. Goodbye." He turned to the others. "You've probably guessed what Harry had to say. He and Janet wanted me to tell you that she spent the night with him and can swear that he wasn't out of the apartment after nine o'clock. He stuttered and stammered and practically blushed through the telephone, but he sounded as if he were telling the truth."

"Does that make Bongiovanni seem more probable to you as the prowler?" asked Moynahan.

"Not to me," Bill said stubbornly.

"I didn't think it would. The reason I asked what you had told the department is that I have a plan. I doubt that it would prove much, except negatively, but it might be worth trying. It's only nine-thirty now, and the guard in Winthrop Hall doesn't go off duty until eleven. If we were to go to your office in a few minutes, we could wait there until after eleven.

"You've asked the department not to go there until the business of the prowler is cleared up, so that whoever went there last night would be sure that he wouldn't run across any of the rest of the faculty. If, as I suspect, he didn't get the job done last night, he'll come back tonight, when he'll be safe from being bothered again. And we'll be there to catch him."

Carrie said sharply, "I don't want Bill getting in any danger again. Once is enough."

"You needn't worry," said Moynahan. "I've got a gun. There won't be any danger for your husband."

"I don't like the idea of setting a trap for one of the men in my own department," Bill said doubtfully.

"Not even for a murderer?" Moynahan lifted his eyebrows.

"All right then."

"Fair enough," Moynahan said. "And I promise you, Mrs. Stratton, that you needn't worry. In the meantime, we at least have photocopies of the papers stolen from the files. By tomorrow the Chicago police should call about the birth certificate of Thomas's daughter, and I've got searches going on in New York and Boston for a record of their marriage. In the meantime I'd appreciate it if you could go ahead with your friends at Columbia to find out what you can about Benson. There's always the possibility that his fiancée is lying to give him an alibi. Do you think that would be possible, Mrs. Stratton?"

"Most women would lie to protect their husbands. Or fiancés. I know darned well I would."

"I thought you said Mrs. Bongiovanni wouldn't lie."

"All right." Carrie looked shamefaced. "I guess even Laura would."

"You go ahead with the Columbia business, then, and on Saturday we can go to Reading to nose around about Moorhead."

"Why don't you just ask them about the papers?" Carrie wondered aloud. "Surely they'd rather tell the truth about Peter's blackmailing them than be suspected of murder."

"Because I want the truth, not a made-up story. The murderer is probably going to lie, anyway, but we can clear the others more easily if we know the truth. We may have to eliminate all but one of the professors. If we tip them off before we have any evidence, even the innocent ones might panic and lie about being blackmailed. Clear?"

Carrie nodded. "Clear."

"Fackler is the one who baffles me," Moynahan said. "October 21, 1964, doesn't mean a blessed thing to me, and neither the local newspapers nor the police blotters around here have anything about him. And you say that he was teaching that Wednesday, so he couldn't have gone far. The man who is looking for a record of Thomas's marriage in New York is also looking for a police record on Fackler, but I don't think he'll find anything. Is there any way you could find out whether he actually taught that Wednesday?"

"There's no official record," said Bill, "but he is so proud of never having missed a seminar, that it's as good as a record. When I first came here, he had never missed one. If he had missed in 1964, we'd have heard about it."

"Did you say a Wednesday seminar?" Carrie asked.

"Yes."

"He's had them on Wednesday nights for years, hasn't he?"

"As long as I can remember."

"Bill, if I got into trouble, would you try hard to keep anyone else from knowing about it?"

"Of course." He frowned with his usual embarrassment at demonstrations of conjugal affection in front of others.

"Perhaps E. W. feels the same way. Margaret Fackler often goes off to Boston on Wednesdays, since E. W. is going to be busy in the evening. She visits a sister there, and it's the day for cheap excursions on the train. Sometimes she goes to the theater. I think she went to a play last month on a Wednesday."

"She told me yesterday at the party," said Bill.

"I don't know of any kind of trouble she could have got into, but if she did, I'll bet she was innocent," Carrie said. "I mean, it wouldn't have been her fault. But that might explain why you can't find out anything around here."

"Mrs. Stratton, I could kiss you," Moynahan said.

"Be my guest," Bill said and had the satisfaction of watching the detective turn red for the second time in their acquaintance.

At ten-thirty Bill and Moynahan parked near Winthrop. As they got out of the car, Bill put the flashlight from the glove compartment into his coat pocket. Feeling absurdly like a character in a grade-B movie, he asked Moynahan, "Got your gun?" In answer the detective patted his side.

The night guard was yawning over a book as he sat inside the glass doors of the building. "Anyone in the English office tonight, Fred?"

"No, sir. I think they all got scared off by last night."

"Then do us a favor and don't say anything about our being here if someone else comes in."

"Right you are." Fred gave him a conspiratorial wink. "Not a word."

Bill opened the door to the stairway and motioned Moynahan through. "It's a long climb, but it doesn't advertise to the whole building that we're here, as the elevator would."

Before they got to the fifth floor, Bill was puffing and wishing that they could stop for a rest, but Moynahan moved beside him in the darkness with the relentless tread of the tireless walker. Bill was glad that he had at least managed to get the post position.

He unlocked the door to the fifth floor. The corridor was black. "Put your hand on my shoulder," he said softly, and guided Moynahan across the hallway to the door of his own office. Once inside, Moynahan took the flashlight and shone it around. Everything seemed to be in place. They walked into Rosie's office and looked. Nothing wrong there. They returned to Bill's office, leaving the door ajar.

"If we talk quietly, no one in the hall can hear us," Moynahan said. "But hold it down. And no overhead lights. They probably couldn't be seen from the hall, but they could from the outside." He handed Bill the flashlight.

Bill went to the personnel file and unlocked it. Without removing Tony's folder, he fanned it open. "The sheet's still there," he said, then shut the drawer and locked the file again.

"I doubt that anyone will show up," Moynahan said in a dispirited whisper. "All the same, we'd better hide now."

The Coromandel screen had been Bill's grandparents' pride, but it was too big to fit easily into the house, and he had kept it in his office ever since he came to Wilton. Its four panels of tiny figures washed with gold, now gone dull, stood against the wall at the end of the office nearest the door to the corridor, facing the desk and files by the windows. "I'll fold it a bit more, so that the cracks will be wider," Bill said. He shone the light on his watch. It was five minutes before eleven. "And it will give us more room. It may be a long wait."

The two men lay stretched out on the floor, their feet protruding at either end of the screen. If there should be any noise, they could quickly sit up and pull in their feet. In the meantime it was more comfortable lying down. For the first time Bill blessed the hated wall-to-wall carpeting. "I feel like something out of a French farce," he said.

"More like a Sheridan play," Moynahan contributed, and Bill smiled to himself. "I don't know what your grandmother would think of our using her screen this way. I'd hate to damage anything as beautiful as this."

Bill folded his hands behind his head. It was strange to whisper to someone lying with the top of his head almost touching one's own. After a long silence he said, "How long do you think we ought to wait?"

"I don't see much sense in staying long after midnight. Anyone who is coming will show up at a time when it would be reasonable for him to be on a legitimate errand."

"The funny thing is that I can't think of anything to say. I guess it's the effect of being so completely out of context. Probably we ought to be swapping dirty stories or limericks, but I can't remember any."

"Except for unprintable ones that I've heard ascribed to Robert Frost, the limerick has pretty much had it," Moynahan said. "I like double dactyls better. More metrically demanding. I even wrote some once."

Bill smiled again at the thought of a detective who wrote poetry. "I've tried them, too."

"Okay, let's have one."

"You brought it up. You first."

"It isn't much, really." Moynahan sounded embarrassed, as if the incongruity of his being a detective had hit him, too. "But here goes:

> Higgledy-piggledy,
> Alfred Lord Tennyson
> Met in the garden a
> Maiden named Maud.
>
> There he behaved to her
> Ultraplatonically,
> Proving conclusively
> Poets are odd.

As I said, it isn't much," he finished lamely. "Your turn."

"You're more literary than I am," Bill said. "My own reflects a dirtier mind. I wrote it after seeing too many movies.

> Tittipy-hittipy,
> G. Lollabrigida,
> Making a movie, met
> Miss Janet Leigh,

Said, 'Anglo-Saxons are
Circummammarily
Grossly inferior to
Loren and me.'"

He had scarcely finished the last word before Moynahan touched his head. "Sssh!"

Through the door Bill heard the low hum of the elevator. The sound increased as it rose in the shaft. Both men sat up and leaned against the wall, their feet hidden by the screen. Bill turned the light onto his watch and showed it to Moynahan. Eleven-forty. He reached to the screen to turn the end panel in further. As he did, it began swaying. Moynahan reached up and steadied it until it sat firmly again. "Thank God," was all he whispered.

The elevator was now clearly audible. Then its sound stopped at their floor, and there was a fraction of a second before its doors opened. Bill was conscious of a slight shiver down his back. The banging of the doors might have covered the sound of someone stepping out, for he heard nothing but the elevator. He sensed Moynahan's alertness, although he would have been puzzled to say how he recognized it, since there was no noise from the detective.

After a time the doors closed again, and the elevator started its descent. For a wild moment Bill wondered whether lying on the floor so long had inverted his senses. Could someone else have been on the fifth floor all the time? If so, the elevator would be taking him down to the first floor, instead of having deposited him outside the office door. He was debating whether to mention it to Moynahan, when he heard the whisper of rubber soles on the terrazzo floor of the corridor. They moved past his own door toward the door of Rosie's office, and then he heard the handle turning quietly, as if to see whether it was locked.

Then came a jingle followed by the sound of a key being inserted carefully into the lock. The door opened, and instead of being allowed to close by itself, it was shut so quietly as to be almost inaudible. Briefly Bill heard nothing but his own breathing and the pounding of his heart. He put his nose into the crook of his arm to muffle the sound of his breathing, but his heart seemed more tell-tale than any Poe ever thought of. Moynahan was as quiet as stone.

The door from Rosie's office squeaked slightly as it was pushed open. Through the crack of the screen Bill could see the doorway, but he could make out little except a vague shadow in the darkness. The rubber soles whished across the rug toward Bill's desk, and now he could see a man's form clearly against the faint light from the windows. He heard his desk chair being moved backward, as if toward the files. The man's figure disappeared below the line of the window sills, and there was no noise until Bill heard a scritch-scritch-scritch, like metal rubbing on metal.

Moynahan took the flashlight from him, then Bill felt the detective rising with infinite care. The scritch continued. Soft as it was, it probably masked any sound Moynahan had made.

"Stay where you are, and don't move!" Moynahan's voice cracked the silence. Bill scrambled to his feet as a beam of light shot out from the flashlight toward the intruder. He heard the click as Moynahan switched on the bright overhead lights.

Through the crack in the screen Bill saw the desk chair turn around. Blinded, first by the flashlight, now by the general illumination, Harry Benson gaped at them. Bill stepped from behind the screen just as Harry picked up the heavy crystal ashtray in one hand and heaved it at them. Bill ducked, but it caught him hard on the shoulder. "Stop it, Harry," he shouted.

Harry blinked and focussed, then crumpled back into the chair. "Oh, my God, Bill, I didn't know it was you."

Moynahan walked toward Benson, his gun pointing at him. "Stand up and put your hands over your head." Benson obeyed. Bill saw that he was trembling. "Now tell us what you're doing here."

"Nothing, nothing. I didn't mean to hit you. I thought it was the prowler, the one who had been in the other offices. You aren't hurt, are you?"

"Not much." He would have a painful bruise, but there had been no real harm done. "What are you doing here, Harry?" Without waiting for an answer, he walked to the file cabinet. Projecting from the top of the "Current" drawer was a flat piece of steel. "What's this?" Even as he asked, he saw that it was a hack-saw blade. "What are you doing here?"

Benson stood silent, as if unable to remember himself why he had come. "Honestly, Bill, I thought it was the man who had robbed the psychology office. I swear I did."

"See if he's got a gun." For the first time Moynahan's voice sounded to Bill like that of a policeman.

He ran his hands over Harry's body, then shook his head. "No, he hasn't."

"Now empty his pockets."

Embarrassed at treating a colleague in this fashion, Bill carefully searched Harry, who stood limply, and put his scanty findings on the desk. There was a key ring, a billfold, a fountain pen, an engagement book, and a pocket handkerchief.

Moynahan motioned Harry to the other end of the room, and with his left hand opened the billfold, then shook out each key individually. Leaving the little pile on the desk, he pulled a chair from under the seminar table and pushed it against a bookcase. "Sit there. And you can put your hands down."

When Harry was seated, rubbing his hands together,

Moynahan asked again, "What were you doing here? Why were you trying to get into that file cabinet?"

Harry's mouth opened and shut, as if he were unable to control his jaw, before he spoke. "I—I was trying to get some papers."

"What papers?" Moynahan's voice was like steel.

"Reports, reports that Professor Jackson wrote," Harry sounded more in control of himself now.

"What kind of reports?"

"Reports about my teaching."

"What did you want them for?"

Benson looked at Bill, then back at Moynahan. "I had decided to go somewhere else to teach as soon as I could, but I knew that Jackson hated me, and I thought he would probably write adverse reports about me."

"Is that possible?" Moynahan looked at Bill.

"I suppose so." He shrugged.

"Was Professor Jackson blackmailing you?"

Harry's mouth worked again. "I don't know what you're talking about."

"Did he know anything discreditable about you?"

"I—I don't think so."

"Were you in this office last night?"

"No, I swear I wasn't. I told you where I was. Janet can tell you, too."

"Why were you filing the lock? Why didn't you use a key?"

"I didn't have one."

"Are you sure?"

Even to Bill, Harry looked totally confused by the question. "I don't think anyone but Bill has a key."

Moynahan looked at Bill. "Anything you want to ask?"

"No, I don't think so."

Moynahan stood thoughtfully for a moment. "All right, then, I guess you can go home tonight. But you'd better be sure to be around. We may want to talk to you again. Have you got a car here?" Harry shook his head. "Then we'll give you a lift home, if Mr. Stratton doesn't mind."

Harry sat in the front seat with Bill. Moynahan sat in the rear. They rode silently until the detective asked, "Where is Miss Coulson tonight?"

"In her hotel," Harry said sullenly. "I took her there before I went to Bill's office. She knew nothing about this, and I don't want you to try to pin anything on her."

"I don't want to pin anything on anyone," Moynahan said tranquilly.

As Harry got out, he turned to Bill. "I'm sorry I threw that ashtray at you. I wouldn't have hurt you intentionally for anything. I thought it was the sneak thief."

"Good night," the detective said brusquely. "Be sure you don't leave town."

"Well, what do you think of all that?" Bill asked when they were alone.

"I'm not sure. All that I feel positive about is that he wasn't the one who stole the other papers. If he had a key, he would have used it."

"Couldn't he deliberately have used a saw, so that it would look as if there were a second prowler, even if he still had the key he used last night?"

"I don't think so. Sawing through a lock is a long business, and he wouldn't have wanted to take a chance on being caught. He didn't have a key on him, and he didn't have a chance to throw it away before we caught him. Even if he were deliberately trying to mislead us by sawing the lock, he'd have taken out the paper first, to be sure he had it."

"That's right." Bill turned into his driveway. "Let's talk a minute before you go. What you say about the key is sensible. I don't believe, though, that he was there to get his hands on reports Peter might have written."

"Neither do I. My guess is that he wasn't the prowler last night, but that he came tonight to get the record of Jackson's having blackmailed him. After all, if he wasn't there last night, he would have no way of knowing that it had already disappeared."

"Come in for a drink?" Moynahan shook his head. "Okay, then, if he was after a paper, he was lying to us about not having been blackmailed. That figures."

"We had to expect that they would all lie about that, so we're not very far ahead on that score, unless we can find out what happened to him on the twenty-eighth of March 1959."

"I'm glad you let him go home," Bill said. "I don't think that throwing him into jail would have made him tell us anything more. He's a stubborn man."

Moynahan shrugged. "What would we throw him into jail for? He may have disobeyed your warning about going into the building, but there was nothing illegal in his being there or in the office. After all, he has his own keys to both of them. Unless he was prosecuted for damaging the file cabinet, there's not much we could hold him for, anyway. But I'd certainly like to know what information Jackson had that was so important to Benson that he went to the office on the chance that there might be a record of it in his file."

"Is there any chance that the other robberies around campus had anything to do with this? Could they have been smoke-screens to fool us about the theft in the English office?"

"Not a chance," Moynahan said. "They began long before Jackson was murdered and before there was any need to get rid of the yellow sheets. And I don't think any member of the English faculty would be the right type to undertake a succession of thefts and muggings. I'll give you ten-to-one that they turn out to be coincidental."

"We may have been wrong in assuming that last night's prowler was the murderer. Maybe he was just someone like

Harry who was being blackmailed, and was worried about being connected with the murder."

"Possibly," Moynahan said, "but the murderer was the one who needed most urgently to destroy the yellow sheets, and I'll bet he was the one who got here first."

CHAPTER FIFTEEN

The next morning Bill found his senior class in eighteenth-century literature more interested in talking about prowlers than about Fielding. Although they had no way of knowing what had happened the previous night, they all knew that Bill and the police had searched Winthrop two nights before.

"I'm sure it was the S.D.S." was the opinion of one tweedily dressed young man waiting outside the classroom when Bill arrived.

"I doubt it," Bill said comfortably. "Probably just someone looking for a typewriter to sell."

Several of his pupils tried to question him about the prowler at the beginning of the hour. Neither Parson Adams, Joseph Andrews, nor a discussion of Fielding's religious views engaged their attention, and it was only when he shamelessly guided them toward talking about the attempted rape of Fanny that the shadow of stealthy entry to the building seemed to dissipate.

Peter's death had taken place during vacation, while most of the undergraduates were gone from the campus, so it had caused less sensation than it would otherwise have done. But this had happened while they were only a few hundred yards away, drinking beer, planning carnal conquest, sleeping, or even, in some cases, studying. The students' excitement, however, rose immediately to the surface, and though it disrupted their work, it would soon die down. What it must be doing to the efficiency of the other teachers in the department, he could hardly imagine. The unacknowledged presence of murder and theft could totally upset the department in a short time.

Dame Millicent was waiting for him when he finished class. "What can I do for you?" he asked. "Is the seminar shaping up?"

"It's taking form adequately. But that isn't what I wanted to talk to you about. I know you deny that Professor Jackson was murdered. Surely, you can't do that any longer. I've given the matter a good bit of thought, and I am sure I know who killed him."

Bill looked inquiringly, but he refused to give any verbal admission of belief in the murder.

"It's Mrs. Fackler!"

"Why in the name of heaven do you think that?"

"It's obvious. She wanted her husband to be chairman, and she was willing to stop at nothing."

Bill passed a hand over his mouth. If this was the reasoning of Deirdre Desiree, her books must rely for their popularity on more than the logic of the detection of crime. "But she wasn't even in Devonport when he was killed."

Consternation spread over her face. "My goodness. I hadn't considered that." Then, with one of her startling flashes of good sense, she said, "And don't think that I'd have made that mistake in one of my books. I'd have caught it in the rewriting. Oh, dear. Oh, dear. Then it must have been her husband."

"Even if Peter Jackson's death had been murder, Fackler couldn't have killed him. In confidence I'll tell you that E. W. was asked to be chairman and that he declined. I'm afraid you're wrong about him."

She considered. "I don't like to accuse him. He's a splendid scholar, and I like what I have seen of him, but I feel quite positive. Surely, after having killed Professor Jackson, he was so bothered by his conscience that he couldn't bring himself to accept the chairmanship, the very thing for which he had been willing to kill. I'm sure it's the only explanation of why such a nice man could be a murderer. I've just got to work out a few details, and then I think I shall be justified in going to the police."

"I'm sorry, Dame Millicent, but I happen to know that the police thought of that motive and then discarded it." How could he tell her tactfully to keep her oar out of a business that might become dangerous for her? Perhaps a direct lie would be best. "I realize that you haven't had any experience with American police, but I should warn you that the worst you have read about them is an understatement. They don't welcome interference, or even suggestions, and they have been known to be . . . well, brutal to people who innocently approached them. I don't want anything like that to happen to you."

"Yes, yes, I *do* see what you mean." For a moment she looked cowed. "Thank you so much for warning me." Then her face brightened. "However, even they would realize that I am a British subject and that they would not dare touch me. But it would be wise, I imagine, for me to be very careful. If I have any other suggestions, I'll come to you, and you can help me in approaching them."

"That's a sound idea, and I'll be glad to help." Even if she wasted his time, that was better than getting her involved in what was already a sufficiently complicated business.

"Thank you again." She started for the door, then turned. "I almost forgot to tell you. Do you remember that I felt sure I had seen Professor Bongiovanni before? Last night, just before I fell asleep, I realized what I had been thinking of. There is an American cinema actor, a Mr. Anthony Curtis, and I suddenly recognized that because of Professor Bongiovanni's likeness to him, I thought I had seen Professor Bongiovanni himself. Stupid of me, wasn't it?" She went through the door in a whirl of scarves.

Immediately she was gone, Rosie brought in Moynahan. "Thanks to your wife, we found out easily by calling the police. We'd better see him now."

"Must I stay?" asked Bill. "Can't you handle this without me? After all, they're friends of mine."

"There's no way of disguising the fact that you found the paper in his folder. You ought to be here."

"All right," Bill said reluctantly. He pushed Rosie's buzzer. "Ask Professor Fackler to come in, please."

Fackler smiled absently as he entered. "Good morning. What can I do for you?"

"I should tell you," Moynahan said, "that the Devonport police are still investigating Professor Jackson's death. And I must ask you some more questions."

"Yes, of course. I thought it was all settled, but if I can help, I'll be glad to."

"What were your relations with Professor Jackson? Did you have any trouble with him?"

"I admit that I never approved of his scholarship. Both slipshod and unimaginative. The kind of thing that gives academic writing a bad name. But I tried not to let him know how I felt."

"Did you like him?"

Fackler squinted, as if he could not remember. "Not really, I suppose. But probably no one did. He was autocratic, but perhaps he would have softened if he had been around here longer. He wasn't likable. No, the more I think of it, I suppose I didn't like him. Not the way I do most of my colleagues." He looked shyly at his shoes, as if embarrassed at the length of his speech.

"How did your wife get along with him?"

"My wife? Oh, yes, Margaret. I'm afraid I don't know. If she didn't like him, she would not have been apt to say so."

He considered. "Besides, she scarcely knew him, except to talk to him at the three or four parties where they met. I doubt that she had even read anything he wrote."

"Then I must ask you bluntly. Was Professor Jackson blackmailing you?"

With a look of transparent disbelief that such things happened, Fackler said, "Oh, no. I didn't like him, but I wouldn't have thought that of him."

"Was there nothing he might have blackmailed you about? Anything at all?"

Fackler turned pink. "He didn't know about *that*, did he? I was sure no one here knew about it."

"What do you mean?"

"I'm sorry you should find out about it this way, Bill. But you know I am retiring year after next, and I have been worried about how we should live then. The pensions are so small. This past autumn I have been corresponding with the University of New York at Utica. They said that if I were to come there next year, instead of finishing out my term here, they would keep me on until I am seventy-five." He waved a hand vaguely in the air. "That is, if my brain cells don't deteriorate before then. I haven't decided yet. I should have told you at once, as soon as I had decided. Now, how did Jackson find that out? It was supposed to be a completely confidential correspondence." He looked as nearly annoyed as Bill could remember.

"No, I don't mean that," Moynahan said quietly. "Does the date of October 21, 1964, mean anything to you?"

"Oh, dear me, yes. But I can't see what it has to do with Utica. That was when Margaret had such a trying time in Boston. I'll not forget that for a long time."

"Would you tell us what happened, please?"

Fackler turned to Bill. "You know how absent-minded she is. I'm sorry, Lieutenant; I know you haven't met her. But she *is* absent-minded, I'm afraid. It doesn't normally bother

182

her much. But on that day she was shopping in Boston, and in one of the big shops—I'm afraid I've forgotten its name now—she was looking at gloves. There was no clerk to help her, and when she found the pair she wanted, she forgot that she had not paid for them. She put them on and started out of the shop. A detective stopped her." He looked apologetically at Moynahan. "Not a police officer, of course. I'm sure they wouldn't have made that mistake. It was very embarrassing for her." He looked as if he were about to continue, but he slowly subsided into his habitual silence, his eyes once more directed to the floor.

Moynahan waited unsuccessfully a moment for Fackler to continue. "And what happened about it?"

Fackler looked at him in wonder. "Didn't you know? I assumed the police knew these things. She had to go before a judge, but he soon saw the truth and only cautioned her to be careful in the future. A sensible man."

Beginning to look nettled at his difficulty in extracting the information he wanted, Moynahan tried again. "Did Professor Jackson know about this?"

"Yes, I think he spoke about it once. I can't remember when, but I'm sure he did mention it."

"How did he find out?"

"That's curious," said Fackler. "I don't think I had the wit to ask him. I should have, I know. But the truth is, I may occasionally be a little absent-minded myself. Margaret says so."

"Did he attempt to blackmail you about it?"

"No, of course not. As I said, he wasn't that kind of man. Not a good scholar, of course, but he was a gentleman. Or very nearly so, I think."

"Didn't you mind his knowing it?"

"Why? It was embarrassing for Margaret at the time, but the judge was quite sensible. After all, she had done nothing wrong."

Another ten minutes of questioning got Moynahan no further. Fackler did not seem surprised that he should know about his wife, and he seemed totally unembarrassed that Bill should know. It came as a surprise when he turned at the door as he was leaving and anxiously asked Moynahan. "Does anyone else have to know about this?"

"Not unless I find that it's connected with Jackson's death."

Fackler sighed, and the anxiety ebbed away. "That's a relief. You know, I should hate to have anyone know about my negotiations with Utica until I had decided about their offer. It could be most embarrassing for them."

"If he is a fair sample of the academic mind," Moynahan said when the door had closed, "I don't envy you your job as chairman."

"Five minutes from now," said Bill, "he may have forgotten he ever talked to us, but there isn't a better, more informed Shakespearean scholar in the country. Or a better teacher. When it comes to the Renaissance, he has a mind like a steel trap."

"He doesn't look guilty to me. Damn it, that's the trouble with this whole case. No one seems capable of murder, or even vulnerable to blackmail. If this goes on, I'll have to include you in the list of suspects again, just to have something to work on." He grinned. "How about Thomas?"

"I feel safe in saying that you won't find him vague."

When Thomas was seated in the chair where Fackler had sat, Moynahan asked what he felt about Jackson.

"I've already told you I didn't like him. Actually, I disliked him thoroughly. I couldn't respect him as a scholar, and he was stupidly arrogant in his relationships with others."

"What did your wife think of him?"

Thomas's face lost its composure. "She scarcely knew him, but I think she would have disliked him as much as I did, had she known him better."

"Did he ever try to blackmail you?"

184

Thomas's eyebrows shot up, but all that he said was, "Never."

"Is there anything he might have used for blackmail if he had known about it?"

"Probably. I doubt that anyone gets through life without having done something that he is ashamed of. But I can't think of anything specific."

"What does September 30, 1939, mean to you?"

"It's the date that I was—no, it was the first anniversary of our marriage."

"Where were you married, Professor Thomas?"

"In London."

Moynahan took a paper from his briefcase. "I have here a copy of the marriage certificate of Gordon Swift Thomas and Barbara Hewlett Proctor in New York on September 30, 1939. Not 1938. Why did you say you had been married in London a year before?"

Thomas's face seemed to sag as they watched. "All right. I lied. I wanted to protect Barbara. But it doesn't matter now, I suppose."

Quickly, Moynahan pulled out another paper. "And here is a record of the telephone conversation I had this morning. Your daughter Cornelia was born in Chicago on April 16, 1940. Is that right?"

"Yes," said Thomas. "What of it? Why bring it up now? My wife isn't the first woman in history to be pregnant when she was married. Why in hell do you want to rake up things like that? It was bad enough for her thirty years ago. Why bother her now?"

"I'm not interested in your private life, Professor Thomas, unless it has something to do with Jackson's death. Where did you meet Mrs. Thomas?"

"She was touring England. She spent a month in Oxford, and I met her there and fell in love. When she got back home, she found that she was pregnant. She was going to come back and get married there, but the war broke out. I came back to this country instead, and we got married in New York. What else do you want to know?" His voice was hostile.

"Did Jackson know about this?"

"Yes. That is, he knew we had to get married. Once I made a slip and said that we had been married in New York. He knew that we had said we were married in England, and he began nosing around until he found how old Connie was. It wasn't any of his business. If you want to know, that's why I disliked him."

"Did he ever threaten to tell what he had found out?"

Thomas sat without answering for a long time. "Yes," he said at last. "That's how I knew how he had found out."

"Then why did you say he had never blackmailed you?"

Thomas threw him the impatient look he usually reserved for slow students. "He threatened me, but he didn't blackmail me. Blackmail involves money or payment. I didn't lie. But I would have done so willingly to keep you from finding out about Barbara."

"How did he threaten you?"

"Bill, do you remember the meeting where we first voted on Evans? Jackson made it clear to me that he would leak out what he knew if I didn't vote for Evans. I was the one who cast the affirmative vote."

"But you spoke against his promotion," said Bill, puzzled.

"I didn't say I wouldn't do that. Maybe honor at such a point doesn't make much sense, but at least I did what I had promised Jackson."

"Why," asked Moynahan, "did it seem so important to you after all these years? You said yourself that such things aren't uncommon."

"You would have to know my wife to understand that. You understand, don't you, Bill?" Bill nodded. "It might not have mattered to most women. But it did to Barbara. A lot."

"Did it matter enough to her for you to kill Jackson to keep him from talking?" Moynahan cut in quickly.

Thomas lifted his head and looked him in the eye. "No, no. I give you my word of honor it didn't."

When Moynahan had indicated that the interview was over, Thomas asked, "May I speak to Mr. Stratton? Alone, I mean."

"Of course. I'll go outside."

While Moynahan was gathering his papers, Thomas wandered to the window and stood looking out. He did not turn even when he heard the sound of the closing door.

"Gordon," said Bill, "I'm sorry I had to be here. Moynahan insisted."

Thomas stood still, as if he had not heard, but he reached out to take the window cord. When he spoke, still looking toward the river, Bill could scarcely recognize his voice. "I know. Don't worry. I don't care. Really." He turned around, and Bill was shocked to see tears running down his face. "I wanted to tell you it doesn't matter any more. I suppose it's almost funny that I tried so long to protect her over—over what we were talking about, and now it doesn't matter. You see, we are separating. Barbara left for New York this morning, and she's not coming back."

Bill went to him and put a hand on his shoulder. Not for the first time, he realized that there is no grief so hard to bear in others as that of the habitually reserved.

"Thanks, Bill. Sorry to make an ass of myself, but I didn't want you to be embarrassed at hearing Moynahan and me. It seemed simplest just to tell you why it didn't matter. I'd have to tell the others soon, anyway. They'll wonder where she is."

There was something touching in the light accent he gave "she." "Why don't you come for dinner with us?" Bill asked. "Stay overnight if you will."

"No, thanks. It won't be easy to live alone after thirty years, but if I have to, I may as well begin at once. Thirty years is a long time. I know I'm a dry old stick, but I didn't think Barbara minded." He went to the door. "Would you mind telling the rest of the department. I don't think I could do it. I'll go feed the birds now."

When Moynahan came back, Bill told him what Thomas had said. There was no breach of confidence, since it would be common knowledge soon.

"I'm sorry," Moynahan said, "that we had to put him through the hoops about her. Why did she leave him?"

"He didn't say, but I think it's fairly obvious. He's a nice man, but he isn't the world's most exciting. Carrie thinks he's dull as ditchwater. He said something about being a dry old stick."

"I'm not surprised, but women don't usually leave their husbands after thirty years just because they are dull. They've known it long before, and they're usually resigned to the fact. Any chance that she has a lover?"

"I sincerely doubt it. They haven't been getting along well for some time. Maybe she just couldn't take it any longer. I'm not trying to be an amateur psychologist, but I should think that the fact of having had to marry him might gnaw at a woman for years. You know, the feeling that she had been trapped into something she wouldn't have chosen freely."

"I suppose so." Moynahan seemed to lose interest in Thomas. "That's two of them. Glad we won't have to talk to any others today."

"What did you think of Fackler and Thomas?" asked Bill.

"I can't see that either of them had any motive for murder. Fackler was open enough, and everything he told us was borne out by the Boston police report. The fact of his wife's being picked up for shoplifting probably wouldn't worry him. I didn't like Thomas's lying, but I can't blame him. He was obviously shaken up by his wife's leaving him. I hope that we can find something juicier about Moorhead or Benson."

188

"I've been thinking," Bill said, "about that party Carrie and I gave the other night before I nearly got brained. Margaret Fackler mentioned going to Boston, but it didn't mean a thing to me. And Barbara got all tearful about June Jackson, whom she's never liked. Probably knowing that her own marriage was going to bust up made her sympathetic to June for the first time. But that didn't click, either."

"You had no way of knowing that either incident was important."

"That's not what I mean. If someone murdered Peter, it was to protect some very important piece of information, and we ought to be able to figure out what that was. I only wonder what I may have missed about Moorhead or Benson. Maybe even at that same party."

"We may have a better idea when you track down your friends at Columbia, and when we have been to Reading."

CHAPTER SIXTEEN

The doorbell rang as Bill was hanging up the telephone. He started for the hall, but he heard a good-natured bellow that made him wince for Carrie. "I'm so dreadfully sorry to come unannounced, and I do hope that you will forgive me, but I was out for my constitutional and passed your house. I couldn't resist ringing your bell, because I want to ask a favor."

"Come in, Dame Millicent." Carrie was fortunately not one of those women who are furious at unexpected callers.

"There you are, Professor Stratton. Good morning, good morning." Bill tried not to flinch. He was seldom at his best at nine, and most of the energy generated by breakfast had already been dissipated by his telephone call from Derek Lawrence of Columbia.

Dame Millicent accepted a cup of coffee from the bottom of the breakfast pot and shed her coat and several scarves. "I want to ask a favor of you. A great favor. And I do hope that you will feel perfectly free to refuse. It's about this creature." She stroked Emma, who had taken up her place on the visiting lap. "You said the other night that you are going to send her to training school."

"I know it's lazy," Bill said, "but I really don't have the time to train her myself. And, God knows, she needs it. How you can stand fifty pounds of Labrador on your lap, I don't know."

190

"I used to ride a great deal when I was young. The farmer on our family place kenneled the local hunt, and as a girl I spent every moment I could with the hounds. The habit became engrained, and I've had dogs ever since. I had a lovely Alsatian bitch that died last year. As a matter of fact, I don't believe that I should have come here if she were still alive. Too much of a wrench to leave her. St. Agatha's was most forbearing about my keeping a bitch in college. Quite unlike most women's colleges. In Oxford, at any rate. But there: all that is quite unimportant. What I wanted to say is that the one thing I am really good at is handling dogs. Would you let me train Emma? I could come every morning after breakfast and take her for a long walk through the university grounds. I need exercise, and I like a good morning blow. It would be much more amusing for me to have her to walk with, she could get exercise too, and I could be training her at the same time. Is that too much to ask?"

Bill nearly shouted with pleasure. "What a wonderful idea. We hated thinking that she would be away for two months in the kennels. But are you sure it isn't too much for you? You have your own work to do."

"Actually, I'm not doing any writing for Deirdre Desiree right now, and I have been teaching medieval literature for half a century. If I can't give a seminar without putting my full mind to it, it's fifty years wasted. To tell the truth, I have lots of spare time. Besides," and she looked shrewdly at Bill, "I got so much more salary from you than I had anticipated, that I feel I should do something in return."

"It isn't my money," said Bill, "it's the university's."

"If you think I am going to give any of it back to them, you are quite mistaken. Not, as I believe Shaw said, bloody likely. Very well, then, that's settled." She threw down the rest of her coffee, reswathed herself, pulled a pristine leash from her pocket, and had Emma out the door before either

Bill or Carrie could say more. From the front sidewalk drifted hoarse shouts of "Sit! Sit, you little monster."

"Carrie," Bill said as soon as the roars of training had faded, "would you please call Moynahan for me and tell him that I talked to Derek Lawrence. Ask him if he can be in my office at eleven. I've got to rush now."

Moynahan, who had already agreed to come to Wilton if Bill turned up any information, arrived promptly. They talked for ten minutes before Bill buzzed Rosie and asked to have Harry Benson come in.

Moynahan went through the preliminaries of explaining to Harry why they had asked to see him. Benson sat stiffly on the edge of his chair, pale but well in control of himself, answering monosyllabically.

At last Moynahan asked whether Harry had liked Jackson.

"Adequately," he answered. "I didn't know him well. He didn't like me, but I've already told you that the other night."

"Did he ever attempt to threaten you, or coerce you?"

"No." Harry's mouth closed tightly.

Moynahan took out the photograph of the paper that had been stolen from Benson's file. "H. B., March 28, 1959," he read, then slid it over so that the other man could see it. "Does that mean anything to you?"

Harry did not change expression as he looked at it, but his face turned dark red. "Those are my initials, if that's what you mean."

"Do you recognize the date?"

"No."

"Would it refresh your memory if I told you that it was the night before Easter of the spring when you took your general examinations?"

Instead of answering the question, Harry asked, "Where did you get that?"

"It was found in your folder in Professor Jackson's personnel files."

"The dirty son of a bitch," escaped before Harry could catch himself.

"I take it you do recognize the date. To save your wondering, I should tell you that Professor Stratton and I know the general circumstances. What we want to know are the particulars. Whatever you tell us will be treated confidentially unless it can be shown to have something to do with Professor Jackson's death."

It took some time to get the information from Harry, but he began talking reluctantly. He had been preparing for his general graduate examinations that spring and had not gone home for Easter. Most of his friends were away, and he had finished his work for that evening about eleven o'clock. For several days he had hardly spoken to anyone except the library staff, and he felt lonely. He went to a bar near the library and ordered a beer. There were few customers in the place, but sitting on the stool next to him was a man of about his own age. They talked about music in a desultory way, and his neighbor introduced himself as a graduate student in anthropology. By midnight they were the only customers in the bar, and the bartender told them that he was closing for the night.

The young man suggested that they continue talking at another bar, but Harry proposed that they go to his apartment for a nightcap and a sample of his new recording of the Berlioz *Requiem*. The young man accepted and they left the bar.

When they reached the sidewalk, the supposed anthropology student pulled out a badge, announced that he was a detective, and arrested Harry for importuning. At first Harry was so surprised that he didn't even know what the detective meant. When he finally recognized his meaning, he protested his innocence. Finally, he accompanied the policeman to the station, struggling all the way to explain.

He was booked, and when he appeared before a judge, he was found guilty and let off with a suspended sentence. At first he planned to say nothing and hope that no one at Columbia heard of it, but there was a small story about the incident in one of the newspapers. Rather than let the story be unchallenged, he went to the head of the English department and to the dean of the graduate school, to tell the truth of what had happened. Afterwards, he talked to the various members of the faculty with whom he worked.

Fortunately, his reputation was so good that all the professors believed his account. In any case, Bill thought as he listened, most of them would have been less shocked than Harry believed, even if he had not been innocent. But their belief in his innocence had undoubtedly been the reason for the repeated assertions of his high moral character in their recommendations.

"Did Professor Jackson know about all this?" Moynahan asked.

"Yes." Harry was reverting to monosyllables.

"How did he find out?"

"He came to Columbia to teach the year that I came here. Someone told him. Probably without intending to harm me. People are damned thoughtless, particularly about gossip."

"Are you sure he never threatened you with what he knew?"

"You win. Yes, he did."

"How?"

"He never did like me, and he would have been happy if I had left Wilton. Probably so that he could promote one of his own toadies if I vacated an associate professorship. A number of times he told me what wonderful opportunities there were for young men in other universities and asked me if I wanted him to recommend me. I kept pretending I didn't realize that he wanted to get rid of me, and told him I was satisfied here.

"In December he and his wife gave a party at their house. I tried to keep away from him, until he asked me to come into his study. I couldn't refuse. When he got me alone, he told

194

me that he was so very, very sorry, but he would have to ask me to give two extra courses this term. He kept telling me how valuable I was, and how he regretted having to give me an extra load, but I got the message. He intended to make it more and more unpleasant, until I would be forced to go somewhere else. So I told him that I'd be damned if he could force me out.

"Then he changed his tune and told me he understood I was going to get married this spring. He said that would be a real change for me. When I asked him what he meant, he said he hadn't realized I was interested in women. I told him he was a dirty-minded bastard, and then he said, 'I wonder what your fiancée thinks about your getting arrested for being a queer. I'll have to ask her.' That was too much. I hit him, and I guess I caught him off-guard, because I knocked him down. I went out of the study, and that's the last time I spoke to him except for a couple of times at the M.L.A. meeting, when I couldn't get out of it."

"Did your fiancée know about this?"

"She knew what happened when I was at Columbia, but she didn't know how Jackson had been acting. There was no point in getting her all upset."

"Were you angry enough to kill Jackson?"

Harry considered. "I knew you were thinking that. Yes, I was at the time. If I could have beaten him to death at his own party, I think I wouldn't have minded. But I didn't poison him. Anyway, I knew from the way the big coward whimpered that he would be afraid to bother me again. I hated him, but I didn't kill him."

"Mr. Benson," said Moynahan, "would you like to tell us now why you were in Mr. Stratton's office when we found you there?"

With sudden anger flaring in his eyes, Harry said, "Why the hell do you keep badgering me? You know why I was there, and you probably knew the other night, too. I went there to see if Peter Jackson had put anything about that Columbia business in my file. It was just the kind of thing the bastard would do. I knew there wouldn't be anyone else from the department in the building, so I took a chance. I had been thinking about it before, but I was afraid I'd be seen. It's the kind of luck I have that it was the one night when you were there. Do you blame me if I wanted to get whatever Jackson had put there?"

"To be frank," Moynahan answered, "I don't blame you very much. Probably most people would feel the same way. Even if I'm a policeman, I suppose I'd probably have tried it in your place."

The rest of the detective's questions elicited nothing new. When Benson was gone, he said, "Somehow, I believe him, and I believe that he's innocent. The curious thing about his story is that he is the only one of your colleagues on whom Jackson had the kind of information that might lead to murder, but he is also the only one with an iron-clad alibi for the night that someone tried to kill you. We couldn't make any of the wives testify against their husbands if that were necessary. Not even if one of them heard her husband go out that night. But being a fiancée isn't enough; Miss Coulson would have to give evidence. The fact is, though, that I think she really spent the night with him and that he didn't leave the apartment."

"Obviously, I don't know whether he killed Jackson," Bill said, "but I believe everything else that he told us. For one thing, he didn't need to tell us about having slugged Peter because he had no way of knowing that anyone else knew about it. If he had been guilty, I think he would have kept quiet about their having a fight. Everybody seems to be clear so far, and I've got a feeling that we're not going to find out anything about Moorehead to indicate that he was our murderer."

"I know," Moynahan said gloomily.

"Harry and Tony Bongiovanni are the only two men in the department whose flash points are sufficiently low for them to kill someone in anger. But I don't see either of them planning a poisoning."

"I should tell you that we did a little more investigating on your friend Bongiovanni. I sent a man to talk to Miss Englander, and her story about spending the night with him tallied exactly with his. I think he's still in the clear."

And there the matter stood until their trip next day to Reading.

CHAPTER SEVENTEEN

The library stood directly across Franklin Street from the Benevolent and Protective Order of Elks. Presumably classical elks, Bill thought as he looked at the library, a gray Greek temple breathing the air of Paestum over the residents of Reading hurrying down the cold sunlit street.

When he had parked the car, he went up the steps to enter the shrine. A librarian sat working over cards at her desk in what should have been either the adytum or the naos; he ought to have paid more attention to the lectures years ago on an uncomfortable bus tour through Greece. "May I help you?" she asked distrustfully.

Bill smiled as charmingly as he knew how. "I do hope you can. I want to find out about a man who lived in Reading a long time ago. He's dead now, but I don't even know when he died."

Faced with a librarian's problem, she looked a degree less suspicious. "That doesn't help much, does it? Who was he?"

"His name was Ralph Moorhead."

She put her forefinger alongside her nose as she thought. "There are several Moorhead families in Reading. I used to know some of them. When did he lived here?"

Since the first had worked, Bill tried another disarming smile. "I know that he lived here in 1907, and I think he was still here in 1913. It isn't much to go on, I know, and I hate to bother you on a Saturday morning, when I realize that you are so busy. But if you could help, I'd appreciate it enormously. I've driven four hours to get here because it is so important to me."

"Don't apologize," she said, smiling now and tossing her gray hair. "We're not busy in the morning. It's the afternoon, when they've done all their shopping and want to get a thriller for the weekend. That's the bad time. Let's see, now."

"I wonder," said Bill helpfully, "if there would be newspapers for those years. I could start there."

"Of course. We have the files. I think the *Eagle* would be best. In the meantime I can be looking at the city directories."

An hour later Bill was dusty to the elbows and discouraged. He had begun looking through the *Eagle* of February 1913, but if there was a mention of any Moorhead, he had missed it. By the time he got to March, he was beginning to lose confidence, but he had at least learned where the *Eagle* was apt to print its crime news. And innocent enough the 1913 crime news seemed, too: several petty thefts, a fight or two, and an investigation of larceny at a local coal company. Either Reading had a particularly lawful past or times really had changed. No murders or rapes, not so much as a mention of a mugging, and he looked in vain for accounts of automobile accidents.

Not until the May issues did he come across the name. A runaway horse had knocked down an old woman, and Dr. Ralph Moorhead, who had been nearby, had given her first aid. It was at least an addition to his information that Roy's father had been a doctor, but that could have been found out easily in a dozen different ways. Not much progress there. He continued wearily through the rest of May and June, then stopped. Surely, anything criminal in which Dr. Moorhead or his family had been concerned would have been mentioned by then. He closed the volumes and dusted his hands. He had failed, but perhaps Moynahan would have found out something from the police.

Despite her prognostications of a calm morning, the librarian was busy stamping books for a line of patrons when he returned. He waited until she was finished before he approached her. She looked up in chagrin. "I'm sorry, but I've been so busy that I haven't had a chance to get to the city directories. Have you found anything? Was the *Eagle* any use?"

"Not much," Bill said, "except that I found out he was a doctor."

Her face lighted. "*Doctor* Moorhead? Of course. He was our family doctor when I was a girl." She paused and flushed. "Of course, I was very young then. Just a tiny girl. He lived a few houses away from us on North Fifth. I've often seen him. My parents knew him too. What was it you wanted to know?"

Bill stopped. He had not really considered what he would say was the object of his search. "What sort of family did he have?"

"I'm afraid I don't remember very well. As I say, I was very small then. I think they had a boy, but I'm not sure whether they had any other children. Isn't it silly, but I really don't remember."

More conversation ensued, but nothing that was suggestive to Bill. He made a move to break away. "Well, thank you very much indeed. I have to be going now." He was meeting Moynahan for lunch.

"Sorry I wasn't able to help more." But it would not matter, if Moynahan had any luck. "Ssssh!" she hissed at a pair of teenagers who had come in, talking in a normal tone of voice.

Bill was almost to the door when he heard a confused sound of "O-o-o! Excuse me!" He turned to see the librarian waving, and he went back. "My father is dead, but my mother knew the Moorheads. We still live on North Fifth. Would you like to see her?"

"Yes, indeed, if it wouldn't be a nuisance." The librarian was at least sixty; her mother could not be less than eighty, and a visit would probably be useless. Nonetheless, it would be foolish to ignore the only lead he had uncovered.

"She's Mrs. Fenstermacher. Here's the address." She handed him a slip with a number written on it. "We live on the first floor. We used to have the whole house, but after my father died, we thought it would be nicer to have a man upstairs at night. Prowlers."

Lunch in a coffee shop was quiet. Moynahan had been no luckier than Bill, although he, too, had discovered that the elder Moorhead was a doctor. If they were to find out anything in Reading, it would have to be from Mrs. Fenstermacher.

At two o'clock they rang her bell. Bill was expecting a wispy little old lady, but a hearty woman, well corseted, with two spots of rouge on her face, answered the door. Perhaps sixty-five, and probably the companion or nurse to Mrs. Fenstermacher. "I wonder if I might see Mrs. Fenstermacher," he asked.

"Are you Mr. Stratton? I heard you would be coming."

"Yes, I am. Is this a convenient time to see Mrs. Fenstermacher?"

"It's fine for me now. Come in. My daughter didn't say there would be two of you coming." Bill introduced Moynahan. "It doesn't matter. I've got the spice cake out, and all I have to do is get another cup for the coffee. There's lots of coffee. Sit down." She bustled out to the kitchen, while Bill and Moynahan leaned cautiously back against the antimacassars, looking in surprise at each other. It was impossible for her to be less than eighty. Perhaps spice cake was the answer in the search for eternal youth.

"Well, now," she said when she sat down after giving them

coffee, cake, and napkins, and passing sugar and thick cream. "Eat up, and tell me what you want."

Cautiously, Bill told her they were trying to find out about Dr. Moorhead. "He was a relative of a friend of mine."

"Is there money involved?" Bill shook his head. "That's a pity. It's always nice to get money. I got to know him about 1903. His wife Orpha and I were in school together, and she and Ralph and my husband Earle and I used to run around together. He was a good man. He was older than Orpha, of course, but he was real good to her. They got married when he got out of medical school in Philadelphia, and then they settled down here. Earle and I got married a year or two later, and we moved into this house. I've lived here ever since. And I'll probably die here," she said happily as she took another large bite of cake.

"Did they have any children?" Moynahan asked disingenuously.

"Just little Leroy. Orpha lost several babies. It was touch and go with Leroy, but with his father a doctor and all, he made it. A good little boy. Too quiet for me, but a nice boy. I hear he's teaching at a school up in New England now. He always was smart."

As cautiously as he could, Bill edged the conversation around to gossip about the Moorheads. "Not them," she said vigorously. "They never had a bit of trouble. Ralph was always good to her, like I said. Now, the Stroheimers, who lived next door to them, that was different. Frank used to cheat on Beulah all the time."

After a highly colored account of the flagrant infidelity of Frank Stroheimer, Moynahan asked about Dr. Moorhead's professional ability. Interspersed with a story of how he had saved her when she had a ruptured appendix was Mrs. Fenstermacher's recurrent paean of praise of his medical brilliance. Nothing there, so far as they could see. Both the elder Moorheads had been dead for years, and the house had been sold to a family from Pottstown, whose children were bringing down the tone of the neighborhood.

Was there anyone with whom they didn't get on well? Orpha was the best housekeeper in the neighborhood, and Ralph the best doctor in town; how could anyone fail to get on with them? Avenue after avenue was pursued, but there was nothing to fasten on. At last, gorged with spice cake, Bill and Moynahan took their leave. A dead end.

"With that sterling success under our belts," Moynahan said as they got to the car, "we may as well go home and chalk up a lost day. I'm sorry for you, Mr. Stratton, but it's an old story to me. We may find out something back in Cartersville, but I don't know how at the moment."

The sun that had made the air crystalline that morning was gone. A few miles out of Reading scattered flakes of snow began falling. In another hour the snow was thick and the road slippery, so that Bill had to slow down to twenty miles an hour. "We'll be late getting back," he said. "I hope you don't have plans for the evening." Moynahan shook his head, but said nothing. It was nearly four o'clock, and the light would soon be gone. Both men stared glumly through the snow ahead.

It was the worst drive Bill could remember. Frequently he had to stick his head out of the window when the snow defeated the wipers, and after dark it was worse. At eight they stopped for coffee and sandwiches. They still had thirty miles to go, and they would not be in Cartersville before ten. Moynahan had left his car in the Strattons' driveway, and he would have to pick it up before going back to Devonport. Even worse than the snow was the realization that the trip had been totally unrewarding.

It was nearly ten-thirty before they pulled up at Bill's house. The front light was burning. "Do you want to stay the night?" Bill asked. "Or haven't you had enough snow driving yet?"

"No, thanks, I have to get back."

"At least come in and have a drink and something warm to eat before you start. You've not had much but spice cake since lunch." Moynahan accepted with alacrity.

Dame Millicent had eaten dinner with Carrie, and she was waiting for a taxi to take her home. Carrie introduced Moynahan, and Bill was relieved to notice that she called him "Mr. Moynahan," without mentioning that he was a detective. Dame Millicent might find out in time who he was, but there was no point in letting her badger Moynahan with her theories while he was so tired.

"I'm the dog trainer," she said cryptically to Moynahan. "Mr. Stratton, I want you to see how well Emma is getting along. She's responding very nicely. Come here, girl." Emma trotted obediently to her. "SIT!" Unabashed by the bellow, Emma obeyed slowly. "She's not very firm yet, but that is a real sit." Emma looked around for approval, her tail sweeping a wide arc in the nap of the rug, and Dame Millicent patted her. "All right, go play." The puppy ran with dizzying speed around the circle of her admirers, giving a passing lick to each, then collapsed with her nose under the sofa and fell instantly asleep. "Not bad for an eight-month-old," Dame Millicent said proudly.

There was scarcely time to begin their drinks before the taxi came. Bill took Dame Millicent out. As she left, she reminded Carrie, "I'll come for her in the morning. I have a pair of stout boots, and I don't mind the snow."

She leaned heavily on Bill's arm as they went down the front walk, and for the first time he was aware of her as an old woman. But there was fire in her eye as she stopped halfway and faced him. "That man is a detective. Mrs. Stratton said he was concerned with your investments, but I know he is a detective. I didn't realize at first, because he is a gentleman. But it showed finally. It always does. I know that he is a policeman. You are going to deny it, but don't bother.

If you want to ignore my offer, please do so, but remember that I'll be glad to help you when you need me." With a quickness that surprised him after her leaning on his arm, she leaped into the taxi, waving goodbye.

"Any luck today?" Carrie asked when she had brought trays into the living room.

"Not a thing." Moynahan looked discouraged.

"What did you have to go on?" she asked.

Bill explained that there was nothing but a date of more than half a century ago to work from.

"What was the date?"

"The twelfth of February, 1913."

"Oh, darling, no!" Carrie looked in disbelief at the men. "Why didn't you ask me, and I might have saved you a trip. Didn't either of you ever consider that E. W. was trying to protect Margaret Fackler, and that Gordon was protecting Barbara? Even Tony was trying not to hurt Laura. Didn't it occur to you that it might be Grace, not Roy? I'm sure Grace's birthday is the twelfth of February. Wait until I get my birthday list, and I can tell you positively."

While she was gone from the room, Bill and Moynahan exchanged sheepish glances. "That's it," she said as she returned. "The twelfth of February, and I must remember to send her a card, too. I'm sure she's five or six years younger than Roy. I'd be willing to bet that she was born in 1913."

"Do you know where?"

"Right here, I think. Her father was president, and since that would have been term-time, I don't think her mother would have gone away to have a baby. Her mother came from Cartersville, too, so she wouldn't have been going away to be with her own family."

"In that case," Moynahan said, "it should be easy enough to check on Monday morning. I congratulate you, Mrs. Stratton."

"Oh, don't be silly. Why didn't you ask your wife? I'll bet she could have told you."

"I haven't got a wife," said Moynahan.

"Then I'd better work on that, too."

"No, Carrie." Bill scowled affectionately at her. "Lieutenant Moynahan has enough to worry about now. Don't start your matchmaking routine."

"Never mind," Carrie said loftily to Bill. "If you had asked your own wife, the pair of you would not have had to mush through the snow from Reading, like a pair of huskies."

CHAPTER EIGHTEEN

The entire East Coast was covered in snow the following morning. In Cartersville it had stopped at eleven the night before, but the wind had whipped the feathery flakes into drifts, and to Bill it seemed a mile to the driveway from the front door. As he stood leaning on the snow shovel, looking at the task before him, Emma began yipping excitedly. In the distance he saw Dame Millicent churning indomitably along the unshoveled walks. At times she appeared to sink waist-deep, but her red hat sailed along in undeterred progress.

In less efficient fashion Emma struggled out to meet her. "Good morning, Mr. Stratton. Invigorating, isn't it? Hello, girl, hello."

"At least," said Bill, "it has stopped. If it had kept on, we might have had to cancel classes tomorrow."

Dame Millicent pulled the leash from her pocket and slipped a training collar over Emma's head. "It's difficult walking, so I shall probably have her back within an hour." She waved a mittened hand and began plowing back down the street, with Emma gallantly leaping through the snow, trying to comply with the encouraging shout of "Heel!"

Bill had worked halfway toward the drive when Carrie came to the door. "Telephone, darling," she called. For a moment, she stood shivering as she watched him stick the shovel into a drift, then hurried inside.

"Professor Stratton," said an unfamiliar voice as he answered the phone, "this is Police Chief McKerrow. I'm calling from the university campus. There's been a serious accident at Winthrop Hall. A man died. Could you come down now?"

"Who is it?"

"I think he's a member of the English faculty. Can you come?"

"Of course," Bill said with a sick feeling in his stomach. "I can't get my car out of the snow, so I'll have to walk. I'll be there in fifteen or twenty minutes."

Lacking Dame Millicent's English bounce, he found walking even harder work than shoveling the snow. It took him half an hour to get to the campus, even though, when he reached the middle of town, the streets had been plowed and some of the sidewalks cleared. As he turned around the corner of the library, he could see, through the fine snow blown painfully into his eyes, two police cars drawn up near the door of Winthrop. No one was in sight.

He had nearly reached the building when another car drew up and parked near the ones already there. Moynahan got out and called, "Glad you could make it. I asked them to get you."

"What happened?"

"I don't know," Moynahan said briskly, almost curtly. "We'll see."

"How did you get here so fast? Or were you already in Cartersville?"

"No, They called me, and I hurried over. The highways are clear."

A university policeman stood inside the main doors of the building. He came out and jerked a thumb to indicate the side of the building. "They're around there."

Bill and Moynahan went around the corner to the side of Winthrop that faced the river. Aside from a few clumps of ornamental evergreen, now symmetrical mounds of white, there was nothing to break the smooth expanse of snow between the building and the river except a group of men standing in a circle six or eight feet away from the wall of Winthrop. Bill recognized a university policeman, and with him were a big man in a heavy tweed overcoat and two uniformed Cartersville policemen. Standing by himself in the shelter of the wall was Mario, an elderly Italian, one of the janitors. The big man was pointing up to the roof, then back at what lay in the center of the ring of men. From a distance it looked like a heap of old clothes dusted with snow.

"Hello, Moynahan," the big man called when he saw them. "Glad you got here. Is that Professor Stratton?"

"Morning, Chief. We got here together. What's up?"

McKerrow beckoned in answer, and they approached the heap of clothes. Arms and legs in distorted abandon, eyes staring past them to the sky, the crumpled body looked half its former size.

"It is Professor Thomas, isn't it?" the Chief asked.

"Yes, it is," Bill said slowly. The import of the pronoun caught at him. "Or it was." In less than a month and a half, he had stood looking at the bodies of two men who a short time before had been colleagues and friends. At least Gordon had been his friend, even though it was a word he would have been hesitant to apply to Peter Jackson. But, somehow, he was less appalled at Gordon's death than he had been at Peter's. Peter had left behind a wife and children. Gordon's daughter was married and living far away, his wife had broken up their marriage after nearly thirty years. There had been little left for him, and presumably he had realized it.

"He probably jumped from the building. The janitor found him this morning and called us."

"Had he been here all night?"

"Yes. His body was covered with snow, and the snow stopped late last night. The janitor, Mr. Angelotti, looked out of a window and saw a foot uncovered by the wind. After he called us, he came out and brushed the snow off the body."

Bill looked around at the little mound of snow surrounding Thomas. "The snow could have drifted over him this morning, but I doubt it. We'll probably be able to tell when the doctor examines the body."

Moynahan intervened. "Were there any other footprints besides Angelotti's?"

McKerrow shook his head. "Even if there had been earlier, they would have been covered by the wind."

"And the building? Anything there?"

"His office lights were still on, and so were the lights in the hall. The janitor said that Thomas sometimes went up to feed birds on the roof. The door to the roof was unlocked. No footprints there, either. They'd all been drifted over. It's going to be hard to tell whether he jumped or fell. Have you ever been up there with him, Professor Stratton?"

"Lots of times."

"Would you mind coming up to have a look?"

As they left Thomas's body, one of the policemen was taking photographs of it. Bill wondered how long it would have to lie there before it was decently taken away.

"Chief," asked Moynahan in the elevator, "did you know that his wife had just left him?"

"No. What do you know about it? Where is she?"

"In New York," Bill answered for Moynahan. "My wife has her address, and I can get it from her."

"I suppose he couldn't take it and jumped off when it got to be too much for him." What sounded like callousness in the Chief's voice, Bill realized, was probably only the reaction of a man who had seen too many accidents, suicides and even murders in a long career.

As they got out of the elevator on the top floor, Bill could see through the open door of Gordon's office. The lights were on, Gordon's hat stood on top of the file cabinet where he habitually put it, there was still a sheet of paper in the typewriter. It looked as if he might return at any moment.

At the end of the hall they climbed the steps to the roof. "Don't go out yet," McKerrow warned. "Just take a look from here. There aren't any footprints, but I want my men to photograph it before we go out. Do you see anything unusual?"

Bill could not help looking beyond the parapet, remembering the last time he had been up here, jogging around the roof. The river that had been filled with the figures of skaters then was now only a flat stretch of white between two hills, and the other campus buildings looked as if they had been covered with dust sheets by a meticulous housekeeper. On the flat roof of Winthrop the snow reached nearly to the top of the low parapet. The elevator housing was capped with it, and so was the bag of grain that Gordon had kept for the birds.

"Sorry," he said at last, "but there's not much to see. It looks all right to me. Shouldn't it? Gordon was a neat man, and I doubt that he would have messed up anything, even just before he was going to die."

The three men went back to Thomas's office. It was as impeccable as usual. Bill thought with chagrin of his own incurable messiness in his office. Even when he was working hardest, Thomas was a model of neatness. There were two or three unanswered letters held upright on a coiled bronze rack, two pencils—one red, one black—laid side by side parallel to the edge of the spotless blotter, and a pile of undergraduate themes whose edges were lined up with the left-hand corner of the desk. Guiltily, Bill hoped that they had already been marked. He leaned over. The top one bore Gordon's small handwriting, and a circled "B plus." Anal compulsive, Gordon's more psychologically minded friends might have said of his neatness. More probably a bastion against the chaos of the world that had eventually taken his life, Bill decided.

"Do you know anyone named Arnold?" asked McKerrow. "Anyone that Thomas could have quarreled with?"

"No, I don't think so."

The Chief stepped behind Gordon's desk and read from the sheet in the typewriter, "Arnold's revisions were ill-advised."

Suddenly Bill laughed, realizing as he did how out of place his amusement was. "That's Matthew Arnold. The poet." He stopped, remembering his contretemps with Peter Jackson over Browning, and almost laughed again. "Gordon was writing an article on the last revisions of his poetry that he made. No clue there."

McKerrow nodded. "I was afraid it was something like that. We'd better get in touch with his wife. Did you say that Mrs. Stratton has her address?"

"Yes, I'll call her now." He reached for the phone, but Moynahan grabbed his arm.

"Better use another phone," he said. "That one hasn't been dusted."

From Carrie he got the telephone number of the friends in New York with whom Mrs. Thomas was staying, then went out of his office while Moynahan telephoned her. Five minutes later the detective rejoined him. "She's coming up here as soon as she can get a train."

"How did she take it?"

"Very well. She didn't even break down."

"That's what I expected. Barbara is a remarkably controlled woman."

"There isn't much for you to do here, Mr. Stratton, unless you want to stay. The guard who was on duty yesterday afternoon is coming down in a few minutes, and Thomas's office has to be gone over. But I doubt that much of it would be interesting to you."

"Very well," said Bill. "But why don't you come for lunch with us, and you can tell me if anything does crop up. Not that I think anything will. It certainly looks like suicide to me. You don't suspect anything else, do you?"

"Not really," Moynahan said. "But when one man in your department has been murdered, and someone has tried to kill you in this building, we've obviously got to check thoroughly. It's routine, anyway."

When he left the building, Bill could not help looking around the corner. He was relieved to see that Gordon's body had been taken away. All that remained was the disturbed snow where it had lain, and the footprints of the janitor and the police. It was a curiously peaceful scene to have witnessed a violent death. Because the snow this Sunday morning was so deep, there were few undergraduates to be seen on campus, and apparently none of them had come to investigate the presence of police cars at Winthrop Hall.

By the time that Moynahan arrived, the walks were shoveled, Emma was resting from her exertions, lunch was ready, and Bill was longing for the only drink that he permitted himself at lunch during the week.

"Nothing out of the ordinary," Moynahan reported as he drank his sherry. (Who would believe, Bill wondered, that policemen drank sherry?) "I talked to the regular janitor. He cleaned Thomas's office yesterday morning. Did a good job, too, because there were no fingerprints but Thomas's. He went off at noon. Thomas came in about three in the afternoon, according to the guard, just as the snow was beginning. The guard went off duty at four and locked the building. Thomas was the only person who had come in during the afternoon, so the guard went up before he left, to be sure that Thomas realized the building would be locked for the weekend. When he went into Thomas's office, he was just sitting there at his desk, with no papers or books in front of him, as if he were thinking, not working. The guard said he looked haggard, but perhaps he only thinks so in retrospect. Lots of witnesses remember ominous symptoms after the event. Anyway, when the guard left, Thomas was alive, and so far as the guard could tell, the only person in the building."

"How about Mario, who found him?"

"Angelotti says that he waxes the halls on Sundays, and that he is the only university employee who comes in. He looked out from a second-floor window and saw the body."

"Poor Gordon," Bill said. "I knew that he was taking Barbara's leaving pretty hard, but I didn't expect this."

"Bill," Carrie said, "do you mind if I invite Barbara to stay with us while she's here? She shouldn't go back to stay in Gordon's house."

"Sure," Bill said. "She oughtn't to stay alone."

"I'm sorry to sound callous," Moynahan interjected, "but it would also be easier for me if she stayed here. I'll have to talk to her."

The only reasonable train from New York on Sunday afternoons got to Cartersville at three-thirty, and Carrie and Bill went to meet it. Barbara had not told them when she was coming, but they guessed correctly. Carrying a small bag, she came down the steps of the train as briskly and erectly as if nothing had happened. When she saw them, she waved and started forward. The only sign of unusual emotion was the kiss she gave Carrie. "Thank you so much for being here. I can't tell you how I dreaded getting off alone."

It was quickly arranged for her to stay with the Strattons, and for her daughter Connie to stay also when she came the following day from San Francisco.

Moynahan arrived at five o'clock with McKerrow.

When Barbara Thomas came down from her room, her eyes were red, but her manner was controlled. "I left for New York on Wednesday, no, Thursday morning," she said in answer to Moynahan.

"Did you intend to come back to live with your husband?"

"No," she said calmly.

"I'm sorry to have to ask, but why did you leave? Had you quarreled?"

"No. At least, not what I think you mean by quarreled. We had been getting farther and farther apart ever since our daughter married. We didn't quarrel, but I sometimes thought it would have been easier if we had. Our marriage had simply dried up, until it was nothing but a formality. We lived in the same house, but we were not really married any longer." Her voice wavered. "At least, it had dried up for me."

"Didn't your husband feel the same way?"

"No, I suppose not. As a matter of fact, I know he didn't. He said that he still—" She looked up at Moynahan, as if asking not to have to say it. "He still loved me."

"Did you intend to divorce him?"

"Probably not. I don't know. All I was sure of was that I couldn't stay here any longer with him."

"After thirty years you decided that?" McKerrow sounded shocked.

"No," she answered slowly. "I didn't decide, really. I had probably known for three or four years that I would have to leave sometime. Last Wednesday I simply knew the time had come, that's all. It wasn't even a decision. It was just there. So I told him, and the next morning I went to stay with the Thorntons."

Moynahan looked at her with pity. "How did he take it when you left?"

Her eyes filled with tears, and her whole face softened, as if the release were welcome. "That was the terrible part. He didn't break down, but he said calmly that life wasn't worth living if I were not here. I—I didn't think he meant it literally." She turned to Carrie. "I must get a glass of water."

"I'll get it," said Bill, rising.

"No, let me get it myself." She went swiftly out of the

room. From the kitchen came the sound of running water, but it was nearly ten minutes before she returned, her face under control again. "Sorry."

"Just one more thing, Mrs. Thomas. Had you heard from him after you left?"

"No, nothing. I stayed in all day yesterday. In the hope, I suppose, that he might call. I had left him, thinking I wouldn't go back, but thirty years is a long time. If he had asked me to come back, I think I might have done so. Now, I only wish that I had called him, instead of waiting for him to take the first step. This wouldn't have happened." Once more she seemed on the verge of losing control. Moynahan and McKerrow stood up, thanked her, and said good night.

At dinner Barbara carried on bravely, but there were too many topics to be avoided for the conversation to be normal. After they had eaten, she and Bill discussed the arrangements for Gordon's funeral while Carrie cleared away the dinner. She had just rejoined them when the doorbell rang.

Bill answered it, cursing inwardly. He was fond of Dame Millicent, who was their only friend who made a practice of dropping in unannounced, but this was no time for her breeziness. He hoped that the news had reached her that Barbara was staying with them, so that she would not be tempted to come in.

Standing on the doorstep was June Jackson, wearing a scarf thrown carelessly over her head, and no makeup. "Is Barbara—Mrs. Thomas here, Bill?"

"Yes, come in, June." In the light he could see that she wore old shoes and slacks.

She looked into the living room and rushed to Barbara. "Mrs. Thomas, I'm so sorry to bother you, but I just heard you were here. I shouldn't have come, but you were so kind to me last week. I wanted you to know how terribly sorry I am about your husband." She took Barbara's hands into hers.

"You're very kind, Mrs. Jackson." Barbara's eyes were luminous. "I wish I had been as generous in the same situation. Can you forgive me?"

"That doesn't matter. Don't say anything about it, please. I came because I want to help you in anyway that I can. I won't stay. I only wanted to be sure that you would ask if there were anything I could do."

"I will. Believe me, I will."

Bill found it almost intolerable to see them together: Barbara, whose husband had thrown himself off a building and lain all night in the snow because she had left him; June, whose husband she believed to have committed suicide because she would not put up with his infidelity.

True to her word, June left in a few minutes. Barbara sat down again, heavily. "I was hoping that no one would come tonight to sympathize with me, but I'm glad she did. Somehow, I feel less guilty about how I treated her. She's very generous. I wish I had seen that before."

CHAPTER NINETEEN

Gordon's death caused considerably more sensation in the national newspapers than Bill had anticipated. His suicide accounted for some of the more lurid stories, but they were less surprising than the lengthy ones in the serious newspapers. *The New York Times* carried a full two-column obituary with a fairly recent photograph. Bill knew the reputation that Gordon had achieved among scholars, but he had not supposed that his name would mean so much to other readers.

While he was still unburied, it seemed incongruous, even wrong, to be plugging away at Peter's blackmail list. Only yesterday afternoon he had met Barbara at the station, and here he and Moynahan were looking at the list again.

"There's no record of Mrs. Moorhead's birth on February 12, 1913, in Cartersville. At least, no record of the birth of Grace Evelyn Henn."

"What do you mean? That was her name."

"So it says in *Who's Who*. The curious thing is that there is a record of the birth that day of Grace Evelyn Wilson."

Bill waited. Moynahan was obviously going to tell his story his own way.

"And the mother's name was Muriel Wilson. President Henn's wife was Evelyn."

"I don't follow you," Bill said, momentarily confused.

"Mrs. Moorhead," Moynahan explained patiently, "was, or says that she was, the daughter of President and Mrs.

Henn. Mrs. Henn, whose name was Evelyn, was a Wilson before she married. But it was Muriel Wilson who was the mother of the Grace Evelyn who was born that day."

"I see," Bill said cautiously. "Do you know who Muriel Wilson was?"

"Not yet. But I suspect that we're going to find that Mrs. Henn had a sister or niece named Muriel, who was not married on February 12, 1913. The space on the birth certificate for the father's name is blank."

"I guess that's that, then." Bill looked chagrined. "We needn't have gone to Reading and eaten all that spice cake. Carrie was right."

"The trip wasn't a total waste. If we hadn't taken it, we might not have mentioned the problem to Mrs. Stratton, and we might still be looking. I think we'd better talk to Moorhead."

Bill reached for the master schedule of teaching assignments. "He's in class now. But he should be out at eleven-thirty. I'll ask him to come in then." He buzzed Rosie and asked for Moorhead to come in when he was free. He turned back to Moynahan. "How about the autopsy on Gordon?"

"Nothing, except that he died of a broken neck when he jumped from the top of the building. That's no surprise. And, as we guessed from the snow on the body, he probably died between seven and nine in the evening. The cold made it difficult to be more sure than that. And that's about what we expected, too."

"What else could you expect?"

"Not much. Still, you have to admit that it's a strange coincidence that Jackson's death looked like suicide because he and his wife had been having trouble. And so does Thomas's death. And don't forget, too, that someone tried to kill you."

"I'm not about to," Bill said grimly. "But the point is that Gordon wasn't blackmailing anyone, and Peter was. At least, I don't think Gordon was."

219

"No, but he might have known something that made him dangerous to the murderer. That's at least a possibility."

"And now the list of suspects is narrowed down even further. Fackler, Moorhead, and Benson." Bill hesitated. "Maybe even Tony Bongiovanni. And I can see why you might even suspect me."

Moynahan looked impatient. "Don't forget that you were with me at the time that Thomas was killed. And that certainly clears you. To tell the truth, for a short time I had wondered whether you might have dropped the copy of *Who's Who* down the stairwell yourself, to make it look as if someone else had tried to kill you. I didn't take it very seriously, but I did wonder."

Bill smiled ruefully. "Then I'll quit complaining about having driven to Reading with you. If nothing else, that trip back in the snow puts me in the clear." He stopped momentarily. "Or does it? I'm clear only if someone killed both Peter and Gordon. But if Gordon committed suicide, I don't have any alibi for Peter's death."

"Nonsense," Moynahan said curtly. "If you were Jackson's murderer, you wouldn't point out that you don't have an alibi. Stop trying to get every possible angle figured out, and stick to what's important. Don't complicate things unnecessarily."

"What do you honestly think about Gordon's death? Was it suicide?"

"It must have been. Between six and midnight Benson and his fiancée were having drinks and dinner with the Bongiovannis. That clears two of them. And the Facklers and the Moorheads were at the president's house for a reception and dinner. I doubt that the president is lying. All the possible people have ironclad alibis, unless the whole campus is in a conspiracy. I think the simple solution is the obvious one: Thomas committed suicide because his wife left him."

The buzzer interrupted them. Moorhead was on his way

in. Moynahan explained to him why he had been called in, then asked the significance of February 12, 1913.

Roy answered at once. "That was the day my wife was born."

Moynahan looked at the paper as if searching for information. "Her father was the president of the university, wasn't he?"

Bill tried to think of the right word for the look that came over Moorhead's face. Shy? Embarrassed? Neither was quite right, but there was an element of each. "What I tell you is confidential, isn't it?"

"Unless it has something to do with Professor Jackson's death."

"The truth is that the president was not her father. It's so long ago now that it doesn't matter much, but the simple fact is that Grace was illegitimate. Her Aunt Muriel, her mother's younger sister, was got in the family way by a man she fell in love with. A married man." He stopped. "It's confusing to tell. You see, her mother wasn't really her mother. That is, Mrs. Henn was not her mother. Mrs. Henn's sister Muriel was Grace's mother. She was Muriel Wilson. When Grace was born, her mother adopted her." Confused, he stopped again, trying to sort out the words.

"You mean president and Mrs. Henn adopted your wife?" Moynahan asked tactfully.

Moorhead gave him a grateful look. "Yes, that's it. They had no children of their own. Grace's Aunt Muriel—"

"Miss Wilson?" Moynahan supplied again.

"Yes. Miss Wilson never married. After the Henns adopted Grace, Miss Wilson came to live with them. Grace was fond of her, but she didn't know that she was her mother. Miss Wilson died when Grace was thirteen. And Grace didn't know that she was adopted until she was twenty-one."

"Did it come as a shock?"

"Not for long. And she had been Grace Henn for so long

221

that it was silly for her to change her name. Besides, we got married not long after that, so that she did change her name, after all."

"Did she tell other people?"

"I don't think so, although there must have been people in Cartersville who knew. She didn't tell me until I had proposed. She thought I should know before we were married. But she wasn't ashamed. It was only that she had loved her Aunt Muriel—her mother—before she knew the relationship, and it didn't seem fair to her memory to tell. Anyway, she really thought of the Henns as her parents." He paused again, but not this time to consider the intricacies of references to her family. "That's a nice point, isn't it? The word *parent* comes from *parere*, meaning to bring forth. Who actually are the parents then, the ones who bring forth? The physical ones or the ones who really give life to a child? What a strange language we have." He chuckled. "Did you know that the portion of a Greek building we call a pediment is really only a corruption of the word *pyramid?*" He seemed already to have forgotten his wife's illegitimacy. "And that *obscene* doesn't actually mean *off-stage*, as most people think. It means *out of filth*. Of course, that is the more sensible derivation, but we are so used to the idea that the language is illogical that we usually prefer the illogical derivation."

Bill watched Moynahan stifle a smile. There were advantages for academics in dealing with policemen who were well educated. At least, they weren't totally unused to the eccentricities that universities seem to foster.

"Do you think your wife minds now the fact that her mother was unmarried?"

"Perhaps a little. As I said, she was so used to thinking of President Henn as her father that it would probably bring her up short if someone were to point out that she was actually illegitimate. That's all."

"I wonder," asked Moynahan, as if musing over the subject, "whether Professor Jackson knew about her parentage?"

"I'm sure he didn't. Why?"

"Did he ever try to coerce you by mentioning it?"

"No. I said I don't think he even knew. Besides, he wouldn't have had any way of knowing. He was a newcomer to Cartersville, and I doubt that any of the few people who knew about Grace even knew him. They weren't apt to," he concluded a touch smugly. Then he smiled. "That sounds intolerably snobbish, doesn't it? I didn't mean it to be. I was an outsider myself when I came here. Until I married Grace. After that everyone forgot that I hadn't been here all my life. Probably that would have happened with him, too."

"You're sure he didn't know, and that he never mentioned it to you?"

Moorhead looked annoyed. Students and young policemen might be encouraged to ask questions, but they were not to question the answers, once *they* were given. "Quite sure."

And that was as much information as they got from Roy Moorhead.

When he was gone, Moynahan groaned. "Everything is so damned inconclusive. I haven't a reason in the world to believe that he was lying. I even said *coerce* deliberately, so that he couldn't say, as Thomas did, that he hadn't been blackmailed, since no money was involved. But it is strange that Jackson hadn't yet made use of his information about Mrs. Moorhead. Of course, Jackson had been here only since summer, but he managed in that time to attempt blackmail—coercion, I mean—on everyone else. Strange that he missed Moorhead."

"Maybe not," said Bill. "He didn't try anything with me."

"True, but getting a little drunk at a party isn't very good basis for blackmail. He was probably looking for something better. Besides, he may have liked you."

"Do you think," Bill asked, "that he might have tried to

blackmail Mrs. Moorhead herself? Roy is so vague that it would probably be hard to get him even to understand that he was being blackmailed."

"It's worth a try. I have to go back to Devonport before long, but I could stop off to see her on the way. I think I'd rather see her before he has a chance to tell her that we were talking to him. Want to come?"

"Not unless you really need me. I felt sufficiently awkward sitting in on the interviews with my colleagues. I don't want them to think I'm badgering their wives, too. Why don't you go without me, in your official capacity?"

After a hasty lunch Bill spent the rest of the day in Winthrop, filling out reports and reviewing for class the following morning. Trying to combine teaching, detecting, and administration was slowly grinding him into the ground. What he really needed was two or three nights of long, uninterrupted sleep. Perhaps it would be possible after Gordon's funeral.

There were several telephone calls but only one major interruption. About three o'clock Dame Millicent asked to see him. When Rosie opened the door for her, she was preceded by a streak of yellow. Emma whizzed around the room, licking Bill in passing, investigating waste baskets, and then settling down for a chew at the tail of his overcoat. "Sit!" thundered her mentor, and she slid into position, immobile except that every muscle was quivering with excitement.

"Good girl," said Dame Millicent. "I wanted to demonstrate her to you. I've had her in my office all afternoon. Mrs. Stratton said it would be all right, but I thought I should say nothing to you until I had seen how she would behave. She was angelic. An absolute lamb. The point is that you might want to bring her here with you one day."

"God forbid," breathed Bill. Then he took another look at the puppy. "Actually, you've done an amazing job in two or three days."

"Well, yes," said Dame Millicent, as if surprised that there could be any doubt of her efficiency.

"Perhaps I could bring her occasionally. She certainly seems to enjoy being here. I can't tell you how much I appreciate what you have done already. It would have taken me months to get her this far."

Dame Millicent beamed with pleasure. Then her face took on a more somber look. "I have been feeling sad ever since I heard of Professor Thomas's death. I have known him over thirty years. Not well, of course, but it is hard to realize that a former pupil is dead." She looked positively gloomy. "Not surprising at my age, perhaps, but hard for all that. I was so happy that I recognized him when we met at your house. And he seemed *most* pleased."

"Yes, it is hard for all of us to realize that he's dead."

"Remorse, I imagine." At the sight of Bill's puzzled face, she amplified her statement. "Over having killed Professor Jackson."

"No," said Bill. This old woman must be stopped. "Not at all. I may as well tell you that Mrs. Thomas had left him. Three or four days ago. That was the reason for his suicide."

He sounded unwontedly stern, and Dame Millicent caught the tone in his voice. "I am truly sorry, Professor Stratton. I *am* a blunderer. But it would have solved so many problems, wouldn't it? However, you can count on my saying nothing more. Come on, Emma."

As soon as she was gone, Bill regretted his manner. After all, she was a good, kind woman and a distinguished scholar. And an excellent dog trainer. A month ago he would not have let his irritation show. The whole business was fraying his nerves.

When he got home that night, Connie Nicholls, the daughter of the Thomases, had arrived from San Francisco. Barbara seemed far less tense once she had come.

After dinner Bill worked until ten in his study. When he

came downstairs again to rejoin the three women, Barbara was speaking of June Jackson. "Caroline, my dear, would you do me a great favor, if it doesn't go against your principles? You remember that when I left here after your party, I went to see her? I didn't quite know how to indicate that I was sorry I had treated her badly in the past. While I was driving there, I was thinking that she wanted very much to join the Garden Club. She had never seemed—well, quite the right sort to me. And I know that she didn't to Grace Moorhead, either. But I have realized since how snobbish I was. When I got there, I asked her if she would like to have me sponsor her for the Club. I haven't talked to Grace, but I am sure she would support her if I asked.

"Well, the thing is, that after what I really intended as a gesture of friendliness to her, I left Cartersville. Caroline, would you sponsor her as a member?"

Carrie did not respond for a moment, and Bill knew that she was thinking of her own past dislike of June, and of her sympathy for her since Peter's death. "Of course, if you want me to. I'd like to sponsor her, anyway. At least, if she stays in Cartersville."

"Thank you, my dear. I appreciate it. And I'll talk to Grace, if you would like me to."

"I may as well confess," Carrie said, "that I knew you didn't like June, but I didn't realize that Grace felt so strongly."

Barbara flushed. "I'm sorry I made it so apparent. Grace tried to be friendly to Mrs. Jackson when she first arrived, but I believe that Mrs. Jackson rebuffed her. Grace didn't seem to bear a grudge about it, though."

"Come on, Emma," said Bill. "Time for your last walk tonight."

CHAPTER TWENTY

Moynahan was waiting for him when he came back to his office from class the following morning.

"I saw Mrs. Moorhead yesterday when I left here. Your wife was right about checking with the women first."

"Had Peter bee bullying her?"

"It may not have been real, bullying, but he certainly indicated to her that he knew she was illegitimate. Not very subtly, either. First he told her that his wife had always admired her, and that her dearest wish was to get into the Garden Club." Moynahan looked whimsically at Bill. "Her words, not mine. When Mrs. Moorhead said that she really had little to do with new memberships, Jackson suggested it would be nice if she were to push the matter a little. I gather that Mrs. Moorhead became a little stubborn and stony at this point. So he began asking about her Aunt Muriel. Had she ever married, or had children? And so on. He didn't say the word *illegitimate*, but he did everything else, and then he repeated that it would be nice for his wife to get into the Garden Club."

"Sweet guy!" Bill said. "Everything we find out about him makes him seem worse. I suppose he only proved how much dirty information it's possible to pick up if you keep your ears open."

"Mr. Stratton," said Moynahan, "you bear up remarkably well. I don't think I could take the departmental in-fighting

227

if I had your job. And I know damned well I couldn't handle the Garden Club aspect of the wives. My hat's off to you that you're still sane. I think I prefer dealing with pimps and pickpockets."

"At least, what you found out doesn't indicate much reason for Moorhead to have killed Peter, does it?"

"I don't know. There are so many little things that mean nothing to me, but which seem to be taken seriously here, that I am beginning to think a professor might commit murder just to keep the lower classes out of the Garden Club. But I admit that anywhere else I wouldn't take Moorhead's motive very seriously. Not for murder."

"What's going to happen about Gordon? Barbara is staying here, waiting for the funeral. Will there be a decision soon about whether it is accident or suicide?"

"That's up to Chief McKerrow, but there isn't much doubt that it was suicide. Even though there wasn't a note or any other indication of his intention of taking his own life. The circumstances are almost conclusive."

The buzzer sounded at Bill's elbow. Rosie's voice was apologetic. "There's a cable here for you. Should I wait until you are finished, or would you like to see it now? I wouldn't have called you, but I thought it might have something to do with Dame Millicent."

"All right, bring it in, please." When he had it in his hand, he realized that Rosie had already opened the envelope. Her remark about Dame Millicent had been a police fiction. Undoubtedly she had read the cable already. It was a night letter, addressed not to him personally but to the Chairman of the English Department. "Read in *Times* of death of Professor Thomas. Please notify executor or solicitor we represent claim of widow, Penelope Thomas, for share of estate. Please ask to get in contact. Gilliatt, Puddifatt, and Gilliatt, solicitors." A Mayfair address followed.

Bill whistled softly and passed the cable to Moynahan, who

read it slowly, then read it again. "I don't see what we can do but talk to Mrs. Thomas. It may be hard on her, but we must."

Bill nodded. In all probability there was a mistake, but to rectify it might cause Barbara unnecessary pain at an already difficult time.

Barbara and her daughter were with Carrie when Bill and Moynahan arrived. "What is it, Lieutenant?" Barbara asked.

"A cable came from London, and I'd like to ask you about it. I'm not certain what it means."

Barbara tilted back her head and stared at the ceiling. "Yes," she said after a time. "Would you like to read it, or do you want me to read it myself?"

Moynahan handed her the cable. She read it through without emotion, then returned it to him. "Yes?"

"Would you rather we talked alone?"

"No, thank you. There is nothing here, and I have nothing to say, that my daughter and the Strattons cannot hear."

Bill saw the cords tighten in Moynahan's neck. He was not a brutal man, and what he had to say could not be easy. "Who is Penelope Thomas?"

She gestured toward the cable. "As it says, she was Gordon's wife."

"Was she his wife when he died?"

"Yes." Her control seemed complete. She looked toward her daughter. "I'm sorry, Connie."

"Mrs. Thomas," Moynahan said quietly, "it would help if you could tell us about it. Unfortunately, we do have to know."

She clasped her hands together, apparently less to hold onto her emotions than to think best how to tell what she had to say. "Very well. In June 1939, I went to stay in Oxford with a cousin of Mother's. I was a junior at Vassar. Cousin Helen asked undergraduates to tennis parties and dinner to entertain me. That's how I met Gordon. We fell in love almost at once.

229

But he had another year to study in Oxford, and I wanted to finish Vassar, so we decided that it would be foolish to marry before the next year was finished.

"I went home late in July. I had already arranged to go to Maine with the family. We were in Maine when I realized that I was pregnant. I didn't know what to do. It seemed impossible to tell my parents, and I didn't think it would be fair to write to tell Gordon. I'm sorry, Connie, but I thought perhaps I could get an abortion after we went back to Boston. All the time Gordon was writing, and I was answering his letters, but I couldn't tell him. I suppose it seems silly, but I couldn't.

"At last I got up my courage to write and tell him I was pregnant. He cabled, asking me to come to England and marry him. I planned on staying in Maine until Labor Day weekend, then taking some of my own money and going to England without telling my parents until I was there. But England went into the war that weekend. Gordon cabled to say that he would come home as soon as possible."

"I know most of that," Moynahan said. "Now could you tell us about Penelope Thomas?"

"Perhaps you knew it, but my daughter didn't. Please let me tell it my way. Gordon got an early boat out of England. I met him in New York, and we were married there. We told my parents that we had been secretly married while I was still in England. I think they believed me. They would have wanted to believe me, in any case, and they never questioned me.

"There isn't much to tell after that until 1952. I know that was the year, because Connie was twelve. Gordon and I both liked being in England, and we spent most of our summers there after the war. He worked in the libraries at his research. We had enough money to travel when we wanted to. Gordon told me that he had inherited a moderate amount, and we used most of the money beyond his salary in travel.

"We were in London in the summer of 1952. Gordon and I were still very much in love. Connie had a governess during the week, but we usually tried to plan expeditions on the weekend that she would like. Picnics or trips to the country. That sort of thing. Do you remember, Connie?"

"Of course. That's what I loved about England."

"Several times on Sundays," Barbara continued, "Gordon said that he was not feeling well and urged me to take Connie out by myself. I knew that his health was good, but I began to worry about his not coming with us. I wondered if he was getting tired of me, or even if he had a mistress somewhere in London. After all, we had come regularly every summer for six or seven years.

"I tried to not show it, but I became more and more unhappy. Even jealous. At last I felt I had to know what he was doing. One Sunday in August, only a few weeks before we were to come back to this country, he asked me to take Connie out alone. I told him that we would go the Tower of London. Instead, I left her with friends who lived nearby, then I went back and sat having coffee in a little restaurant across the street from our flat near Park Lane.

"After a time Gordon came out of the door and walked toward Park Lane. I followed him. When he got into a taxi, I got another and asked the driver to follow his. We went to Chelsea and his taxi stopped in front of a large building near the river. When he had gone in, I got out and walked past the door of the building. There was a brass plate that said it was a nursing home.

"I waited a few minutes, then went in. I asked the girl at the desk if Mr. Thomas had come in. She said that he had, and that he was with his wife." Barbara pulled out her handkerchief and blew her nose. "I can't tell you what I felt when she said that. My dear Bill, would you get me a glass of water, please?"

Connie came over and put her hand on her mother's

shoulder. "Thank you, darling," Barbara said, "but please don't. I'll not be able to finish if I don't hang onto myself. Later."

Bill brought her the water, then sat down on the sofa beside Carrie and took her hand.

"The nurse asked me if I would like to wait for him," Barbara continued, "but I said no and asked her not to mention that I had been there. The next day I made inquiries about the nursing home. It was a private hospital for the incurably insane.

"It's hard to explain why I didn't say anything to Gordon. It's even hard to remember myself. Partly, I suppose, because I was sorry for him. Partly because I loved him, whether we were married or not. And mostly because of you, Connie. It took some time, but I finally found the record of his first marriage in Somerset House. He had married her only a few months after he first came to England. I found out afterward that her parents were dead, and that she had a small fortune of her own. Two or three months after they were married, she was in an automobile accident and came out of it with brain injuries that permanently destroyed her mind. That was over a year before he met me.

"I don't even know whether he could have got a divorce in England. Certainly he could have in this country. But, as her husband, he was in charge of the income from her inheritance. If she had died, it would have come to him. I hadn't realized it at the time, of course, but he had been too poor to marry me without that money. When he found that I was pregnant, all that he could think of to do was to marry me anyhow. And we had been married for nearly thirteen years before I ever suspected anything.

"As I told you, I said nothing to him when I found out about his first wife. His wife, I suppose I should say; he never had a second wife legally. The following summer I hired a private investigator in London and found out most of what I have just told you, about her accident and the fact that the poor woman would never recover from her injuries.

"I lived with the knowledge that I was not really married until you had been married yourself, Connie. I didn't want you to get hurt until you had a life of your own to help you out. For a time I hoped that his wife would die, so that we could get married. But she didn't. The longer it went on, the harder it was. I pitied Gordon for what he must have gone through for me, but I couldn't help being hurt that he had never trusted me enough to confide in me. It's not surprising that we grew farther and farther apart.

"Finally, about three years ago, I told him what I knew. I had gone so long after I knew most of the truth that I had no grounds for reproaching him, and I agreed to continue pretending that I was Mrs. Thomas. We jogged along, not quarreling, but I felt continually more estranged. Perhaps he even resented me, at least subconsciously, because my pregnancy had forced him into the whole thing. But he was kind, even if he did resent me. It went along like that until last November, when he came home and told me that Peter Jackson had found out. He didn't tell me how Mr. Jackson had found out, and maybe he didn't know himself.

"I had never liked the Jacksons, but after that I couldn't bear to go to their Christmas party. After Christmas Gordon went to the meeting of the M.L.A. He had packed his bag that morning, but before I left, I checked as I usually did to be sure he had remembered handkerchiefs. In the bag was a bottle of weed killer. I closed up the bag and said nothing.

"I know how cruel it will sound to you, but I thought that he intended to commit suicide. By then it seemed the only answer I could think of. I would have done it myself if it would have helped. But if I had been dead, he would still have been guilty of bigamy. All I could think of was my daughter.

"I was nearly insane myself while he was in Devonport,

expecting to get the news of his death at any moment. But when the news came, it was of Mr. Jackson's death, not his. And it was death by weed killer.

"When Gordon came home from Devonport, I told him I knew that he had killed Mr. Jackson. I didn't intend to tell the police, but I felt the end had come at last for us. I simply couldn't live with him any longer; I could have carried on for a long time as we were before, but murder changed the situation completely. I couldn't, I simply couldn't live on money that he kept by murder. Our marriage, if that is the word for it, had not hurt that poor woman, his wife. This was totally different.

"I had to stay for two or three weeks to clear up my affairs. When I had done so, I went to New York, and I never wanted to come back to this town for the rest of my life. I hoped to get a job there and stay. I lied to you, Lieutenant, when I said that I might have come back if he had asked me. I never would have. Never."

Her voice ran out into a thin note as she finished, almost as if she had conserved her strength until the end, only to have it fail her when it was no longer necessary.

There was a long silence in the room. Barbara Thomas sat with downcast eyes, and no one moved.

Moynahan spoke at last. "Couldn't you have told me this before, Mrs. Thomas?"

"Please don't call me that name. I don't know what I shall call myself, but it will not be Mrs. Thomas. I couldn't tell you. There was no use. It wouldn't have brought back either Gordon or Mr. Jackson. What purpose would it have served to make a scandal about Gordon after he was dead?"

"It would have helped us solve Jackson's murder."

She shook her head slowly from side to side. "Perhaps it would have solved the problem for you, but aside from that, it wouldn't have done any good. It wouldn't even have helped

Jackson's poor widow." She looked at Carrie. "Now you know why I felt so terrible at having been unkind to her."

In a subdued voice Moynahan spoke again. "I know how hard this must have been on you, and I just want to ask one more question. When I asked you whether Professor Thomas had been in all night when there was a prowler in Winthrop Hall, why did you tell me that he had not gone out of the house all evening?"

"Because it was the truth." Her eyes met his candidly. "I didn't go to sleep until three or four in the morning. I was awake reading. Gordon's room was at the end of the hall, and he would have had to pass my open door to get to the stairs. He didn't. Actually, I heard him snoring most of the time that I was reading. He didn't leave his own room, let alone the house."

"Couldn't you possibly be mistaken? I believe that he tried to kill Mr. Stratton that night. Are you sure?"

Before she answered, she looked at Bill. "Oh, no! Bill, I didn't know that." She turned again to Moynahan. "I know I'm not mistaken. I swear he was in the house all night."

CHAPTER
TWENTY-ONE

"She was certainly telling the truth," Bill said. "And if she didn't lie about the marriage, she wouldn't about Gordon's killing Peter. I've felt it in my bones ever since Gordon said he had voted for Evans. But just in my bones; it's hard to give a rational explanation of why I took that so seriously. Maybe because we academics agonize so much over promotions that I felt anyone who would throw in his vote might be guilty of worse things. But it wasn't more than a premonition."

"You bones must be more sensitive than mine," Moynahan said. "I thought it had to be Thomas or Fackler or Moorhead, but I couldn't get closer than that. You convinced me that Benson and Bongiovanni blew off their steam when they lost their tempers, and that they weren't dangerous after that." He paused and looked around Bill's office.

How many times had the detective been there, Bill wondered. His own time in the office in the past month seemed to have been more taken up with police matters than with teaching or being chairman. Peter had left the legacy of a deeply unhappy department, and so far there had been no chance to begin building up the mutual confidence to make it contented and efficient. "At least we know that Gordon had even more reason to commit suicide than we had suspected."

"What I don't understand," said Moynahan, "is his wife's statement that he was home all evening when that copy of *Who's Who* was thrown at you."

"After all, we thought that the murderer had come to the office to get the papers out of the file, but we didn't know which one of the men it was. Now we know that Gordon was the murderer. But it doesn't follow that he had to be the man in the office that night. Fackler, Benson, or even Tony Bongiovanni could have been there. If Roy Moorhead was telling the truth, he couldn't have come to steal the papers because he wasn't aware that Peter knew Grace was illegitimate. So he wouldn't even have known that there were papers to steal. But Peter had let the others know that he was aware of what they were trying to conceal. So, any one of them might have been here, in spite of their having alibis."

"And tried to kill you?"

"That's less likely," Bill admitted, "particularly as the information he had about them wasn't so serious that they would murder to keep it from being known. Gordon Thomas was another matter, because he stood to lose all his money, to be publicly exposed, and perhaps wind up in prison for bigamy if Peter opened his mouth."

"We were fooled about Thomas because we knew part of the truth about him, and so we thought that was all there was to know. Maybe we're making the same mistake about one of the others."

The buzzer sounded at Bill's elbow. "Damn," he said without passion as he picked up the telephone. "Yes?"

"Dame Millicent would like to see you," Rosie said.

"I'm busy now." A touch of annoyance crept into his voice. After all, Rosie had seen Moynahan come in with him. "Tell her I'll see her later if she wants to wait. Otherwise, I'll call her when I'm finished."

"She says it's very important," Rosie sounded unusually

cowed, as if she were shrinking from Dame Millicent's over-powering presence.

"Then I'll come out in a few minutes and see her in your office."

He was about to hang up when Rosie spoke again. Deference was seldom her long suit, but she sounded as if she were afraid of both Bill's anger and that of Dame Millicent. "She says it's *very* important to see you both."

"All right. Give me two minutes." Resignedly, he explained to Moynahan that she was sure to be full of theories about Gordon's death. "But be gentle with her. I don't want to hurt her feelings."

Dame Millicent's entrance into a room always gave one the sense of unleashed energy that came with opening a door to a howling northwest wind. Perhaps it was heightened on this occasion by her being preceded once more by Emma, who was incapable of making a sedate entrance.

When the dog had been reduced to a state of relative docility, Bill said, "Dame Millicent, I believe you have met Mr. Moynahan."

"Indeed we have met," she said. "What is your rank, young man? Sergeant, lieutenant, captain? I'm not certain about police titles out here."

Moynahan obviously realized that equivocation would be pointless. "Lieutenant." He hesitated, then added, "Ma'am." Bill was unsure whether it was a tribute to her title, her age, or her sheer physical energy.

"Very well, Lieutenant. I'm delighted to find you. Professor Stratton's secretary told me that you were here. It's lucky to find you both together."

"What can I—what can we do for you?" Bill asked.

"You remember that I thought Professor Thomas had committed suicide out of remorse for having killed Professor Jackson?"

Bill nodded.

"Well," she said triumphantly, "I was wrong."

"Perhaps," Moynahan suggested, "you weren't too far off the mark."

"Oh but I was, and I have proof." She nodded her head up and down vehemently, making her hat wobble perilously.

Bill said nothing,. Her constant theories, while occasionally diverting, were becoming tiresome. Moynahan, who had certainly had less experience with them, surveyed her with interest. "Would you mind telling us what the proof is?" Bill was surprised at the gravity with which the detective treated her suggestion.

Her left hand had been in the pocket of her coat since she had come into the office. With a dramatic flourish she drew it out. It was clasped, as if holding something. "This!" Even Moynahan winced at the explosion of air that accompanied the monosyllable. She brandished the closed fist before their faces.

"May we see what you have, please?" Moynahan asked quietly.

For a moment Dame Millicent covered her fist with her other hand, then slowly, as if reluctant to give her secret away too easily, opened her left hand. In the palm lay a motley collection of seeds. Bill recognized only the largest, sunflower seeds. "What are they?" he asked. As he spoke, he noticed Moynahan nodding his head as if in confirmation.

"Bird seed, of course. Professor Thomas's bird seed."

"And where did you find it?" Moynahan sounded almost conspiratorial.

"Near Winthrop Hall." As she spoke, Emma trotted over to sniff at her palm. "Sit!" she thundered, and the puppy obeyed with alacrity. "Where his body was found."

"I thought so," Moynahan said. "You'd better tell us about it."

"I went to get Emma this noon," she began. "That was just after you had left, I fancy. Mrs. Stratton said you had been there. She seemed busy, so I didn't go into the house. Instead, I brought Emma to the campus for her walk. I put her through her paces on the library plaza, but there were so many undergraduates watching that I began to worry that she might become more interested in them than in her training. That would be disastrous, of course. You do understand, don't you?"

"Yes, indeed." Moynahan nodded gravely. "It's very distracting to a puppy to have too many spectators."

"Exactly. With such a young puppy, it's important never to neglect the romp, so I walked her toward Winthrop Hall. When we got there, I thought it might be interesting to see where Professor Thomas had fallen. I thought I might discover something the police had missed." She looked inquiringly toward Moynahan. "Perhaps you didn't know that I am Deirdre Desiree?"

"Indeed I did, Dame Millicent, and I have often wanted to tell you how much I admire your work."

"Thank you so much. Very kind. As a matter of fact, you are the first—well, the first person in your calling—with whom I have talked about my books." Her face broke into a glow of enthusiasm, and for a moment she appeared to be forgetting her story. "However, all that is unimportant now. But I should like to talk to you at greater length about them sometime. Now, to get back to what I was saying. And I do think that is the important thing, don't you? I didn't *really* think the police would have neglected anything important. I poked around for a bit, most unsuccessfully. Meanwhile, Emma was rushing about through the snow, and I was afraid she might get away, so I called her back. She came at once. Professor Stratton, you have a remarkably intelligent little bitch. She picks up almost everything at the first try.

"Now, let's see. Where was I? Ah, yes. Emma. She came bounding back to me, and when she did, she began burrowing at my feet. It seemed somehow quite wrong, digging on

240

the very spot where poor Professor Thomas had lain throughout the night. Most disrespectful. Suddenly I realized that she was after something. You know, I really wonder sometimes whether you feed her sufficiently; she seems to be constantly hungry. Her paws were going in a regular fury. Then she began mouthing what she had found. I made her give it up, although she didn't like to do so. It was a sunflower seed, and the truth flashed on me like a thunderclap. No, that metaphor is totally confused. Like lightning."

"I'm afraid it hasn't flashed on me yet," Bill began, but Moynahan held up a hand for him to be quiet, his eyes still on Dame Millicent.

"Of course, I knew at once that Professor Thomas had not committed suicide. You do see, don't you, Lieutenant Moynahan?" The detective nodded, and she turned back to Bill. "I began looking in the snow myself then. It had melted considerably, so it was much easier for me than for the police. And I found all these seeds. Probably there are more, but I thought these would be adequate to show that he had either fallen from the roof of Winthrop Hall or had been pushed."

"I'm sorry," Bill said, aware that the other two were far ahead of him, "but I still don't see."

"Surely you have visited Professor Thomas when he was feeding birds. I have several times. Most instructive. Your birds are so different out here from ours at home. Professor Thomas always fed them from the bag of seeds near the door of the stairway to the roof. He would reach into the bag and then scatter the seeds. Then he would close the bag and replace the plastic cover. But he never went near the parapet. Nor was there any reason for him to do so." She stopped. "Oh, dear, I feel that I am getting confused. You do understand, don't you, Lieutenant Moynahan?" She was pink with embarrassment.

"Perfectly." Moynahan nodded again. "You're admirably lucid."

She flushed more deeply. "Thank you. You know, you are most kind to me. I feel sometimes that I'm a silly old woman, but I do feel positive about this. The point is, that a man doesn't suddenly decide to commit suicide, and then, without dropping whatever he is doing, rush to throw himself off a roof. Certainly not a scholar so admirable as Professor Thomas. Someone must have interrupted him as he was feeding the birds, called him to the parapet, and then—" Her face crumpled. "It's so easy to write about murder, but I don't know how to talk about it." Suddenly, disconcertingly, she broke into tears. "I've never seen a body or been involved with a murder before," came out in a loud wail. "It's horrible."

To Bill's surprise, Moynahan leaned over and patted her hand. "Of course it is. And I can tell you that it never becomes less horrible."

"Then you don't think I'm a silly old woman?"

"How ridiculous. Of course not. I've been on the same track ever since Professor Thomas's death, Dame Millicent, but I couldn't get the proof. I don't know how to thank you enough. Without you, we might never have found it." Dame Millicent's eyes were still cast down to conceal her tears, and she could not see, as Bill did, Moynahan's gulp for the courage to continue: "You know, I think the police too often neglect the help of writers like you. You are the ones who have the imagination to see what we so often miss."

Her film of tears burgeoned into a flood, and she could scarcely find her way out of the door to which Moynahan led her, with a firm hand under her elbow. She recovered in time to shout, "Emma, COME!" and disappeared.

"Were you just being kind to her?" Bill asked when she was gone.

"Of course not. She's absolutely right, bless her heart. Now, Mr. Stratton, would you like to come with me?"

"Where are you going?"

"To the Cartersville police station, to get a search warrant and a policeman to come with me to make the arrest."

"But—?"

"Just come along. We can talk some other time."

Half an hour later Bill was climbing into the back seat of a police car. Moynahan and one of the local force were in the front. They drove down Scott Street, turned right on Grafton, and then picked up speed. No one spoke. Two miles along Grafton Road, Sergeant Brooks began slowing down, and a block later they stopped before the house the Jacksons had bought from the Todhills. Moynahan turned to Bill. "You might as well come along and see the end of this." Bill nodded silently and followed the two policemen to the door.

A cleaning woman answered the bell and looked at them distrustfully. "May we see Mrs. Jackson?" Moynahan asked.

Without answering, she shut the door and left them standing on the porch. In a minute June Jackson opened the door again. Her face was white. "Yes?"

"Mrs. Jackson," said Brooks, "I have a warrant to search your house."

"What the hell do you mean? What are you after?" Her face was still white, but her voice was controlled under the anger.

Brooks looked at Moynahan. "Mrs. Jackson," he said, "we're looking for keys and for overshoes."

"Overshoes? Keys? What keys? You're out of your mind."

"The keys to Winthrop Hall, to the office that your husband used to occupy and that is now Professor Stratton's, and to the files in that office."

"I don't know what you're talking about. You can't come in. Go away, or I'll call the—"

"No, Mrs. Jackson," Moynahan said in the same gentle voice that he had used to Dame Millicent. "*We* are the police. I'm afraid that we must come in."

She stood without moving, and at last Moynahan went past

her, careful not to brush against her. Brooks followed. Only Bill, to whom she had not spoken, still stood on the porch. "I'm sorry, June," he began.

"Oh, shut up," she interrupted and ran after the policemen, leaving the door open.

Bill hesitated between remaining painfully outside in the cold, and going into the house. Then the thought of freezing for an indefinite time made up his mind for him, and he sat on a chair in the hallway. June and the policemen had disappeared, but he could hear an occasional word from upstairs. The cleaning woman was nowhere to be seen.

In another five minutes Moynahan and Brooks came down the stairs with June at their heels. "What of it?" she was shouting. "They were Peter's keys. There's nothing criminal in my still having them here. I forgot to give them back to the English office, that's all."

"No," said Moynahan a shade too calmly, "nothing criminal in that. But it may be harder to explain why you were on the roof with Thomas just before he died." He waved the pair of overshoes that he had been carrying under his arm, then handed them to Brooks.

"June Jackson," said Brooks solemnly, "I arrest you for the murder of Gordon Swift Thomas."

CHAPTER
TWENTY-TWO

"I knew from the beginning," said Moynahan, "there was something fishy about Mrs. Jackson. It was the note she showed the police after her husband's death." He pulled a slip of paper from his pocket. "'I can face death,'" he read, 'better than your going to the president. Peter.' It began at the top of the page, without a date or solution. I realized that there was a possibility it was the last page of a leter that wasn't even concerned with suicide."

He took a cup of coffee from Carrie. "Thank you. Telling about all this isn't a good way to top off a splendid dinner like that."

"No modesty, Lieutenant, please," said Dame Millicent. "You know perfectly well we want every detail. I'm sure I could work them out for myself, if I were to put my mind to it, but I much prefer to have you tell us."

"Okay. You remember that Jackson had specified that she was to get nothing but a widow's portion of the estate if he died by either murder or manslaughter. That could mean only that she had threatened to kill him, presumably for his infidelity. But the fact that she was innocent of his murder is what kept us from suspecting her as the prowler.

"She was, of course, right in this house when he was murdered, so she was clear of the killing. And we didn't even know positively that her husband had told her about the provision in his will. But, of course, he had told her. We know now that her willingness to show the letter, to prove that he had committed suicide, meant that she was willing to let the murderer go free so long as she could keep the money."

Bill looked chagrined. "Even though I was Peter's executor, I missed the essential point of the case. Since the provision in the will was so clearly the result of his fear of June, I neglected the fact that she would lose the money if someone else killed him. When we knew that she had not killed him and assumed that his death was a suicide, I forgot that his murder by another person would cut off her legacy just as effectively as if she had killed him. And that's why she had to keep us from suspecting Gordon as the murderer."

Moynahan nodded. "Exactly. Most of us refuse to think that we could be murdered unless we are directly threatened, as Jackson was by his wife. He didn't believe that anyone else might kill him. And the result was that his will, which was intended to direct suspicion at his wife if he died, drew our attention away from her."

"I'm not sure," said Carrie, "how you knew that she wasn't in a conspiracy with one of the other members of the department to kill Peter."

"The usual reason for conspiracy is an attempt to get money. Nobody in the department seemed to need it that badly. Not even Bongiovanni. The other possibility was the official verdict, that Jackson really had committed suicide. Perhaps he had reason to do so if his wife was going to ruin his life. But, as you pointed out, that was out of character. Besides, he probably wouldn't have chosen such a painful way to die.

"The truth was, of course, that Mrs. Jackson had no part in his murder, but when she heard of his death, she produced one page of his letter in order to prove that he had committed suicide. The note was the end of a letter written from Devonport, in which he promised to reform; there wasn't much else for him to do since he faced the alternatives of her going to the President or killing him."

"Did you suspect Professor Thomas of the murder?" asked Dame Millicent, stroking Emma, who was once more asleep on her capacious lap. "I certainly suspected him, but Professor Stratton refused resolutely to listen, in spite of the fact that he knew I'm not an amateur at this sort of thing. I hadn't yet worked out all the details, but I could have done that, I'm sure."

"Sorry about that," Bill murmured.

"Until Mr. Stratton found the papers in the files, I had little to go on. But Mrs. Jackson knew at once who the murderer was, because Thomas was the only one who had a compelling reason to kill her husband. If the truth of Thomas's past were found out, his marriage would be ruined, he would lose his first wife's money, and he would be known as a bigamist. That was enough for her to figure out who had killed her husband.

"Like you, Mrs. Stratton, and your husband, I assumed it was the murderer who rifled the files and tried to kill your husband. The reason seemed obvious, and any single one of the suspects might have slipped out of his house that night without his wife's knowing it. Or his wife might have lied to protect him. I didn't stop to think that Mrs. Jackson would probably still have her husband's keys.

"I didn't suppose she was aware of her husband's blackmailing activities, although I should have realized that she knew when we found out that he had tried to force Mrs. Moorhead into getting her into the Garden Club. He wouldn't have done that kind of thing without her prompting. By the time I found that out this morning, I was so busy I failed to put two and two together at once. Not that it would have made a difference of more than an hour or two at most.

"Mrs. Jackson assumed that the papers wouldn't mean anything to anyone else who read them accidentally, so at first it was safer for her to leave them in the files than to steal them. But then Mrs. Thomas went to her and offered to support her as a candidate for the Garden Club. Mrs. Jackson is not a fool, and the suddenness of the offer made her realize that Mrs. Thomas was feeling remorse about Jackson's death. The remorse meant that Mrs. Thomas had discovered her husband's guilt. Mrs. Jackson knew enough about Mrs. Thomas to realize that she wouldn't connive at murder, and that she would probably leave Thomas. And Thomas loved his wife so much he would break up if she left; he might even confess to the police. I'm sure Mrs. Jackson was right in assuming that he would confess."

"Then why did she change her mind and decide to steal the papers?" Bill asked.

"Because she intended to kill Thomas before he could go to the police. She expected us to assume, as we did, that he had killed himself because his wife had left him. Mrs. Thomas would assume the same thing, but she wouldn't be apt to tell us that he was a murderer, after his death. Mrs. Jackson stole the papers, and then you interrupted her. No one else had seen her because she had used the key to the stair door of the building to come in after the guard was gone. Once the papers were destroyed, there would be no evidence after Thomas's death that he had killed Jackson."

"I don't see why she tried to kill Bill," Carrie said. "All she had to do was wait until he was gone, then slip out the way she had come."

"Mr. Stratton was the only person who could possibly have noticed that the papers were gone from the files. It was improbable he would know what they meant, but he might notice their absence."

"Not a very charming woman," Dame Millicent said quietly.

"When Mrs. Thomas left her husband, Mrs. Jackson

knew she must act quickly. She called Thomas at home that Saturday afternoon, but she got no answer, so she guessed he would be at his office. When she got there, he was out of his office, although he had clearly not left the building, since his hat was still on the file cabinet and the lights were burning.

"His coat was gone, however, so she assumed correctly that he had gone to the roof to put out extra food for the birds because of the snowfall. When she went up there, he was scattering the food on top of the snow. She told him that she had come to look for some books belonging to her husband that had never been returned. He said he would help her look for them. As he was putting out the last of the bird seed, she went to the parapet and looked over. She gave a little scream and called him. He came running as fast as he could through the snow. She is a big woman, and he was a small man. She threw out a hand as he got even with her and took advantage of his momentum. It didn't take too much strength to give him a push. The parapet was low, and he went over. The rest you know."

"How did you find out all this?" Carrie looked as if she were going to cry.

"She confessed finally. At first she kept denying that she had deliberately kept her husband's keys. So we had to try something else." Moynahan looked embarrassed. "To tell the truth, we suggested that her hard-packed footprints were found under the loose snow that later fell on the roof. It would have been illegal to say positively that we had done so, since it wasn't the truth, but we talked around the subject so that she could make her own assumption that we had found them. It seemed the only way to make her talk. Perhaps you don't approve of the method, but it did bring a murderer to justice. She broke down and told us everything that had happened."

There was a long silence. At last Dame Millicent spoke.

"You know, I am glad that at least one of my theories worked. It did, didn't it, Lieutenant."

"It certainly did. We might have made the connection when the snow melted, but, as it was, we didn't have the sense to brush the snow off the seed bag on the roof of the building. When we did, after your discovery, we found that Thomas had not replaced the plastic cover. At the very least, you saved us a lot of time. I could have kissed you for finding those seeds."

In answer she picked up Emma and plopped her onto the floor. "There. It's still not late for you to kiss me, but I refuse to have a dog on my lap at the time. When you have done so, would you be so kind as to motor me home? I don't have an automobile, although I have always thought it might be amusing to learn to drive." She held up her cheek and Moynahan bent over. "Thank you. A woman shouldn't thank a man under these circumstances, but it *has* been a long time."

"It was my pleasure," said Moynahan. "While I'm taking you home, I'd like to ask you about some things that have always bothered me in the Tristram legend."

"Very well, and in exchange I shall ask your criticism of *The Mistress of Muddlethorp Hall*. Do you think, Lieutenant, that you wouldn't like to collaborate with me on a suspense novel?"